CASTILE FOR ISABELLA

Due to illness, Jean Plaidy was unable to go to school regularly and so taught herself to read. Very early on she developed a passion for the 'past'. After doing a shorthand and typing course, she spent a couple of years doing various jobs, including sorting gems in Hatton Garden and translating for foreigners in a City café. She began writing in earnest following marriage and now has a large number of historical novels to her name. Inspiration for her books is drawn from odd sources – a picture gallery, a line from a book, Shakespeare's inconsistencies. She lives in London and loves music, second-hand book shops and ancient buildings. Jean Plaidy also writes under the pseudonym of Victoria Holt.

CONDITIONS OF SALE

The Ferdinand and Isabella Trilogy

CASTILE FOR ISABELLA

JEAN PLAIDY

UNABRIDGED

PAN BOOKS LTD : LONDON

First published 1960 by Robert Hale and Company
This edition published 1974 by Pan Books Ltd,
33 Tothill Street, London SW1

ISBN 0 330 23830 2

Printed in Great Britain by
Richard Clay (The Chaucer Press), Ltd, Bungay, Suffolk

CONTENTS

FLIGHT TO AREVALO

THE Alcazar was set high on a cliff from which could be seen the far-off peaks of the Guadarrama Sierras and the plain, watered by the Manzanares River. It was an impressive pile of stone which had grown up round what had once been a mighty fortress erected by the Moorish conquerors of Spain. Now it was one of the Palaces of the Kings of Castile.

At a window of this Palace, a four-year-old child stood looking towards the snow-topped peaks of the distant mountains, but the grandeur of the scenery was lost to her, for she was thinking of events inside the granite walls.

She was afraid, but this was not apparent. Her blue eyes were serene; although she was so young, she had already learned to hide her emotions, and fear above all must be kept hidden.

Something extraordinary was happening in the Palace, and it was something quite alarming. Isabella shivered.

There had been much coming and going in the royal apartments. She had seen the messengers hurrying through the *patios*, stopping to whisper with others in the great rooms and shake their heads as though they were prophesying dire disaster, or wearing that excited look which, she knew, meant that they were probably the bearers of bad news.

She dared not ask what was happening. Such a question might bring a reproof, which would be an affront to her dignity. She must constantly remember her dignity. Her mother had said so.

'Always remember this,' Queen Isabella had told her daughter more than once. 'If your stepbrother Henry should die without heirs, your little brother Alfonso would be King of Castile; and if Alfonso should die without heirs, you, Isabella, would be Queen of Castile. The throne would be yours by right, and woe betide any who tried to take it from you.' Little Isabella remembered how her mother clenched her fists and shook them, how her whole body shook, and how she herself wanted to cry out, 'Please, Highness, do not speak of these things,' and yet dared not. She was afraid of every subject which excited her mother, because there was something terrifying in her mother's excitement. 'Think of that, my child,' she would proceed. 'Indeed, you must never forget it. And when you are tempted to behave in any manner but the best, ask yourself: Is this worthy of one who could become Queen of Castile?'

Isabella always said on such occasions: 'Yes, Highness, I will. I will.' She would have promised anything to stop her mother shaking her fists, anything to drive the wild look out of her mother's eyes.

And for this reason she always did remember, for when she was tempted to lose her temper, or even to express herself too freely, she would have a vision of her mother, veering towards one of those terrifying moods of hysteria, and that was all that was needed to restrain her.

Her thick chestnut hair was never allowed to be disordered; her blue eyes were always serene; and she was learning to walk as though there was already a crown on her head. The attendants in the royal nursery said: 'The Infanta Isabella is a good child, but she would be more natural if she would learn to be a little *human*.'

Isabella could have explained, if it had not been beneath her dignity to do so: 'It is not for me to learn to be human. I must learn to be a Queen, because that is what I may one day be.'

Now, much as she longed to know the reason for the tension in the Palace, this hurrying to and fro, these expectant looks on the faces of courtiers and messengers, she did not ask; she merely listened.

Listening was rewarding. She had not *seen* the end of her

father's friend, the great Alvaro de Luna, but she had *heard* that he had ridden through the streets, dressed as an ordinary criminal, and that people, who had once hated him so much that they had called for his death, had shed tears on seeing such a man brought low. She had heard how he had mounted the scaffold with a demeanour so calm and haughty that he might have been arriving at the Palace for an interview with Isabella's father, the King of Castile. She knew that the executioner had thrust his knife into that proud throat and cut off the haughty head; she knew that de Luna's body had been cut into pieces and set up for the people to shudder over, to remind themselves that this was the fate of one who, such a short time before, had been the King's dearest friend.

All this one could learn by listening.

The servants said: 'It was the Queen's doing. The King ... why, he would have taken de Luna back at the last moment. Yes ... but he dared not offend the Queen.'

Then Isabella had known that she was not the only one who was afraid of her mother's strange moods.

She loved her father. He was the kindest of men. He wanted her to learn her lessons so that she might, as he said, appreciate the only worthwhile things in life.

'Books are a man's best friends, my child,' he told her. 'I have learned this too late. I wish I had learned it earlier. I think you are going to be a wise woman, daughter; therefore when I pass on this knowledge to you I know that you will remember it.'

Isabella, as was her custom, listened gravely. She wanted to please her father, because he seemed so weary. She felt that they shared a fear of which neither of them could ever speak.

Isabella would be good; she would do all that was expected of her, for fear of displeasing her mother. It seemed that her father, the King, would do the same; he would even send his dearest friend, de Luna, to the executioner's knife because his wife demanded it.

Isabella often felt that if her mother had been always as

calm and gentle as she could be sometimes, they could have been very happy. She loved her family dearly. It was so pleasant, she thought, to have a baby brother like Alfonso, who was surely the best-tempered baby in the world, and a grown-up brother like Henry – even though he was only a stepbrother – who was always so charming to his little stepsister.

They ought to have been happy, and could so easily have been, apart from the ever-present fear.

'Isabella!' It was her mother's voice, a little harsh with that strident note which never failed to start the alarm signals within Isabella's brain.

Isabella turned without haste. She saw that her governess and attendants were discreetly leaving. The Queen of Castile had intimated that she wished to be alone with her daughter.

Slowly, and with the utmost dignity that a child of four could possibly display, Isabella came to the Queen and sank to the floor in a graceful curtsy. Etiquette at Court was rigid, even within the family circle.

'My dear daughter,' murmured the Queen; and as Isabella rose she embraced her fervently. The child, crushed against the jewel-encrusted bodice, endured the discomfort, but she felt her fear increasing. This, she thought, is something really terrible.

The Queen at length released the little girl from that violent embrace and held her at arms' length. She studied her intently, and tears welled into her eyes. Tears were alarming, almost as alarming as the fits of laughter.

'So young,' murmured the Queen, 'my four-year-old Isabella, and Alfonso but an infant in the cradle.'

'Highness, he is very intelligent. He must be the most intelligent baby in the whole of Castile.'

'He'll need to be. My poor ... poor children! What will become of us? Henry will seek some way to be rid of us.'

Henry? wondered Isabella. Kind, jovial Henry, who always had sweetmeats to offer his little sister and would pick her up and give her a ride on his shoulder, telling her that she would be a pretty woman one day! Why should Henry want to be rid of them?

'I am going to tell you something,' said the Queen. 'We will be ready ... when the time comes. You must not be surprised if I tell you that we are to leave at once. It will be soon. It cannot be long delayed.'

Isabella waited, fearful of asking another of those questions which might win a rebuke. Experience told her that if she waited attentively she could often discover as much as, or even more than, if she asked questions.

'We may leave at a moment's notice ... a moment's notice!' The Queen began to laugh, and the tears were still in her eyes. Isabella prayed silently to the saints that she would not laugh so much that she could not stop.

But no, this was not to be one of those terrifying scenes, for the Queen stopped laughing and put a finger to her lips. 'Be prepared,' she said. 'We will outwit him.' Then she put her face close to the little girl's. 'He'll never get a child,' she said. 'Never ... never!' She was close to that terrifying laughter again. 'It is the life he has led. That is his reward. And well he deserved it. Never mind, our turn will come. My Alfonso shall mount the throne of Castile ... and if by some chance he should not reach manhood, there is always my Isabella. Is there not, eh? Is there not?'

'Yes, Highness,' murmured the little girl.

Her mother took the plump cheek between thumb and forefinger, and pinched it so hard that it was difficult to prevent the tears coming to those blue eyes. But the little girl knew it was intended as a gesture of affection.

'Be ready,' said the Queen.

'Yes, Highness.'

'Now I must be back with him. How can one know what plots are hatched when one's back is turned, eh? How can one?'

'How can one, Highness,' repeated Isabella dutifully.

'But you will be ready, my Isabella.'

'Yes, Highness, I will be ready.'

There was another embrace, so fierce that it was an effort not to cry out in protest against it.

'It will not be long,' said the Queen. 'It cannot be long now. Be ready and do not forget.'

Isabella nodded, but her mother went on with the often repeated phrase: 'One day you may be Queen of Castile.'

'I will remember, Highness.'

The Queen seemed suddenly calm. She prepared to leave, and once more her little daughter gave her a sweeping curtsy.

Isabella was hoping that her mother would not go into that room where Alfonso lay in his cradle. Alfonso had cried in protest last time his mother had embraced him so fiercely. Poor Alfonso, he could not be expected to know that he must never protest, that he must not ask questions but merely listen; soon he would be old enough to hear that one day he could be King of Castile, but as yet he was only a baby.

When she was alone, young Isabella took the opportunity of slipping into the room where Alfonso lay in his cradle. He was clearly unaware of the tension in the Palace. He lay kicking joyously, and he crowed with pleasure as Isabella appeared.

'Alfonso, baby brother,' murmured Isabella.

The baby laughed at his sister and kicked more furiously.

'You do not know, do you, that one day you could be King of Castile?'

Surreptitiously, Isabella bent over the cradle and kissed her brother. She looked furtively about her. No one had noticed that little weakness, and she made excuses to herself for betraying her emotion. Alfonso was such a pretty baby and she loved him very much.

The Queen of Castile was on her knees beside her husband's bed.

'What hour is it?' he asked her, and as she dropped her

hands from her face he went on: 'But what matters the hour? My time has come. It is now for me to say my farewells.'

'No!' she cried, and he could hear the rising hysteria in her voice. 'The time has not yet come.'

He spoke gently, pityingly. 'Isabella, my Queen, we should not deceive ourselves. What good will it do? In a short time there will be another King of Castile, and your husband, John II, will begin to be a memory – a not very happy one for Castile, I fear.'

She had begun to beat her clenched fist lightly on the bed. 'You must not die yet. You must not. What of the children?'

'The children, yes,' he murmured. 'Do not excite yourself, Isabella. I shall arrange that good care is taken of them.'

'Alfonso...' muttered the Queen, 'a baby in his cradle. Isabella ... just past her fourth birthday!'

'I have great hopes of our sturdy Isabella,' said the King. 'And there is Henry. He will be a good brother to them.'

'As he has been a good son to his father?' demanded the Queen shrilly.

'This is no time for recriminations, my dear. It may well be that there were faults on both sides.'

'You ... you are soft with him ... soft.'

'I am a weak man and I am on my death-bed. You know that as well as I do.'

'You were always soft with him ... with everybody. Even when you were well, you allowed yourself to be governed.'

The King lifted a weak hand for silence. Then he went on: 'I believe the people are pleased. I believe they are saying "Good riddance to John II. Welcome to Henry IV. He will be a better king than his father was." Well, my dear, they may be right in that, for they would have to search far and wide for a worse.'

John began to cough and the Queen's eyes widened in fear. She made an effort to control herself. 'Rest,' she cried. 'For the love of the saints, rest.'

She was afraid that he would die before she had made her plans. She distrusted her stepson Henry. He might seem to be good-natured, a less intellectual, a more voluptuous replica of his father, but he would allow himself to be ruled by favourites who would not easily tolerate rivals to the throne. They would impress upon him the fact that if he displeased his subjects they would rally round young Alfonso and Isabella. Therefore he would be watchful.

She trusted no one, and she was growing more and more determined that her own son should inherit the throne.

And what shall I do? the Queen asked herself; and her fist began to beat once more upon the bed. I, a weak woman, surrounded by my enemies!

Her wild gaze rested on the dying man in the bed.

He *must* not die until she was ready for him to do so; he must remain King of Castile until she was prepared to whisk her little son and daughter from Madrid.

They would go to a place where they could dwell in peace, where there was no danger of a morsel of poison being slipped into their food or drink, where it would be impossible for an assassin to slip into their sleeping chamber and press a pillow over their baby mouths as they slept. They should go where they might bide their time until that moment – and the Queen was sure it would come – when Henry should be ousted from the throne and little Alfonso – or Isabella – triumphantly take it, King – or Queen – of Castile.

King John lay back on his pillows watching his wife.

Poor Isabella, he thought, what will become of her – she who was already tainted with the terrible scourge of her family? There was madness in the royal house of Portugal; at the moment it had not completely taken possession of Isabella, his Queen, but now and then there were signs that it had not passed her by.

He was by no means stupid, bad King though he had been, and he wondered whether that tendency to insanity had been inherited by their children. There was no sign of it as yet. Isabella had inherited none of the hysteria of her mother; there could rarely have been a more serene child than his sedate little daughter. Little Alfonso? It was early to say as yet, but he seemed to be a normal, happy baby.

He prayed that the terrible disease of the mind had passed them by and that Isabella had not brought its taint into the royal house of Castile to the detriment of future generations.

He should never have married Isabella. Why had he? Because he was weak; because he had allowed himself to be led.

When Maria of Aragon, Henry's mother, had died, it had naturally been necessary for John to find a new wife, and he had believed it would be an admirable gesture to ally himself with the French. He had considered marriage with a daughter of the King of France; but his dear friend and adviser, Alvaro de Luna, had thought differently. He had seen advantages to Castile, he said – and to himself, which he did not mention – through an alliance with Portugal.

Poor misguided de Luna! Little did he realize what this marriage was going to mean to him.

The dying John allowed himself to smile as he thought of de Luna in the early days of their friendship. Alvaro had first come to Court as a page – handsome, attractive, he had been a dazzling personality, a skilled diplomat, a graceful courtier, under whose spell John had immediately fallen. He asked nothing more than to stay there, and, in return for the pleasure this man's company brought him, John had bestowed on him all the honours for which he craved. De Luna had been not only Grand Master of St James but Constable of Castile.

Oh yes, thought John, I was a bad king, for I gave myself completely to pleasure. I had no aptitude for statecraft and, because I was not a stupid man, because I had some intellectual leanings, my behaviour was the more criminal. I have not the excuse of inability to rule; I failed through indolence.

But my father, Henry III, died too young. And there was I, a minor, King of Castile. There was a Regency to rule in my stead. And how well! So well that there was every excuse why I should give myself to pleasure and not concern myself with the government of my country.

But regrettably there had come the day when John was old enough to be King in more than name. And there he had been, young, good-looking, accomplished in the arts, finding that there were so many more interesting things to do than govern a kingdom.

He had been frivolous; he had loved splendour; he had filled his Court with poets and dreamers. He was a dreamer himself. He had been touched perhaps by the Moorish influence of his surroundings. He had lived rather like a Caliph of some Arabic legend. He had sat, with his friends around him, reading poetry; he had staged colourful pageants; he had roamed about the brilliant gardens of his Madrid Alcazar with his tamed Nubian lion for companion.

The splendour of the Palace was notorious; so was the extravagance and frivolity of the King. And side by side with royal extravagance was the hardship and poverty of the people. Taxes had been imposed to provide revenue for favourites; there was misery and privation throughout the land. These were the inevitable results of his misrule and, if the country had been split by civil war and his own son Henry had taken sides against him, he blamed himself, because here on his death-bed he saw more clearly where he had failed.

And always beside him had been his beloved Alvaro de Luna, who, having begun life humbly, could not resist the opportunity to flaunt his possessions, to show his power. He had made himself rich by accepting bribes, and wherever he went he was surrounded by lackeys and trappings of such magnificence that the King's retinue was put in the shade.

Some said that de Luna dabbled in witchcraft, and it was to this cult that he owed his power over the King. That was untrue, John told himself now. He had admired the brilliant, dashing courtier, this illegitimate son of a noble Aragonese family, because he was possessed of the strong character which John himself lacked.

John was the sort of man who seemed willingly to accept the domination of others. He had been as docile as usual when he agreed to his marriage with Isabella of Portugal.

If that marriage had brought him little peace, it had brought disaster to de Luna, for the bride was a woman of strong character in spite of her latent taint. Or was it that he himself was so weak and feared her outbursts of hysteria?

'Who,' she had demanded, 'is King of Castile, you or de Luna?'

He had reasoned with her; he had explained what good friends he and the Constable had always been.

'Of course he flatters you,' she had retorted scornfully. 'He coaxes you as he would a horse he was riding. But he holds the reins; he decides which way you shall go.'

It was when she was pregnant with Isabella that the real wildness had begun to show itself. It was then that he began to suspect the taint might exist in her blood. Then he had been ready to do anything to calm her in order not to have to face the terrifying fear that he might have introduced madness into the royal blood stream of Castile.

She had fretted and worked for the disgrace of de Luna, and now he felt bitterly ashamed of the part he had played; he tried to shut this out of his thoughts, but he could not do so. Some perversity in his dying self forced him to face the truth as he had never done before.

He remembered the last time he had seen de Luna; he remembered what friendship he had shown the man, so that poor Alvaro had reassured himself, had told himself that he cared nothing for the enmity of the Queen while the King was his friend.

But he did not save his friend; he loved him still, yet he had allowed him to go to his death.

That, he thought, is the kind of man I am. That action was characteristic of John of Castile. He entertained warm

feelings for his friends, but he was too indolent, too much of
a coward to save one whom he had loved more than any. He
had been afraid of angry scenes, of being forced to face that
which he dared not; and so the Queen, balanced very deli-
cately between sanity and insanity, had achieved in a few
months what his ministers had plotted for thirty years: the
downfall of de Luna.

John felt tears in his eyes as he thought of de Luna's brave
walk to the scaffold. He had heard how gallantly his friend
had gone to death.

And up to the moment of de Luna's execution he, the
King, who should have been the most powerful man in Castile, had promised himself that he would save his friend, had
longed to quash the sentence of death and bring de Luna
back to favour; but he had not done so, for he, who had once
been dominated by the charm of de Luna, was now the thrall
of the latent madness of his wife.

All I wanted was peace, thought the dying King. All? It
was more difficult to find than anything else in turbulent
Castile.

In his tapestried apartment of the Palace, Henry, heir to the
throne, was waiting to hear the news of his father's death.

The people, he knew, were eager to acclaim him. When he
rode through the streets they shouted his name; they were
tired of the disastrous rule of John II and they longed to
welcome a new King who could bring a new way of life to
Castile.

As for Henry, he was very eager to feel the crown on his
head, and he was determined to keep the popularity which
was his. He had no doubt that he could do this, for he was
fully aware of his charm. He was good-tempered, easy-going,
and he had the art of flattering the people, which never failed
to delight them. He could condescend to be one of them
without apparent condescension; that was the secret of the
people's love for him.

He was determined to dazzle his subjects. He would raise armies and achieve victories; he would go into battle against the Moors, who for centuries had remained in possession of a large part of Spain. The Moors were perennial enemies, and the proud Castilians could always be brought to a wild enthusiasm by talks of campaigns against them. He would give them pageants to delight their eyes, spectacles and entertainments to make them forget their miseries. His reign should be one of continual excitement and colour.

And what did Henry want? He wanted more and more pleasure – that meant new pleasures. They would not be easy to find, for he was a man of great erotic experience.

While he was waiting, his wife, Blanche, came to him. She too was expectant, for would she not be Queen of Castile when the news was brought to them? She would wish to receive the homage, to stand beside Henry and swear with him to serve the people of Castile with every means at her disposal.

He took her hand and kissed it. Always affectionate in public, even when they were alone he did not show his indifference; he was never actively unkind, for it was against his nature to be so. Now the look of affection he gave her disguised the distaste which she was beginning to rouse in him.

It was twelve years since Blanche of Aragon became his wife. At first he had been delighted to have a wife, but she was not his kind; she could not share his pleasures as his many mistresses could; and since the union had proved fruitless he had no further use for her.

He needed a child – never more than at this time – and he had recently been considering what action he might take to remedy matters.

He had been a voluptuary from boyhood, when there had always been pages, attendants, and teachers to encourage a very willing pupil; and the exploitation of the senses had appealed to him so much more than book-learning.

His father had been an intellectual man who had filled the Court with literary figures, but Henry had nothing in common with men such as Iñigo Lopez de Mendoza, Marquis of Santillana, the great literary figure, nor for the poet John de Mena.

What had such men done for his father? Henry asked himself. There had been anarchy in the Kingdom and unpopularity for the King – civil war, with a large proportion of the King's subjects fighting against him. If he had pursued pleasure as indefatigably as his son he could not have been more unpopular.

Henry was determined to go his own way and now, looking at Blanche, he was making up his mind that since she could not please him she must go.

She said in her gentle way: 'So, Henry, the King is dying.'

'It is so.'

'Then very soon...'

'Yes, I shall be King of Castile. The people can scarcely wait to call me King. If you look out of the window you will see that they are already gathering about the Palace.'

'It is so sad,' she said.

'Sad that I shall soon be King of Castile?'

'Sad, Henry, that you can only be so because of the death of your father.'

'My dear wife, death must come to us all. We must take our bow at the end of the performance and move on, so that the next player may strut across the stage.'

'I know it, and that is why I am sad.'

He came to her and laid an arm about her shoulders. 'My poor, sweet Blanche,' he said, 'you are too sensitive.'

She caught his hand and kissed it. Temporarily, he deceived even her with his gentle manners. Later she might wonder what was going on in his mind as he caressed her. He was capable of telling her that she was the only woman he really loved at the very moment when he was planning to rid himself of her.

Twelve years of life with Henry had taught her a great deal about him. He was as shallow as he was charming, and she would be a fool to feel complacent merely because he implied that she still held a high place in his affections. She was aware of the life he led. He had had so many mistresses that he could not have been sure how many. He might, even at a moment when he was suggesting that he was a faithful husband, be considering the pursuit and seduction of another.

Lately she had grown fearful. She was meek and gentle by nature, but she was not a fool. She was terrified that he would divorce her because she had failed to bear a child, and that she would be forced to return to her father's Court of Aragon.

'Henry,' she said on impulse, 'when you are indeed King it will be very necessary that we have a son.'

'Yes,' he replied with a rueful smile.

'We have been so unfortunate. Perhaps . . .' She hesitated. She could not say: Perhaps if you spent less time with your mistresses we might be successful. She had begun to wonder whether it was possible for Henry to beget a child. Some said that this could be a result of a life of debauchery. She could only vaguely visualize what went on during those orgies in which her husband indulged. Was it possible that the life he had led had rendered him sterile?

She glanced at him; did she imagine this or had his gaze become a little furtive? Had he really begun to make plans to rid himself of her?

So she was afraid. She realized that she was often afraid. She dared not state frankly what was in her mind.

Instead she said: 'There is trouble at my father's Court.'

He nodded and made a little grimace. 'It would seem that there must be trouble when a King has children by two wives. We have an example here at home.'

'None could prevent your taking the crown, Henry.'

'My stepmother will do her utmost, never fear. She is already making plans for her little Alfonso and Isabella. It is a dangerous thing when a King's wife dies and he takes another ... that is, when there are children of both first and second unions.'

'I think, Henry, that my stepmother is even more ambitious than yours.'

'She could scarcely be that; but let us say that she has as high hopes for her little Ferdinand as mine has for Alfonso and Isabella.'

'I have news from home that she dotes on the child, and that she has influenced my father to do the same. Already I hear that he loves the infant Ferdinand more than Carlos, myself and Eleanor combined.'

'She is a strong woman and your father is her slave. But never fear, Carlos is of an age to guard that which is his – as I am.'

Blanche shivered. 'Henry, I am so glad I am not there ... at my father's Court.'

'Do you never feel homesick?'

'Castile became my home when we were married. I have no other home than this.'

'My dear,' he said lightly, 'it makes me happy that you should feel thus.'

But he was not looking at her. He was not a man who cared to inflict cruelty; indeed he would go to great lengths to avoid anything which was unpleasant. That was why he found it difficult to face her now.

She was trembling in spite of her endeavours to appear calm. What would happen to her if she were sent back to her father's Court, she wondered. She would be disgraced, humiliated – a repudiated wife. Carlos would be kind to her, for Carlos was the kindest of men. Eleanor would not be there, for her marriage with Gaston de Foix had taken her to France. Her father would not be her friend, for his affection was all for the brilliant and attractive Joan Henriquez who had given him young Ferdinand.

Carlos had inherited the Kingdom of Navarre from his mother; and, should Carlos die without heirs, Navarre would fall to Blanche herself as her mother, who had been the widow of Martin, King of Sicily, and daughter of Charles III of Navarre, had left Navarre to her children, excluding her husband from its possession.

She had, however, stated in her will that Carlos should, in governing the Kingdom, seek the good will and approbation of his father.

On his inheritance Carlos, since his father had not wished to give up the title of King of Navarre, had allowed him to keep it, but insisted that it was his own right to rule Navarre, which he did as its Governor.

So at this time Blanche was the heir of Carlos; and if he should die without issue, the right to govern Navarre would be hers, as also would be the crown.

She was foolish perhaps to let these fancies upset her; but she had a premonition that some terrible evil would befall her if she were ever forced to return to Aragon.

Here she felt safe. Henry was her unfaithful husband; she had failed to give him children, which was the whole purpose of marriages such as theirs; yet Henry was kind to her. Indolent, lecherous, shallow, he might be, but he would never use physical violence against her. And how could she know what would befall her if she returned to her father's Court?

Now he was smiling at her almost tenderly.

Surely, she thought, he could not smile at me like that unless he had some affection for me. Perhaps, like myself, he remembers the days when we were first married; that must be why he smiles at me so kindly.

But Henry, although he continued to smile, was scarcely aware of her. He was thinking of the new wife he would have when he had rid himself of poor, useless Blanche; she would naturally be young, this new wife, someone whom he could mould to his own sensual pleasure.

Once my father is dead, he told himself, I shall have my freedom.

He took Blanche's hand and led her to the window. They looked out and saw that he had been right when he had said the people were beginning to gather down there. They were waiting impatiently. They longed to hear that the old King was dead and that a new era had begun.

The King asked his physician, Cibdareal, to come closer.

'My friend,' he whispered, 'it cannot be much longer.'

'Preserve your strength, Highness,' begged the physician.

'Of what use? That I may live a few minutes more? Ah, Cibdareal, I should have lived a happier life, I should be a happier man now if I had been born the son of a mechanic, instead of the son of the King of Castile. Send for the Queen. Send for my son Henry.'

They were brought to his bedside and he looked at them quizzically.

The Queen's eyes were wild. She does not regret the passing of her husband, thought the King; she regrets only the passing of power. 'Holy Mother,' he prayed, 'keep her sane. Then she will be a good mother to our little ones. She will look after their rights. Let not the cares, which will now be hers, drive her the way her ancestors have gone . . . before her children are of age to care for themselves.'

And Henry? Henry was looking at him with the utmost compassion, but Henry's fingers he knew were itching to seize the power which would shortly be his.

'Henry, my son,' said John, 'we have not always been the best of friends. I regret that.'

'I too regret, Father.'

'But let us not brood on an unhappy past. I think of the future. I leave two young children, Henry.'

'Yes, Father.'

'Never forget that they are your brother and sister.'

'I will not forget.'

'Look after them well. I have made provision for them, but they will need your protection.'

'They shall have it, Father.'

'You have given me your sacred promise and I can now go to my rest content. Respect my children's mother.'

'I will.'

The King said that he was tired, and his son and second wife moved away from the bed while the priests came forward.

Within half an hour the news was spreading through the Palace:

'King John II is dead. Henry IV is now King of Castile.'

The Queen was ready to leave the Palace.

Her women were clustered about her; one carried the baby in her arms; another grasped the hand of Isabella.

Muffled in her black cloak the little girl waited – listening, watching.

The Queen was in a mood of suppressed excitement, which caused Isabella great anxiety.

She listened to her mother's shrill voice. 'Everything must appear to be normal. No one must guess that we are going away. I have my children to protect.'

'Yes, Highness,' was the answer.

But Isabella had heard the women talking: 'Why should we go as though we are fugitives? Why should we run from the new King? Is she mad ... already? King Henry knows we are leaving. He makes no effort to detain us. It is of no consequence to him whether we stay here or go away. But we must go as though the armies of Castile are in pursuit of us.'

'Hush ... hush.... She will hear.' And then, the whispers: 'The little Isabella is all ears. Do not be deceived because she stands so quietly.'

So he would not hurt us, thought Isabella. Of course dear Henry would never hurt us. But why does my mother think he would?

She was lifted in the arms of a groom and set upon a horse. The journey had begun.

So the Queen and her children left Madrid for the lonely castle of Arevalo.

Isabella remembered little of the journey; the movement of the horse and the warm arms of the groom lulled her to sleep, and when she awoke it was to find herself in her new home.

Early next day her mother came into that apartment in which Isabella had slept, and in her arms she carried the sleeping Alfonso, and with her were two of her trusted attendants.

The Queen set Alfonso on the bed beside his sister. Then she clenched her fists together in the well-remembered gesture and raised her arms above her head as though she were invoking the saints.

Isabella saw her lips move and realized that she was praying. It seemed wrong to be lying in bed while her mother prayed, and Isabella wondered what to do. She half rose, but one of the women shook her head vigorously to warn her to remain where she was.

Now the Queen was speaking so that Isabella could hear her.

'Here I shall care for them. Here I shall bring them up so that when the time comes they will be ready to meet their destiny. It will come. It will surely come. He will never beget a child. It is God's punishment for the evil life he has led.'

Alfonso's little fingers had curled themselves about Isabella's. She wanted to cry because she was afraid; but she lay still, watching her mother, her blue eyes never betraying for a second that this lonely place which was now to be her home, and the rising hysteria in her mother, terrified her and filled her with a foreboding which she was too young to understand.

JOANNA OF PORTUGAL, QUEEN
OF CASTILE

JOHN PACHECO, Marquis of Villena, was on his way
to answer a summons from the King.

He was delighted with the turn of events. From the time
he had come to Court – his family had sent him to serve with
Alvaro de Luna and he had entered the household of that
influential man as one of his pages – he had attracted the
notice of the young Henry, heir to the throne, who was now
King of Castile.

Henry had delighted in the friendship of Villena, and
John, Henry's father, had honoured him for his service to the
Prince. He had been clever and was in possession of great
territories in the districts of Toledo, Valencia and Murcia.
And now that his friend Henry was King he foresaw greater
glories.

On his way to the council chamber he met his uncle, Alfonso Carillo, Archbishop of Toledo, and they greeted each
other affectionately. They were both aware that together they
made a formidable pair.

'Good day to you, Marquis,' said the Archbishop. 'I believe we are set for the same destination.'

'Henry requested me to attend him at this hour,' answered
Villena. 'There is a matter of the greatest importance which
he desires to discuss before making his wishes publicly
known.'

The Archbishop nodded. 'He wants to ask our advice,
nephew, before taking a certain step.'

'You know what it is?'

'I can guess. He has long been weary of her.'

'It is time she returned to Aragon.'

'I am sure,' said the Archbishop, 'that you, my wise nephew, would wish to see an alliance in a certain quarter.'

'Portugal?'

'Exactly. The lady is a sister of Alfonso V, and I have heard nothing but praise of her personal charms. And let us not dismiss these assets as frivolous. We know our Henry. He will welcome a beautiful bride; and it is very necessary that he should welcome her with enthusiasm. That is the best way to ensure a fruitful union.'

'There must be a *fruitful* union.'

'I agree it is imperative for Castile ... for Henry ... and for us.'

'You have no need to tell me. I know our enemies have their eyes on Arevalo.'

'Have you heard news of events there?'

'There is very little to be learned,' Villena replied. 'The Dowager is there with her two children. They are living quietly, and my friends there inform me that the lady has been more serene of late. There have been no hysterical scenes at all. She believes herself to be safe, and is biding her time; and, while this is so, she devotes herself to the care of her children. Poor Isabella! Alfonso is too young as yet to suffer from such rigorous treatment. I hear it is prayers ... prayers all the time. Prayers, I suppose, that the little lady may be good and worthy of any great destiny which may befall her.'

'At least the Dowager can do little mischief there.'

'But, uncle, we must be ever watchful. Henry is ours and we are his. He must please his people or there will be those ready to call for his abdication and the setting up of young Alfonso. There are many in this kingdom who would be pleased to see the crown on Alfonso's baby brow. A Regency! You know how seekers after power could wish for nothing better than that.'

'I know. I know. And our first task is to rid the King of his present wife and provide him with a new one. When the heir is born a fatal blow will have been struck at the hopes of the Dowager of Arevalo. Then it will matter little what she teaches her Alfonso and Isabella.'

'You have heard of course . . .' began Villena.

'The rumours . . . indeed yes. The King is said to be impotent, and it is due to him – not Blanche – that the marriage is unfruitful. That may be. But let us jump our hurdles when we reach them, eh? And now . . . here we are.'

The page announced them, and Henry came forward to meet them, which was characteristic of Henry; and whilst this show of familiarity pleased both men they deplored it as unworthy of the ancient traditions of Castile.

'Marquis! Archbishop!' cried Henry as they bowed before him. 'I am glad you are here.' He waved his hand, signifying to his attendants that he wished to be entirely alone with his two ministers. 'Now to business,' he went on. 'You know why I have asked you here.'

The Marquis said: 'Dearest Sire, we can guess. You wish to serve Castile, and to do this you have to take steps which are disagreeable to you. We offer our respectful condolence and assistance.'

'I am sorry for the Queen,' said Henry, lifting his hands in a helpless gesture. 'But what can I do for her? Archbishop, do you think it will be possible to obtain a divorce?'

'Anticipating your commands, Highness, I have given great consideration to this matter, and I am sure the Bishop of Segovia will support my plan.'

'My uncle has solved our problem, Highness,' said Villena, determined that, while the Archbishop received the King's grateful thanks, he himself should not be forgotten as chief conspirator.

'My dear Archbishop! My dear, dear Villena! I pray you tell me what you have arranged.'

The Archbishop said: 'A divorce could be granted *por impotencia respectiva.*'

'Could this be so?'

'The marriage has been unfruitful, Highness.'

'But...'

'There need be no slur on the royal virility, Highness. We might say that some malign influence brought about this unhappy state of affairs.'

'Malign influence?'

'It could be construed as witchcraft. We will not go too deeply into that, but we feel sure that all would agree, in the circumstances, that Your Highness should repudiate your present wife and take another.'

'And Segovia is prepared to declare the marriage null and void!'

'He will do that,' said the Archbishop. 'I myself will confirm it.'

Henry laughed. 'There could surely not be a better reason.' He repeated. '*Por impotencia respectiva....*' And then: 'Some malign influence.'

'Let us not worry further on that point,' said Villena. 'I have here a picture of a delectable female.'

Henry's eyes became glazed as he looked at the picture of a pretty young girl, which Villena handed him; his lips curved into a lascivious smile. 'But ... she is enchanting!'

'Enchanting and eligible, Highness, being none other than Joanna, Princess of Portugal, sister of Alfonso V, the reigning monarch.'

'I can scarcely wait,' said Henry, 'for her arrival in Castile.'

'Then, Sire, we have your permission to go ahead with these arrangements?'

'My dear friends, you have not only my permission; you have my most urgent command.'

The Marquis and the Archbishop were smiling contentedly as they left the royal apartments.

The Queen begged an audience with the King. One of her

women had brought the news to her that the Marquis and the Archbishop had been closeted with the King, and that their discussion must have been very secret, as the apartments had been cleared before it began.

Henry received her with warmth. The fact that he would soon be rid of her made him almost fond of her.

'Why, Blanche my dear,' he said, 'you look distressed.'

'I have had strange dreams, Henry. They frightened me.'

'My dear, it is folly to be afraid of dreams in daylight.'

'They persist, Henry. It is almost as though I have a premonition of evil.'

He led her to a chair and made her sit down, while he leaned over her and laid a gentle and caressing hand on her shoulder.

'You must banish these premonitions, Blanche. What harm could come to the Queen of Castile?'

'There is a feeling within me, Henry, that I may not long be the Queen of Castile.'

'You think there is a plot afoot to murder me? Ah, my dear, you have been brooding about the Dowager of Arevalo. You imagine that her friends will dispatch me so that her little Alfonso shall have my crown. Have no fear. She could not harm me, if she would.'

'I was not thinking of her, Henry.'

'Then what is there to fear?'

'We have no children.'

'We must endeavour to remedy that.'

'Henry, you mean this?'

'You fret too much. You are over-anxious. Perhaps that is why you fail.'

She wanted to say: 'But am I the one who fails, Henry? Are you sure of that?' But she did not. That would anger him, and if he were angry he might blame her; and who could say what might grow out of such blame?

'We must have a child,' she said desperately.

'Calm yourself, Blanche. All will be well with you. You have allowed your dreams to upset you.'

'I dream of going back to Aragon. Why should I dream that, Henry? Is not Castile my home!'

'Castile is your home.'

'I dream of being there ... in the apartment I used to occupy. I dream that they are there ... my family ... my father, Eleanor, my stepmother holding little Ferdinand – and they approach my bed. I think they are going to do me some harm. Carlos is somewhere in the Palace and I cannot reach him.'

'Dreams, my dear Blanche, what are dreams?'

'I am foolish to give them a thought, but I wish they did not come. The Marquis and the Archbishop were with you, Henry. I hope they had good news for you.'

'Very good news, my dear.'

She looked at him eagerly; but he would not meet her gaze; and because she knew him so well, that fact terrified her.

'You have a great opinion of those two,' she said.

'They are astute – and my friends. I know that.'

'I suppose you would put their suggestions to a Council ... before you accept them.'

'You should not worry your head with state affairs, my dear.'

'So it was state affairs that they discussed with you.'

'It was.'

'Henry, I know I have been an unsatisfactory wife to you because of my inability to bear children, but I love you and I have been very happy in Castile.'

Henry took her hands and drew her to her feet. He put his lips to her forehead and then, putting an arm about her shoulders, he led her to the door.

It was her dismissal.

It was kindly; it was courteous. He could not treat me thus, she assured herself, if he were planning to rid himself of me. But as she went back to her own apartments she felt very unsure.

When she had gone, Henry frowned. He thought: One of them will have to break the news to her. The Archbishop is the more suitable. Once she knows, I shall never see her again.

He was sorry for her, but he would not allow himself to be saddened.

She would return to her father's Court of Aragon. She had her family to comfort her.

He picked up the picture of Joanna of Portugal. So young! Innocent? He was not sure. At least there was a promise of sensuality in that laughing mouth.

'How long?' he murmured. 'How long before Blanche goes back to Aragon, and Joanna is here in her place?'

The procession was ready to set out from Lisbon, but the Princess Joanna felt no pangs at leaving her home; she was eager to reach Castile, where she believed she was going to enjoy her new life.

Etiquette at the Court of Castile would be solemn, after the manner of the Castilians, but she had heard that her future husband entertained lavishly and that he lived in the midst of splendour. He was a man devoted to feminine society and, if he had many mistresses, Joanna assured herself that that was due to the fact that Blanche of Aragon was so dull and unattractive.

But she had no intention of putting too strong a curb upon him. She was not herself averse to a little amorous adventuring; and if Henry strayed now and then from the marriage bed she would not dream of reproaching him, for if she were lenient with him so must he be with her, and she foresaw an exciting life in Castile.

Here in Lisbon she was, in her opinion, too well guarded.

Therefore it was with few regrets that she prepared to

leave. She could look from the windows of the castle of São
Jorge on to the town and say goodbye quite happily. She had
little love for the town, with its old cathedral, close to which
it was said that St Anthony was born. The saints of Lisbon
meant little to her. What cared she if after his martyrdom
Saint Vicente's body was brought to Lisbon along the Tagus
in a boat which was guided by two black crows? What did
she care if the spirit of St Anthony was supposed to live on
and help those who had lost something dear to them to recover it? These were merely legends to her.

So she turned away from the window and the view of olive
and fig trees, of the Alcaçova where the Arab rulers had once
lived, of the mossy tiles of the Alfama district and the glistening stream of the Tagus.

Gladly would she say farewell to all that had been home,
for in the new land to which she was going she would be a
Queen – Queen of Castile.

Soon they would depart, travelling eastwards to the
border.

Her eyes were glistening as she took the mirror which was
held to her by her maid of honour; she looked over her
shoulder at the girl, whose eyes danced as merrily as her
own.

'So, Alegre, you too are happy to go to Castile?'

'I am happy, my lady,' answered the girl.

'You will have to behave with decorum there, you know.'

Alegre smiled mischievously. She was a bold creature, and
Joanna, who herself was bold and fond of gaiety, had chosen
her for this reason. Her nickname, Alegre, had been given
her some years before by one of the Spanish attendants: the
gay one.

Alegre had had adventures; some she recounted; some she
did not.

Joanna grimaced at the girl. 'When I am Queen I must
become very severe.'

'You will never be that with me, my lady. How could you

be severe with one who is as like yourself in her ways as that
reflection is like your own face?'

'I may have to change my ways.'

'They say the King, your husband, is very gay . . .'

'That is because he has never had a wife to satisfy him.'

Alegre smiled secretly. 'Let us hope that, when he has a
wife who satisfies him, he will still be gay.'

'I shall watch you, Alegre, and if you are wicked I shall
send you home.'

Alegre put her head on one side. 'Well, there are some
charming gentlemen at your brother's Court, my lady.'

'Come,' said Joanna. 'It is time we left. They are waiting
for us down there.'

Alegre curtsied and stood aside for Joanna to pass through
the apartment.

Then she followed her down to the courtyard, where the
gaily-caparisoned horses and the loads of baggage were ready
to begin the journey from Lisbon to Castile.

Before Joanna began the journey Blanche had set out for
Aragon.

It seemed to her that the nightmare had become a reality,
for in her dreams she had feared exactly this.

It was twelve years since she had left her home to be the
bride of Henry; then she had been fearful, even as she was
now. But she had left Aragon as the bride of the heir to
Castile; her family had approved of the match, and she had
seen no reason why her life should end in failure.

But how different it had been, making that journey as a
bride, from returning as a repudiated wife, one who had
failed to provide the necessary heir to a throne.

She thought now of that moment when she had been no
longer able to hide the truth from herself, when the Archbishop had stood before her and announced that her marriage
was annulled *por impotencia respectiva*.

She had wanted to protest bitterly. She had wanted to cry

out: 'What use to throw me aside? It will be the same with any other woman. Henry cannot beget children.'

They would not have listened to her, and she could have done her cause no good. What was the use of protesting? She could only listen dully and, when she was alone, throw herself upon her bed and stare at the ceiling, recalling the perfidy of Henry who, at the very time when he was planning to be rid of her, had implied that they would always be together.

She was to return to her family, who would have no use for her. Her father had changed since his second marriage; he was completely under the spell of her stepmother. All they cared for was the advancement of little Ferdinand.

And what would happen to her ... she who would have no friend in the world but her brother Carlos? And what was happening to Carlos now? He was at odds with his father, and that was due to the jealousy of his stepmother.

What will become of me at my father's Court? she asked herself as she made the long and tedious journey to the home of her childhood; and it seemed to her then that the nightmares she had suffered had been no dreams; when she had been tortured by them she had been given a glimpse of the future.

Life in the Palace of Arevalo had been going smoothly.

We are happier here, thought young Isabella, than we were in Madrid. Everybody here seems serene and not afraid any more.

It was true. There had been none of those frightening interludes when the Queen lost control of her feelings. There was even laughter in the Palace.

Lessons were regular, of course, but Isabella was quite happy to receive lessons. She knew she had to learn if she were to be ready for her great destiny. Life ran to a set of rules. She rose early and retired early. There were many prayers during the day, and Isabella had heard some of the women complaining that to live at Arevalo was to live in a nunnery.

Isabella was contented with her nunnery. As long as they could live like this and her mother was quietly happy and not frightened, Isabella could be happy.

Alfonso was developing a personality of his own. He was no longer a gurgling, kicking baby. It was a great pleasure to watch him take his first steps, Isabella holding out her arms to catch him should he stumble. Sometimes they played these games with one of the women; sometimes with the Dowager Queen herself, who occasionally would pick up the little boy and hug him tightly. Then the ever alert Isabella would watch her mother for the tell-tale twitching of the mouth. But Alfonso would utter lusty protests at being held too tightly, and often an emotional scene was avoided in this way.

Isabella missed her father; she missed her brother Henry; but she could be happy like this if only she could keep her mother quiet and contented.

One day she said: 'Let us stay like this . . . always. . . .'

But the Dowager Queen's lips had tightened and begun to twitch, so that Isabella realized her mistake.

'You have a great destiny,' began the Dowager Queen. 'Why, this baby here . . .'

That was when she picked up Alfonso and held him so tightly that he protested, and so, fortunately, his protests diverted the Queen from what she was about to say.

This was a lesson. It showed how easily one could stumble into pitfalls. Isabella was aghast on realizing that she, whose great desire was to avoid hysterical scenes, had almost, by a thoughtless remark, precipitated one of them.

She must never cease to be watchful and must not be deceived by the apparent peace of Arevalo.

There came a terrifying day when their mother visited the two children in the nursery.

Isabella knew at once that something unfortunate had occurred, and her heart began to hammer in an uncomfortable way. Alfonso was, of course, unaware that anything was wrong.

He threw himself at his mother and was picked up in her arms. The Queen stood holding him strained against her, and when Alfonso began to wriggle she did not release him.

'Highness . . .' he cried, and because he was proud to be able to say the word he repeated it. 'Highness . . . Highness. . . .'

It seemed to Isabella that Alfonso was shouting. That was because everything was so quiet in the apartment.

'My son,' said the Queen, 'one day you will be King of Castile. There is no doubt of it.'

'Highness . . . you hurt me . . .' whimpered Alfonso.

Isabella wanted to run to her mother and explain that she was holding Alfonso too tightly, and to remind her how much happier they were when they did not talk about the future King or Queen of Castile.

To Isabella it seemed that the Queen stood there a long time, staring into the future, but it could not have been more than a few seconds, or Alfonso's whimper would have become a loud protest.

Meanwhile the Queen said nothing; she stared before her, looking angry and determined, as Isabella remembered so well to have seen her in the past.

Then the little girl could bear it no longer; perhaps because it was so long since she had had to restrain herself, or because she was so very eager to preserve the peace of Arevalo.

She went to her mother and curtsied very low. Then she said: 'Highness, I think Alfonso is hungry.'

'Hungry, Highness,' wailed Alfonso. 'Highness hurts Alfonso.'

The Queen continued to stare ahead, ignoring their appeal.

'He has married again,' she resumed. 'He thinks he will

beget a child. But he never will. How could he? It is impossible. It is the just reward for the life he has led.'

It was the old theme which Isabella had heard many times before; it was a reminder of the past; it warned her that the peace of Arevalo could be shattered in a moment.

'Alfonso hungry,' wailed the boy.

'My son,' the Queen repeated, 'one day you shall be King of Castile. One day . . .'

'Don't want to be King,' cried Alfonso. 'Highness squeezing him.'

'Highness,' whispered Isabella earnestly, 'shall we show you how far Alfonso can walk by himself?'

'Let them try!' cried the Queen. 'They will see. Let them try! The whole of Castile will be laughing at them.'

Then, to Isabella's relief, she set Alfonso on his feet. He looked at his arms and whimpered.

Isabella took his hand and whispered: 'Walk, Alfonso. Show Highness.'

Alfonso nodded gleefully.

But the Queen had begun to laugh.

Alfonso looked at his mother and crowed with pleasure. He did not understand that there were more kinds of laughter than one. Alfonso only knew about laughing for amusement or happiness, but Isabella knew this was the frightening laughter. After the long peace it had returned.

One of the women had heard and came into the apartment. She looked at the two children, standing there watching their mother. Then she retired and very soon a physician came into the room.

Now the Queen was laughing so much that she could not stop. The tears were running down her cheeks. Alfonso was laughing too; he turned to Isabella to make sure that she was joining in the fun.

'Highness,' said the physician, 'if you will come to your bedchamber I will give you a potion which will enable you to rest.'

But the Queen went on laughing; her arms had begun to wave about wildly. Another physician had now joined them.

With him was a woman, and Isabella heard his quiet order. 'Take the children away ... immediately.'

But before they went, Isabella saw her mother on the couch, and the two doctors holding her there, while they murmured soothing words about rest and potions.

There was no escape, thought Isabella, even at Arevalo. She was glad Alfonso was so young that, as soon as he no longer saw his mother, he forgot the scene they had just witnessed; she was glad that he was too young to understand what it might mean.

Henry was happy in those first weeks of his marriage. He had arranged ceremonies and pageants of such extravagance as had rarely been seen before in Castile. So far he had not displeased his subjects, and when he rode among them at the head of some glittering cavalcade, towering above most of his retinue, his crown on his red hair, they cheered him vociferously. He knew how to dispense smiles and greetings so that they fell on all, rich and poor alike.

'There is a King,' said the people of Castile, 'the like of whom we have not seen for many a year.'

Some had witnessed the departure of Blanche and had pitied her. She looked so forlorn, poor lady.

But, it was agreed, the King had his duties to Castile. Queen Blanche was sterile, and however virtuous queens may be, virtue is no substitute for fertility.

'Poor Henry!' they sighed. 'How sad he must be to have to divorce her. Yet he considers his duty to Castile before his own inclination.'

As for Henry he had scarcely thought of Blanche since she had left. He had been delighted to dismiss her from his thoughts, and when he saw his new wife his spirits had soared.

He, who was a connoisseur of women, recognized something beyond her beauty ... a deep sensuality which might match his own, or at least come near to it.

During those first weeks of marriage he scarcely left her. In public she delighted his subjects; in private she was equally satisfactory to him.

There could not have been a woman more unlike poor Blanche. How glad he was that he had had the courage to rid himself of her.

Behind the sparkling eyes of the new Queen there was a certain purpose, but that was not evident as yet. Joanna was content at first merely to play the wife who was eager to please her husband.

Attended by the maids of honour whom she had brought with her from Lisbon, she was always the centre of attraction. Full of energy, she planned balls and pageants of her own to compete with those which the King gave in her honour, so that it appeared that the wedding celebrations would go on for a very long time.

Always to the fore among those who surrounded the new Queen was Alegre. Her dancing, her spontaneous laughter, her joy in being alive, were already beginning to attract attention.

Joanna watched her with some amusement.

'Have you found a Castilian lover yet?' she asked.

'I think so, Highness.'

'Pray tell me his name.'

'It would scarcely be fair to him, Highness, for he does not yet know of the delights in store for him.'

'Am I to presume that this man has not yet become your lover?'

'That is so,' answered Alegre demurely.

'Then he must be a laggard, for if you have decided, why should he hold back?'

'Who shall say?' murmured Alegre. Then she laughed and went on: 'It is a great pleasure to all of us who serve Your Highness to note how devoted the King is to you. I have heard that he has had hundreds of mistresses, yet when he is with you he is like a young man in love for the first time.'

'My dear Alegre, I am not like you. I would not tolerate laggards in love.'

Alegre put her head on one side and went on: 'His Highness is so enamoured of you that he seems to have forgotten those two cronies of his, Villena and the Archbishop ... almost.'

'Those two!' said the Queen. 'They are for ever at his elbow.'

'Whispering advice,' added Alegre. 'I wonder if they have advised him how to treat *you*. It would not surprise me. I fancy the King does little without their approval. I believe he has become accustomed to listening to his two dear friends.'

Joanna was silent, but she later remembered that conversation. She was faintly irritated by those two friends and advisers of the King. He thought too highly of them and she considered he was ridiculously subservient to them.

That night, when she and the King lay together in their bed, she mentioned them.

'I fancy those two are possessed of certain conceits.'

'Let us not concern ourselves with them,' the King answered.

'But, Henry, I would not see you humbled by any of your subjects.'

'I ... humbled by Villena and Carillo! My dear Joanna, that is not possible.'

'They sometimes behave as though they are the masters. I consider that humiliating for you.'

'Oh ... you have been listening to their enemies.'

'I have drawn my own conclusions.'

He made a gesture which indicated that there were more interesting occupations than discussing his ministers. But Joanna was adamant. She believed those two were watching her too intently, that they expected her to listen to their advice, or even instructions, simply because they had played some part in bringing her to Castile. She was not going to tolerate that; and now, while Henry was so infatuated with her, was the time to force him to curb their power.

So she ignored his gestures and sat up in bed, clasping her knees, while she told him that it was absurd for a King to give too much power to one or two men in his kingdom.

Henry yawned. For the first time he was afraid she was going to be one of those tiresome, meddling women, and that would be disappointing, as in many ways she was proving to be satisfactory.

It was the next day when, making his way to his wife's apartment, he encountered Alegre.

They were alone in one of the ante-rooms and Alegre dropped a demure curtsy at his approach. She remained with her head bowed, but as he was about to pass on she lifted her eyes to his face, and there was a look in them which made him halt.

He said: 'You are happy here in Castile?'

'So happy, Highness. But never so happy as at this moment when I have the undivided attention of the King.'

'My dear,' said Henry with that characteristic and easy familiarity, 'it takes little to make you happy.'

She took his hand and kissed it, and as she did so she again raised her eyes to his. They were full of provocative suggestion which it was impossible for a man of Henry's temperament to ignore.

'I have often noticed you in the Queen's company,' he said, 'and it has given me great pleasure to see you here with us.'

She continued to smile at him.

'Please rise,' he continued.

She did so, while he looked down at her neat, trim figure with the eyes of a connoisseur. He knew her type. She was hot-blooded and eager. That look was unmistakable. She was studying him in a manner which he might have considered insolent if she had not possessed such superb attractions.

He patted her cheek and his hand dropped to her neck.

Then suddenly he seized her and kissed her on the lips. He had not been mistaken. Her response was immediate, and that brief contact told him a good deal.

She was ready and eager to become his mistress; and she was not the sort of woman who would seek to dabble in state matters; there was only one thing of real importance in her life. That short embrace told him that.

He released her and went on his way.

Both of them knew that, although that was their first embrace, it would not be their last.

Under the carved ceiling in the light of a thousand candles the King was dancing, and his partner was the Queen's maid of honour.

Joanna watched them.

The woman would not dare! she told herself as she recalled a conversation concerning Alegre's lover, who had not then known the role which was waiting for him. The impudence! I could send her back to Lisbon tomorrow. Does she not know that?

But she was mistaken. Alegre was by nature lecherous, and so was Henry; they betrayed it as they danced, and when two such people danced together ... But that was the point. When two such people as Alegre and Henry were together there could be but one outcome.

She would speak to Henry tonight. She would speak to Alegre.

She was not aware that she was frowning, nor that a young man whom she had noticed on several occasions had come to take his stand close to her chair.

He was tall – almost as tall as Henry, whose height was exceptional. He was strikingly handsome with his blue-black hair, and eyes which were brilliantly dark; and yet his skin was fairer than red-headed Henry's. Joanna had considered him as one of the handsomest men at her husband's Court.

'Your Highness is troubled?' he asked. 'I wondered if there was aught I could do to take the frown from your exquisite brow.'

She smiled at him. 'Troubled! Indeed I am not. I was thinking that this is one of the most pleasant balls I have attended since coming to Castile.'

'Your Highness must forgive me. On every occasion when I have had the honour to be in your company I have been deeply conscious of your mood. When you smiled I was contented; when I fancy I see you frown I long to eliminate the cause of that frown. Is that impertinence, Highness?'

Joanna surveyed him. He spoke to her with the deference due to the Queen, but he did not attempt to disguise the admiration she aroused in him. Joanna hovered between disapproval and the desire to hear more from him. She forgave him. The manners of Henry's Court were set by the King; as a result they had grown somewhat uninhibited.

She glanced towards the dancers and saw Henry's hand was laid on Alegre's shoulder caressingly.

'She is an insolent woman ... that!' said the young man angrily.

'Sir?' she reproved.

'I crave Your Highness's pardon. I allowed my feelings to get the better of me.'

Joanna decided that she liked him and that she wanted to keep him beside her.

'I myself often allow my feelings to get the better of the dignity expected of a Queen,' she said.

'In such circumstances ...' he went on hotly. 'But, what amazes me is – how is this possible?'

'You refer to the King's flirtation with my woman? I know him; I know her. I can assure you there is nothing to be amazed about.'

'The King has always been devoted to the ladies.'

'I had heard that before I came.'

'It was once understandable. But with such a Queen. . . . Highness, you must excuse me.'

'Your feelings have the upper hand again. They must be strong and violent indeed to be able to subdue your good manners.'

'They are very strong, Highness.' His dark eyes were warm with adoration. She forgave Henry; she even forgave Alegre, because if they had not been so overcome by desire for each other she would not at this moment be accepting the attentions of this very handsome young man.

He was, she congratulated herself, far more handsome than the King; he was younger too, and the marks of debauchery had not yet begun to show on *his* features. Joanna had always said that if she allowed the King to go his own way, she would go hers, and she could imagine herself going along a very pleasant way with this young man.

'I would know the name,' she said, 'of the young man of such powerful passions.'

'It is Beltran de la Cueva, who places himself body and soul in the service of Your Highness.'

'Thank you,' she said. 'I am tired of looking on at the dance.' She stood up and put her hand in his; and while she danced with Beltran de la Cueva, Joanna forgot to watch the conduct of the King and her maid of honour.

The Queen was in her apartment, and her ladies were preparing her for bed.

She noticed that Alegre was not among them.

The sly jade! she thought. But at least she has the decency not to present herself before me tonight.

She asked one of the others where the girl was.

'Highness, she had a headache, and asked us, if you should notice her absence, to crave your pardon for not attending. She felt so giddy she could scarce keep on her feet.'

'She is excused,' said the Queen. 'She should be warned though to take greater care on these occasions.'

'I shall give her your warning, Highness.'

'Tell her that if she becomes careless of her ... health, it might be necessary to send her back to Lisbon. Perhaps her native air would be beneficial to her.'

'That will alarm her, Highness. She is in love with Castile.'

'I thought I had noticed it,' said the Queen.

She was ready now for her bed. They would lead her to it and, when she was settled, leave her. Shortly afterwards the King, having been similarly prepared by his attendants, would come to her as he had every night since their marriage.

But before her ladies had left her, the King's messenger arrived.

His Highness was a little indisposed and would not be visiting the Queen that night. He sent her his devoted affection and his wishes that she would pass a good night.

'Pray tell His Highness,' she said, 'that I am deeply concerned that he should be indisposed. I shall come along and see that he has all he needs. Although I am his Queen, I am also his wife, and I believe it is a wife's duty to nurse her husband through any sickness.'

The messenger said hastily that His Highness was only slightly indisposed, and had been given a sleeping draught by his physician. If this were to be efficacious he should not be disturbed until morning.

'How glad I am that I told you of my intentions,' declared Joanna. 'I should have been most unhappy if I had disturbed him.'

The King's messenger was ushered out of the Queen's bedchamber, and her ladies, more silently than usual, completed the ceremony of putting her to bed and left her.

She lay for some time contemplating this new state of affairs.

She was very angry. It was so humiliating to be neglected for her maid of honour; and she was sure that this was what was happening.

What should she do about it? Confront Henry with her discovery? Make sure that it did not occur again?

But could she do this? She had begun to understand her husband. He was weak; he was indolent; he wanted to preserve the peace at all costs. At all costs? At almost all costs. He was as single-minded as a lion or any other wild animal when in pursuit of his lust. How far would he allow her to interfere when it was a matter of separating him from a new mistress?

She had heard the story of her predecessor. Up to the last poor Blanche had thought she was safe, but Henry had not scrupled to send her away. Blanche had had twelve years' experience of this man and she, Joanna, was a newcomer to Castile. Perhaps she would be unwise to unleash her anger. Perhaps she should wait and see how best she could revenge herself on her unfaithful husband and disloyal maid of honour.

She was, however, determined to discover whether they were together this night.

She rose from her bed, put on a wrap and went into that apartment next to her own where her women attendants slept.

'Highness!' Several of them had sat up in their beds, alarm in their voices.

She said: 'Do not be alarmed. One of you, please bring me a goblet of wine. I am thirsty.'

'Yes, Highness.'

Someone had gone in search of the wine, and Joanna returned to her room. She had made her discovery; the bed which should have been occupied by Alegre was empty.

The wine was brought to her, and she gazed absently at the flickering candlelight playing on the tapestried walls, while she drank a little and began to plot some form of retaliation.

She was very angry to think that she, Joanna of Portugal, had been passed over for one of her servants.

'She shall be sent back to Lisbon,' she muttered. 'No matter what he says. I shall insist. Perhaps Villena and the Archbishop will be with me in this. After all, do they not wish that I shall soon be with child?'

And then she heard the soft notes of a lute playing beneath her window, and as she listened the lute-player broke into a love song which she had heard at the ball on this very night.

The words were those of a lover, sighing for his mistress, declaring that he would prefer death to repudiation by her.

She took the candle and went to the window.

Below was the young man who had spoken to her so passionately at the ball. For a few moments they gazed at each other in silence; then he began to sing again in a deep voice, vibrating and passionate.

The Queen went back to her bed.

What was happening in some apartment of this Palace between her husband and her maid of honour was now of small importance to her. Her thoughts were full of Beltran de la Cueva.

THE BETROTHAL OF ISABELLA

ISABELLA was aroused from her sleep. She sat up in bed telling herself that surely it was not morning yet, for it was too dark.

'Wake up, Isabella.'

That was her mother's voice and it sent shivers of apprehension through her. And there was her mother, holding a candle in its sconce, her hair flowing about her shoulders, her eyes enormous in her pale wild face.

Isabella began to tremble. 'Highness . . .' she began. 'Is it morning?'

'No, no. You have been asleep only an hour or so. There is wonderful news – so wonderful that I could not find it in my heart not to wake you that you might hear of it.'

'News . . . for me, Highness?'

'Why, what a sleepy child you are. You should be dancing for joy. This wonderful news has just arrived from Aragon. You are to have a husband, Isabella. It is a great match.'

'A husband, Highness?'

'Come. Do not lie there. Get up. Where is your wrap?' The Dowager Queen laughed on a shrill note. 'I was determined to bring you this news myself. I would let no one else break it to you. Here, child. Put this about you. There! Now come here. This is a solemn moment. Your hand has been asked in marriage.'

'Who has asked it, Highness?'

'King John of Aragon asks it on behalf of his son Ferdinand.'

'Ferdinand,' repeated Isabella.

'Yes, Ferdinand. Of course he is not the King's elder son,

but I have heard – and I know this to be the truth – that the
King of Aragon loves the finger nails of Ferdinand more
than the whole bodies of his three children by his first
marriage.'

'Highness, has he such different finger nails from other
people then?'

'Oh, Isabella, Isabella, you are a baby still. Now Ferdinand is a little younger than you are ... a year, all but a
month. So he is only a little boy as yet, but he will be as
delighted to form an alliance with Castile as you are with
Aragon. And I, my child, am contented. You have no father
now, and your enemies at Madrid will do their utmost to
keep you from your rights. But the King of Aragon offers you
his son. As soon as you are old enough the marriage shall take
place. In the meantime you may consider yourself betrothed.
Now, we must pray. We must thank God for this great good
fortune and at the same time we will ask the saints to guard
you well, to bring you to a great destiny. Come.'

Together they knelt on the *prie-Dieu* in Isabella's apartment.

To the child it seemed fantastic to be up so late; the flickering candle-light seemed ghostly, her mother's voice sounded wild as she instructed rather than prayed God and his
saints what they must do for Isabella. Her knees hurt; they
were always a little sore from so much kneeling; and she felt
as though she were not fully awake and that this was some
sort of dream.

'Ferdinand,' she murmured to herself, trying to visualize
him; but she could only think of those finger nails so beloved
of his father.

Ferdinand! They would meet each other; they would talk
together; make plans; they would live together, as her
mother and the King had lived together, in a palace or a
castle, probably in Aragon.

She had never thought of living anywhere other than in
Madrid or Arevalo; she had never thought of having other

companions than her mother and Alfonso, and perhaps Henry if they ever returned to Madrid. But this would be different.

Ferdinand. She repeated the name again and again. It held a magic quality. He was to be her husband, and already he had the power to make her mother happy.

The Queen had risen from her knees.

'You will go back to your bed now,' she said. 'We have given thanks for this great blessing.' She kissed her daughter's forehead, and her smile was quiet and contented.

Isabella offered silent thanks to Ferdinand for making her mother so happy.

But the Queen's mood changed with that suddenness which still startled Isabella. 'Those who have thought you of little account will have to change their minds, now that the King of Aragon has selected you as the bride of his best-loved son.'

And there in her voice was all the anger and hate she felt for her enemies.

'Everything will be well though now, Highness,' soothed Isabella. 'Ferdinand will arrange that.'

The Queen smiled suddenly; she pushed the little girl towards the bed.

'There,' she said, 'go to bed and sleep peacefully.'

Isabella took off her wrap and climbed into the bed. The Queen watched her and stooped over her to arrange the bedclothes. Then she kissed Isabella and went out, taking the candle with her.

Ferdinand, thought Isabella. Dear Ferdinand of the precious finger nails, the mention of whose name could bring such happiness to her mother.

Joanna noticed that Alegre did not appear on those occasions when it was her duty to wait on the Queen. She sent one of her women to the absent maid of honour with a command to present herself at once. When Alegre arrived,

Joanna made sure that no others should be present at their interview.

Alegre surveyed the Queen with very slightly disguised insolence.

'Since you have come to Castile,' said Joanna, 'you appear to take your duties very lightly.'

'To what duties does your Highness refer?' The tone reflected the insolence of her manner.

'To what duties should I refer but those which brought you to Castile? I have not seen you in attendance for more than a week.'

'Highness, I had received other commands.'

'I am your mistress. It is from me only that you should take orders.'

Alegre cast down her eyes and managed to look both brazen and demure at the same time.

'Well, what do you say?' persisted the Queen. 'Are you going to behave in a fitting manner or will you force me to send you back to Lisbon?'

'Highness, I do not think it would be the wish of *all* at Court that I should return to Lisbon. I hear, from a reliable source, that my presence is very welcome here.'

Joanna stood up abruptly; she went to Alegre and slapped her on both sides of her face. Startled, Alegre put her hands to her cheeks.

'You should behave in a manner fitting to a maid of honour,' said Joanna angrily.

'I will endeavour to emulate Your Highness, who behaves in the manner of a Queen.'

'You are insolent!' cried Joanna.

'Highness, is it insolent to accept the inevitable?'

'So it is inevitable that you should behave like a slut at my Court?'

'It is inevitable that I obey the commands of the King.'

'So he commanded you? So you did not put yourself in the way of being commanded?'

'What could I do, Highness? I could not efface myself.'

'You shall be sent back to Lisbon.'

'I do not think so, Highness.'

'I shall demand that you are sent back.'

'It would be humiliating for Your Highness to demand that which would not be granted.'

'You should not think that you know a great deal concerning Court matters merely because for a few nights you have shared the King's bed.'

'One learns something,' said Alegre lightly, 'for even we do not make love all the time.'

'You are dismissed.'

'From your presence, Highness, or from the Court?'

'Go from my presence. I warn you, I shall have you sent back to Lisbon.'

Alegre curtsied and left. Joanna was very angry; she cursed her own folly in bringing Alegre with her; she should have guessed the creature would make trouble of some sort; but how could she have foreseen that she would have the temerity to usurp her own place in the royal bed?

She was thoughtful while her maids were dressing her. She felt she could not trust herself to speak to them, lest she betray her feelings.

It would be so undignified to let anyone know how humiliated she felt, particularly as her common sense told her that if she did not want trouble with the King she would have to accept the situation.

Her seemingly indolent husband, while he remained indifferent to the affairs of the kingdom, would commit any folly to please his mistress of the moment. She would never forget the sad story of Blanche of Aragon, and she knew she would be foolish to let herself believe that, because he appeared to have an affection for herself, he would hesitate to send her back to Lisbon if she displeased him.

After all, she was no more successful than Blanche had

been in achieving the desired state of pregnancy. She was alarmed too by the whispers she had heard. Was it really true that Henry was unable to beget children? If so, what would be the fate of Joanna of Portugal? Would it be similar to that of Blanche of Aragon?

She listened to the chatter of her women, which was clearly intended to soothe her.

'They say he was magnificent.'

'I consider him to be the handsomest man at Court.'

Joanna said lightly: 'And who is this magnificent and handsome personage?'

'Beltran de la Cueva, Highness.'

Joanna felt her spirits lifted, but studying her face in the mirror she saw with satisfaction that she gave no sign of this.

'What has he done?'

'Well, Highness, he defended a passage of arms in the presence of the King himself. He was victorious; and rarely, so we hear, has a man shown such valour. He declared that he would uphold the superior charms of his mistress against all others at this time or any time, and that he would challenge any who denied his words.'

'And who is this incomparable woman? Did he say?'

'He did not. It is said that his honour forbade him to. The King was pleased. He said that Beltran de la Cueva's gallantry had so impressed him that he would build a monastery which should be dedicated to St Jerome to celebrate the occasion.'

'What a strange thing to do! To dedicate a monastery to St Jerome because a courtier flaunts the charms of his mistress?'

'Your Highness should have seen this knight. He was as one dedicated. And the King was so impressed by his devotion to the unknown lady.'

'And have you any notion who this unknown lady is?'

The women looked at each other.

'Well?' prompted Joanna.

'Highness, all know that this knight is devoted only to one who could not return his love, being so highly placed. There could only be one lady at Court to answer that description.'

'You mean . . . the Queen of Castile?'

'Yourself, Highness. It is thought that the King was so pleased by this man's devotion to yourself that he made this gesture.'

'I am grateful,' said Joanna lightly, 'both to Beltran de la Cueva and to the King.'

Joanna felt that in some measure her dignity had been restored, and she was conscious of infinite gratitude towards Beltran de la Cueva.

Joanna had retired; she did not sleep. She knew that very soon the man who was clearly asking to become her lover would be standing below her window.

It would be so easy. She need only give one little sign.

Was it dangerous? It would be impossible to keep such an affair entirely secret. It seemed that there were few actions of Kings and Queens which could be safe from the light of publicity. Yet he had made that magnificent gesture for her.

Moreover she had a notion that the King would not object to her taking a lover. Henry wanted to go his own promiscuous way, and she believed that what had irritated him in his first wife was her virtue. To a man such as Henry the virtue of one whom he was deceiving could be an irritation. What if the rumours were true and Henry was sterile? Would she be blamed as Blanche had been? Henry would be more likely to keep her as his wife if she remained charming and tolerant in spite of his scandalous way of life.

There was another point; she had always been aware of her own sexual needs. The second Queen of Henry of Castile was quite different from the first.

She felt reckless as she went slowly but deliberately towards the window.

The night was dark and warm, soft with the scent of flowers. He was standing there as she had known he would be, and the sight of him excited her. None could say she would demean herself by taking such a lover. He was surely not only the handsomest but the bravest man at Court.

She lifted a hand and beckoned.

She could almost feel the waves of exultation which flowed from him.

Beltran de la Cueva was well pleased with himself, but he was too clever not to understand that this new path on which he was embarking was full of dangers.

The Queen had attracted him strongly since the time he had first seen her, and it had been one of his ambitions to make her his mistress; but he knew that his advancement would have to come from the King. He was pondering now how he could continue in the King's good graces while at the same time he enjoyed his intimacy with the Queen.

It was an odd state of affairs, since he was hoping to enjoy the King's favour while he was the lover of the Queen. But Henry was a meek husband; he was a man who, while devoting himself to the lusts of the flesh, liked to see those about him acting in like manner. He was not one to cherish the virtuous; they irritated him, because he was a man with a conscience which he was trying to ignore, and the virtuous stirred that conscience.

The future was hopeful, thought Beltran de la Cueva. He really did not see why he should not profit doubly from this new relationship with the Queen.

It was impossible to keep it secret.

The Queen had invited him to her bedchamber, and it was inevitable that one of her women would discover that these nightly visits were taking place; and one woman would pass on the secret to another, and sooner or later it would become Court gossip.

He hid his anxiety from the Queen.

He told her in the quiet of her bedchamber: 'If the King should discover what has taken place between us, I do not think my life would be worth very much.'

Joanna held him to her in a gesture of mock terror. It gave an added charm to their love to pretend it was dangerous.

'Then you must not come here again,' she whispered.

'Do you think the fear of sudden death would keep me away?'

'I know you are brave, my love, so brave that you do not consider the danger to yourself. But I think of it constantly. I forbid you to come here again.'

'It is the only command you could give me which I would not obey.'

Such conversations were stimulating to them both. He enjoyed seeing himself as the invincible lover; her self-esteem was reinstated. To be so loved by one who was reckoned to be the most attractive man at Court could make her quite indifferent to the love affair between her husband and maid of honour.

Moreover she had heard that Henry was now dividing his attentions between Alegre and another woman of the Court; and this was gratifying.

Henry must have heard of her own attachment to Beltran, and he showed not the slightest rancour; in fact he seemed a little pleased. Joanna was delighted with this turn of events. It showed that she had been right when she had decided that, if she allowed Henry to take his mistresses without a reproach from her, he would raise no objection if she occasionally amused herself with a lover.

A very satisfactory state of affairs, thought the Queen of Castile.

Beltran de la Cueva was also relieved. Henry had become more friendly than ever with him. A fascinating situation, he reassured himself, when he might expect advancement through the Queen and the King.

* * *

Meanwhile the little girl was growing up in the Palace at Arevalo.

When she looked back she thought pityingly of that Isabella who had lacked her Ferdinand, for Ferdinand had become as real to her as her brother, her mother or anyone within the Palace. Occasionally she heard scraps of news concerning him. He was very handsome; he was the delight of the Court of Aragon; the quarrel between his father and Ferdinand's half-brother was all on account of Ferdinand. It was a continual regret to the royal House of Aragon that Ferdinand had not been born before Carlos.

Often when she was in a dilemma she would say to herself: 'What would Ferdinand do?'

She talked about him so much to Alfonso that her young brother said: 'One would think he was really here with us. No one would believe that you had never seen Ferdinand.'

Those words had their effect on Isabella. It was almost a shock to have it brought home to her that she had never seen Ferdinand. She believed too that she had departed from her usual decorum by talking of him so much. She must remedy that.

But if she did not talk to him, that did not stop her thinking of him. She could not imagine life without Ferdinand.

Because of him she determined to be a perfect wife, a perfect Queen, for she believed that one day Ferdinand would be King of Aragon in spite of his brother Carlos. She mastered the art of the needle and was determined not only to become an expert in fine needlework but to be a useful seamstress as well.

'When I am married to Ferdinand,' she once told Alfonso, 'I shall make all his shirts. I shall not allow him to wear one that is made by another hand.'

She was interested in affairs of state.

She was no longer a child, and perhaps, when she was fifteen or sixteen, she would be married. Ferdinand was a year younger, which could cause some delay, for she would be the one to wait for him to reach a marriageable age.

'Never mind,' she consoled herself, 'I shall have a little longer to perfect myself.'

Now and then she heard news of her half-brother's Court. Henry was a very bad King, she feared, and her mother had been right, no doubt, to insist that herself and her brother should go away and live like hermits. This was the best way to prepare herself for marriage with Ferdinand.

As she had even as a very small child, she listened and rarely interrupted when she heard the conversation of grown-up people; she tried to hide her interest, which was the surest way of making them forget she was present.

One day she heard a great deal of whispering.

'What a scandal!'

'Who ever heard of such behaviour by an Archbishop!'

'And the Archbishop of St James at that!'

Eventually she discovered what this misdemeanour of an Archbishop had been. It appeared that he had been so struck by the charms of a young bride that he had attempted abduction and rape as she left the church after her marriage.

The comments on this scandal were so illuminating.

'What can one expect? It is merely a reflection of the manners of the Court. How can the King censure the Archbishop when he behaves equally scandalously? You have heard, of course, that his chief mistress is the Queen's own maid of honour. They say she keeps an establishment which is as splendid as that of the Queen, and that people such as the Archbishop of Seville seek her favour.'

'It is not as though she is the King's only mistress. The latest scandal is that one of his ladies wished to become an abbess, if you please! And what does our loving King do? He dismisses the pious and high-born abbess of a convent in Toledo and sets up his paramour in her place. It is small wonder that there are scandals outside the Court when they so blatantly exist inside it.'

Isabella began to learn from her mother and her teachers

how the state of Castile was being governed; she was made aware of the terrible mistakes which were being made by her half-brother.

'My child,' said her pastor, 'take a lesson from the actions of the King, and, if ever it should be your fate to assist in the government of a kingdom, make sure that you do not fall into like pitfalls. Taxes are being imposed on the people. For what reason? That the King may sustain his favourites. The merchants, who are one of the means of providing a country with its riches, are being taxed so heavily that they are prevented from giving the country of their best. Worst of all, the coinage has been adulterated. You must try to understand the importance of this. Where we had five mints we now have one hundred and fifty; this means that the value of money has dropped to a sixth of its previous value. My child, try to understand the chaos this can bring about. Why, if matters do not mend, the whole country will be on the verge of insolvency.'

'Tell me,' said Isabella earnestly, 'is my brother Henry to blame for this?'

'The rulers of a country are often to be blamed when it falls on evil times. It is their duty to efface themselves for the love of their country. The duty of Kings and Queens to their people should come before their pleasure. If ever it should be your destiny to rule ...'

Isabella folded her hands together and said, 'My country would be my first consideration.' And she spoke as a novice might speak when contemplating the taking of her vows.

And always on such occasions she imagined herself ruling with Ferdinand; she began to realize that this prospective bridegroom, who was so real to her in spite of the fact that she had never seen him, was the dominating influence in her life.

Later came news that Henry had decided to lead a crusade against the Moors. There was nothing which could win the approval of the people so surely as an attempt to conquer the

Moors. Spaniards smarted in the knowledge that for centuries the Arabs had remained in Spain, and that large provinces in the south were still under their domination. Since the
days of Rodrigo Diaz of Bivar, the famous Castilian leader
who had lived in the eleventh century and had been known as
the Cid Campeador, Spaniards had looked for another great
leader; and whenever one appeared who proposed to lead a
campaign which was calculated to drive the Moors from the
Iberian Peninsula the cry went up: 'Here is the Cid reborn
and come among us.'

Thus, when Henry declared his intention of striking
against the Moors, his popularity increased.

He needed money for his campaigns, and who should provide it but his long-suffering people? The riches of the
countryside were seized that armies might be equipped for
the King's campaign.

Henry, however, was a soldier who could make a brave
show, marching through the streets at the head of his troops,
but was not so successful on the battlefields.

Again and again his troops were routed; he returned from
the wars, with his dazzling cavalcade making a brave show;
but there were no conquests, and the Moors remained as
strongly entrenched as ever.

He declared that he was chary of risking the lives of his
soldiers, for in his opinion the life of one Christian was worth
more than those of a thousand Mussulmans.

This was a sentiment which he hoped would find favour
with the people; but they grumbled, particularly those in
whose districts the fighting had taken place.

It would seem, said these people, that the King makes war
on us, not on the Infidel.

And each day in the schoolroom at Arevalo Isabella would
hear of the exploits of Henry, and must learn her lessons
from them.

'Never go to war,' she was told, 'unless you have a well-
founded hope of victory. Fine uniforms do not necessarily

make good soldiers. Before you go to war make sure that your cause is just and that it is wholeheartedly yours.' 'Never,' said their preceptor, instructing Isabella and Alfonso, 'had a prospective ruler a better opportunity of profiting from the folly of a predecessor.'

The children were told why, on every count, Henry was a bad King. They were not told of his voluptuous adventures, but these were hinted at, and mistresses and ministers were spoken of under one category as Favourites.

He was extravagant almost to the point of absurdity. His policy was to give bribes to his enemies in the hope of turning them into friends, and to his friends that they might remain friendly.

Mistaken policies, both of them, Isabella and Alfonso were warned. Friends should be kept by mutual loyalty, and enemies met by the mailed fist and not by placatory gold.

'Learn your lessons well, children. There may come a time when you will need them.'

'And we *must* learn our lessons, Alfonso,' said Isabella. 'For it may well be that one day the people will have had enough of Henry; and if he has no son they will call upon you to take the throne of Castile. As for myself, one day I shall help Ferdinand to rule Aragon. We must certainly learn our lessons well.'

So, gravely, they listened to what was told to them; and it seemed to them both that the years at Arevalo were the waiting years.

Isabella sat thoughtfully over her needlework.

At any moment, she thought, there may be change. At any moment the people may decide that they will have no more of Henry; then they will march to Arevalo and take away Alfonso to make him King.

She had heard that the debasing of the coinage had caused chaos among certain sections of the community; and the result was that robbery had increased.

Some of the noblest families in Castile, declaring themselves to be on the verge of bankruptcy, lost all sense of decency and took to robbery on the roads. Travelling was less safe than it had been for centuries; and castles, which had once been the homes of noble families, were now little less than robbers' dens. Some of these nobles even attempted to put right their reverses by selling Christian men and women, whom they seized during raids on villages, as slaves to the Moors.

Such conduct was quite deplorable, and it was clear that anarchy reigned in Castile.

Much reform was needed; but all the King seemed to care about was his fancy-dress parades and the pleasure of his Favourites.

Isabella prayed for the well-being of her country.

'Ah,' she told herself, 'how different we shall be – Ferdinand and I – when we rule together!'

One day her mother came to her in a mood of great excitement, and Isabella was reminded of the night when she had been called from her bed to give thanks because the King of Aragon had asked that she might be given in marriage to his son Ferdinand.

'Isabella daughter, here is wonderful news. The Prince of Viana is asking for your hand in marriage. This is a brilliant offer. Not only is Carlos heir to Aragon, but Navarre is his also. My dear Isabella, why do you stare at me so blankly? You should rejoice.'

Isabella had grown pale; she lifted her head and held herself at her full height, for once losing her sense of decorum. 'You have forgotten, Highness,' she said. 'I am already betrothed to Ferdinand.'

The Dowager Queen laughed. 'That . . . oh, we will forget it. Ferdinand of Aragon? A very good match, but he is only a younger brother. Carlos, the heir of Aragon, the ruler of Navarre, is asking for your hand. I do not see why the marriage should be long delayed.'

On one of the few occasions in her young life Isabella lost control. She knelt and, seizing her mother's skirts, looked up at her imploringly. 'But, Highness,' she cried, 'I have been *promised* to Ferdinand.'

'The promise was not binding, my child. This is a more suitable match. You must allow your elders to know what is good for you.'

'Highness, the King of Aragon will be angry. Does he not love the finger nails of Ferdinand better than the whole body of his elder son?'

That made the Dowager Queen smile. 'Carlos has quarrelled with his father, but the people of Aragon love Carlos, and he is the one whom they will make their King. The territories of Navarre are also his. Why, there could not be a better match.'

Isabella stood rigid and for the first time showed distinct signs of a stubborn nature.

'It is a point of honour that I marry Ferdinand.'

Her mother laughed, not wildly nor excitedly, merely with faintly amused tolerance; but now Isabella was past caring about the state of her mother's emotions.

The Dowager Queen said once more: 'Leave these matters to your elders, Isabella. Now you should go on your knees and give thanks to God and his saints for the great good fortune which is to be yours.'

Wild protests rose to Isabella's lips, but the discipline of years prevailed, and she said nothing.

She allowed herself to be led to her *prie-Dieu* and, while her mother prayed for the speedy union of her daughter and the Prince of Viana, heir to the throne of Aragon, she could only murmur: 'Ferdinand! Oh Ferdinand! It must be Ferdinand. Holy Mother of God, do not desert me now. Let anything happen to me or the Prince of Viana or the whole world, but give me Ferdinand.'

SCANDAL AT THE COURT OF CASTILE

In the Palace at Saragossa Joan Henriquez, Queen of Aragon, was discussing the effrontery of Carlos with her husband, John.

'This,' declared Joan, 'is meant to insult you, to show you how little this son of yours cares for your authority. He knows it is a favourite project of ours that Ferdinand shall mate with Isabella. So what does he do but offer himself!'

'It shall not come to pass,' said the King. 'Do not distress yourself, my dear. Isabella is for Ferdinand, and we shall find some means of outwitting Carlos ... as we have in the past.'

He smiled fondly at his wife. She was much younger than he was, and from the date of their marriage he had become so enamoured of her that his great desire was to give her all she wished. She was, he was sure, unique. Handsome, bold, shrewd – where was there another woman in the world to compare with her? His first wife, Blanche of Navarre, had been the widow of Martin of Sicily when he had married her. She had been a good woman, possessed of a far from insignificant dowry, and he had been well pleased with the match. She had given him three children: Carlos, Blanche and Eleanor, and he had been delighted at the time; now, having married the incomparable Joan Henriquez and having had issue by her in the also incomparable Ferdinand, he could wish – because Joan wished this – that he had no other children, so that Ferdinand would be heir to everything he possessed.

It was small wonder, he assured himself, that he should

dote on Ferdinand. What of his other children? He was in continual conflict with Carlos; Blanche had been repudiated by her husband, Henry of Castile, and was now living in retirement on her estates at Olit, where, so Joan insisted, she gave assistance to her brother Carlos in his disagreements with his father; and there was Eleanor, Comtesse de Foix, who had left home many years before when she married Gaston de Foix, and was a domineering woman of great ambitions.

As for Joan, she doted on Ferdinand with all the force of a strong nature, and was resentful of any favours which fell to the lot of the other children.

In the first days of their union she had been gentle and loving, but from that day – it was the 10th March in the year 1452, some eight years ago – when her Ferdinand had been born in the little town of Sos, she had changed. She had become as a tigress fighting for her cub; and John, being so devoted to her, had become involved in this battle for the rights of the adored son of his second wife against the family of his first.

It was a sad state of affairs in any family when there was discord between its members; in a royal family this could be disastrous.

John of Aragon, however, could only see through the eyes of the wife on whom he doted, and therefore to him his son Carlos was a scoundrel.

This was not the truth. Carlos was a man of great charm and integrity. He was good-natured, gentle, honourable, and in the eyes of many people a perfect Prince. He was intellectual and artistic; he loved music; he could paint and was a poet; he was something of a philosopher and historian, and would have preferred to live quietly and study; it was the great tragedy of his life that he found himself drawn, against his will, into a bloody conflict with his own father.

The trouble had begun when Joan had asked that she might share the government of Navarre with Carlos, who had inherited this territory on the death of his mother, the daughter of Charles III of Navarre.

Joan's intention was to oust Carlos from Navarre that she might preserve it for her darling Ferdinand, who was only a baby as yet but for whom her ambitions had begun to grow from the day of his birth. Joan's manner was arrogant, and her policy was to create disturbance, so that the people would become dissatisfied with the rule of Carlos.

Joan was considerably helped in her desire to cause trouble by two ancient Navarrese families who for centuries had maintained a feud – concerning the origin of which neither was absolutely sure – which gave them the excuse to make forays into each other's territory from time to time.

These families were the Beaumonts and the Agramonts. They saw, in the conflict between the Prince and his step-mother, an excuse to make trouble. The Beaumonts therefore allied themselves with Carlos, which meant that automatic-ally the Agramonts gave their support to the Queen; as a result war had broken out and the Agramonts, being the stronger party, took Carlos prisoner.

Carlos was confined for some months, the prisoner of his father and stepmother; but eventually he escaped and sought refuge with his uncle, Alfonso V of Naples. Unfortunately for Carlos, shortly after his arrival there, Alfonso died and it was necessary for Carlos to attempt reconciliation with his father.

Joan was eager to keep the King's heir in disgrace, and Carlos lingered in Sicily, where he became very popular, but when news of his popularity was brought to the Court of Aragon, Joan was disturbed. She saw a possibility of the Sicilians setting up Carlos as their ruler; and of course Joan had long ago decided that Sicily, together with Navarre and Aragon, should become the domain of her darling little Fer-dinand.

It was necessary, she said, to recall Carlos to Aragon. So Joan and the King met Carlos at Igualada, and the meeting appeared to be such an affectionate one that all those who witnessed it rejoiced, for Carlos was popular wherever he went, and it was the desire of the majority that the family quarrel should cease and Carlos be declared without any doubt his father's heir.

This was exactly what Joan intended to prevent, as in her opinion there was but one person who should be declared his father's heir; and the people must be brought to accept this. She prevailed upon her husband to summon the Cortes and, there before it, declare his unwillingness to name Carlos his successor.

Carlos, bewildered and unhappy, listened to his advisers, who assured him that his best place, since his royal house of Aragon was against him, was to ally himself with that of Castile.

This could be done through marriage with the half-sister of Henry of Castile, little Isabella, who was now being carefully guarded at the Palace of Arevalo.

She was as yet a child, being some nine years old; and in addition she had been destined for Ferdinand. But the King of Castile and the child's mother would be far more likely to smile on a match with the elder son of John of Aragon than the younger. Moreover, nothing could be calculated to flout the authority of his stepmother so completely as to snatch the bride she had intended for Ferdinand.

This was the plot, reports of which had reached Joan Henriquez; and it was on this account that she raged against Carlos, to her husband, and determined to bring about his destruction.

'That poor child,' she cried. 'She is nine years old and Carlos is forty! It will be at least another three years before she is of an age to consummate the marriage. By that time he will be forty-three. Ferdinand is now eight years old. What a charming pair they would make! I hear she is a handsome girl; and Ferdinand ... our dearest Ferdinand ... surely, John, you must agree that there is not a more perfect child in

Aragon, in Castile, in Spain, in the whole world!'

John smiled at her fondly. He loved her more deeply in those moments when her habitual calm deserted her and she showed the excessive nature of her love for Ferdinand. Then she became like another woman, no longer the Joan Henriquez who had such a firm grasp of state matters; then she was the predatory mother. Surely, thought John, there cannot be another child in Aragon who is loved as fiercely and deeply as our Ferdinand.

He laid his hand on her shoulder. 'Dearest,' he said, 'we will find some means of preventing this calamity. Isabella shall be for Ferdinand.'

'But, husband, what if Henry of Castile decides to accept Carlos' offer? What if he says Carlos is the rightful heir of Aragon?'

'It is for me to decide who shall succeed me,' said John.

'There would be trouble if you should choose any other than the eldest son. Ferdinand is young yet, but when he grows up, what a warrior he will be!'

'Alas, my dear, he is not grown up yet; and if Carlos married and there were children of the marriage. . . .'

Joan's eyes flashed with purpose. 'But Carlos is not yet married. It will be some years before he can marry, if he waits for Isabella. She could not possibly bear a child for another four years at least. A great deal can happen in four years.'

The King looked into her face, and it seemed as though deep emotions within him were ignited by the passion he read in her eyes.

Ferdinand was the fruit of their union. For Ferdinand she was ready to give all that she possessed – her honour, her life itself.

There was exultation in her voice when she said: 'I believe that I have been blessed with second sight, John. I believe a great destiny awaits our son. I believe that he will be the saviour of our country and that in years to come his name will be mentioned with that of the Cid Campeador. Husband, I believe that we should deserve eternal damnation if we did not do all within our power to lead him to his destiny.'

John grasped his wife's hand. 'I swear to you, my dearest wife,' he said, 'that nothing ... *nothing* shall bar Ferdinand's way to greatness.'

In her retreat at Olit, Blanche lived her quiet life.

She had two desires; one was that she might be allowed to pass her time in peace at this quiet refuge, the other that her brother Carlos might triumph over his stepmother and win his way back into their father's good graces.

Occasionally she heard news of Castile. Henry had had no more good fortune with his new wife than he had had with Blanche. There was still no sign of an heir for Castile, and it was seven years since he had married the Princess of Portugal. She knew that Castile was almost in a state of anarchy; that there were armed bands of robbers on the roads and that rape and violence of all sorts were accepted in a light-hearted fashion, which could only mean that the country was bordering on chaos. She had heard rumours of the King's scandalous way of life, and that his Queen was by no means a virtuous woman. Stories of her liaison with Beltran de la Cueva were circulated. Blanche feared that affairs in Castile were as chaotic and uncertain as they were in Aragon.

But Castile was no longer any great concern of hers. Henry had repudiated her, and she would ignore Henry.

Aragon was a different matter.

Who was there left in her life to love but her brother Carlos? Dear Carlos! He was too good, too gentle and kindly to understand the towering ambition, the jealousy and frustration of a woman such as Joan Henriquez. And there could be no doubt that their father was completely under the influence of Joan.

She longed to help Carlos, to advise him. Strange as it

might seem, she felt she was in a position to do so; she believed that, from her lonely vantage point, she could see what was happening more clearly than her brother could, and she was sure that now was the time for him to be on his guard.

Every time a messenger approached her palace she was afraid that he might be bringing bad news of Carlos. She experienced that premonition of evil which she had known during that period when Henry was preparing to discard her.

When her father had gone to Lerida to hold the Cortes of Catalonia – soon after Carlos had asked for the hand of Isabella of Castile – he had asked Carlos to meet him there.

She had warned Carlos, and she knew his faithful adherents had done the same. 'Do not go to Lerida, dear Carlos,' she had implored. 'This is a trap.'

But Carlos had reasoned: 'If I will not negotiate with my father, how can I ever hope for peace?'

And so he had gone to Lerida where his father had immediately ordered his arrest and incarceration, accused, falsely, of plotting against the King.

But the people of Catalonia adored their Prince and demanded to know why the King had imprisoned him; they murmured against the unnatural behaviour of a father towards his son, and they accused the Queen of vindictiveness and the scheming design to have the rightful heir disinherited in favour of her own son.

Deputations arrived from Barcelona. and as a result it was necessary for John to leave Catalonia for the safer territory of Aragon without delay, and in a manner which was far from dignified. And the result: rebellion in Catalonia.

Back in Saragossa, John had gathered together an army, but meanwhile the revolt had spread, and Henry of Castile, who now looked upon Carlos as his sister's prospective husband, invaded Navarre on the side of Carlos against the King of Aragon. Carlos up to this time had been held prisoner, but in view of the state of the country John saw that his only course was to release his son.

The people blamed Joan for what had happened and, in order to win back their love for his beloved wife, John declared that he had released Carlos because she had begged him to do so.

Carlos, the kindest of men, bore no grudge against his stepmother, and allowed her to accompany him through Catalonia on his way to Barcelona, where John had hoped his presence would restore order; and the fact that his stepmother accompanied him led the people to believe that Carlos had returned to the heart of the family.

Blanche shook her head over these events. Now was the time for Carlos to beware as never before.

What would Joan be thinking during that ride to Barcelona, when she saw the people coming out in their thousands to cheer their Prince and having only sullen looks for his stepmother?

But Carlos seemed unable to learn from previous experience. Perhaps he was weary of strife; perhaps he wished to leave the arena and return to his books and painting, perhaps he so hated strife that he deliberately deluded himself.

He refused to listen to warnings. He preferred to believe that his father and his stepmother were genuine in their assertions that they desired his friendship. But the Queen was warned that she would be unwise to enter Barcelona, where a special welcome was being prepared for Carlos.

And now the Catalans all stood behind their Prince. Blanche had heard of the great welcome they had given him when he entered Barcelona.

'It is Catalonia today,' it was said; 'tomorrow it will be Aragon. Carlos is the rightful heir to the throne and wherever he goes is loved. "We will have Carlos," the people cry. "And the King of Aragon must either accept him as his heir or we will see that there is a new King of Aragon. King Carlos!" And King John? He has deeply offended the people of Catalonia. They will never allow him to enter their province unless he craves and obtains the permission of his people.'

Triumph for Carlos, thought Blanche. Oh, but Carlos, my brother, this is your most dangerous moment!

And so she waited, with that fearful premonition of evil.

She was even at the window watching when the messenger arrived.

'Bring him to me immediately,' she told her attendants. 'I know he brings news of the Prince, my brother.'

She was right; and she saw by the messenger's expression the nature of the news.

'Highness,' said the messenger, 'I crave your pardon. I am the bearer of bad news.'

'Please tell me without delay.'

'The Prince of Viana has fallen ill of a malignant fever. Some say he contracted this during his stay in prison.'

She said: 'You must tell me everything ... quickly.'

'The Prince is dead, Highness.'

Blanche turned away and went silently to her apartment; she locked her door and lay on her bed, without speaking, without weeping.

Her grief as yet was too overwhelming, too deep for outward expression.

Later she asked herself what this would mean. Little Ferdinand was now the heir of Aragon. His rival had been satisfactorily removed. Removed? It was an unpleasant word. But Blanche believed it to be the correct one to use in this case.

It was a terrifying thought. If her suspicion were true, could her father have been cognizant of a plot to murder his own son? It seemed incredible. Yet he was the blind slave of his wife, and she had coaxed him to worship, with her, the beloved Ferdinand.

'My only true friend!' she murmured; and she thought of her brother, who, had he been allowed to reach the throne, would have been a good ruler of Aragon – just, kindly, generous, learned.

'Oh my dear brother!' she cried. And later she said: 'And what will now become of me?'

She remembered, when the first shock of her loss had diminished, that Carlos' death left her the heiress of Navarre, and she knew that greedy hands would be waiting to snatch what was hers.

Her sister, Eleanor de Foix, would be eager to step into her shoes, and how could she do that except through the death of her elder sister? Carlos had been removed. Would the same fate fall upon her?

'Holy Mother of God,' she prayed, 'let me stay here, where at least I know peace. Here in this quiet spot, where I can watch over the poor people of Olit, who look to me for the little I am able to do for them, I can, if not find happiness, be at peace. Let me stay here. Preserve me from that battlefield of envy and ambition which has destroyed my brother.'

Navarre was a dangerous possession. Joan Henriquez would want it for Ferdinand; Eleanor would want it for her son, Gaston, who had recently married a sister of Louis XI of France.

'If my mother had known how much anxiety this possession would bring to me, she would have made a different will,' she told herself.

So Blanche continued to wait. Nor did she have to wait long.

There arrived a letter from her father, in which he told her he had great news for her. She had been too long without a husband. Her marriage to Henry of Castile had been proved null and void; therefore she was at liberty to marry if she wished.

And it was his desire that she should marry. Moreover, he had a brilliant prospect to lay before her. Her sister Eleanor enjoyed the favour of the King of France, and she believed that a match could be arranged between Blanche and the Duc de Berri, Louis' own brother.

'My dear daughter,' wrote the King, 'this is an opportunity of which we have not dared dream.'

Blanche read and re-read the letter.

Why is it, she asked herself, that when life has treated one badly and seems scarcely worth living, one still fought to retain it?

She did not believe in this talk of marriage with the Duc de Berri. If Carlos had met his death by poison, why should not she, Blanche? And if she were dead, Eleanor would take Navarre. What a great gift that would be to her son; and since he was the husband of the French King's sister, Blanche did not believe that Louis would raise any objection if such a crime were committed in his territory.

'You must not go to France!' There were warning voices within her which told her that. Her servants, who loved her, also warned her against going. So, she thought, I am not the only one who suspected the manner in which Carlos died.

'Marriage is not for me,' she wrote to her father. 'I have no wish to go to France, even for this brilliant marriage. I intend to spend the rest of my days here in Olit, where I shall never cease to pray for the soul of my brother.'

Perhaps the mention of her brother angered her father. How much, she wondered, was there on his conscience? He wrote in extreme irritation that she was foolish to dream of casting aside such a wonderful opportunity.

'Nevertheless,' was her reply, 'I shall stay at Olit.'

But she was wrong.

Late one night there was a clattering of horses' hoofs in the courtyard, followed by a hammering on the door.

'Who goes there?' called the guards.

'Open up! Open up! We come in the name of King John of Aragon.'

There was nothing to be done but let them in. Their leader, when he was taken to Blanche, bowed low with a deference which contained a hint of authority.

'I crave your pardon, Highness, but the King's orders are that you prepare to leave Olit at once.'

'For what destination?' she asked.

'For Béarn, Madam, where your noble sister eagerly awaits you.'

So Eleanor eagerly awaited her – yes, with a burning ambition for her son Gaston which equalled that of Joan Henriquez for the young Ferdinand!

'I have decided to stay in Olit,' she told him.

'I am sorry to hear you say that,' was the answer, 'for the King's orders are, Highness, that, if you will not consent to go, you must go by force.'

'So,' she cried, 'it has come to that!'

'These are the King's orders.'

She said: 'Allow me to go to my women that I may make my preparations.'

'Holy Mother of God,' she prayed, 'why should there be this desire to cling to a life which is scarcely worth the living?'

But the desire was there.

She said to her most trusted women: 'Prepare. We have to leave Olit. We must escape. It is imperative that we are not taken to Béarn.'

But where could she go? she asked herself. To Castile? Henry would befriend her. He had repudiated her, but he had never been actively unkind. For all his faults she did not believe Henry would connive at murder. She would explain to him her suspicions of Carlos' end; she would implore him to save her from a like fate.

To Castile ... and Henry. It was the answer.

If she could slip out of the Palace by some secret way ... if a horse could be ready for her. . . .

She whispered instructions. 'We must be swift. My father's men are already in the Palace. Have the horses ready. I will slip out, and my head groom and one of my ladies will accompany me. Quick ... there is not a moment to lose.'

As she was being dressed for the ride she could hear the sound of voices outside her door, and the tramp of her father's soldiers' feet in her Palace.

With madly beating heart she left the Palace by a secret door. The groom was waiting, and silently he helped her into the saddle. Her favourite woman attendant was with her.

'Come,' she cried.

Lightly she touched her horse's flank, but before he could spring into action, his bridle was caught in a pair of strong hands.

'Our grateful thanks, Highness,' said a triumphant voice at her side. 'You have dressed with great speed. Now we will not delay. We will leave at once for the border.'

And through the night they rode. It was dark, but not darker than the sense of foreboding in Blanche's heart as she rode towards Béarn.

A great event had burst upon the Court of Castile. That which most Castilians had begun to believe would never happen was about to come to pass.

The Queen was pregnant.

'It cannot be by the King,' was the comment. '*That* is an impossibility.'

'Then by whom?'

There was only one answer. Joanna's faithful lover was Beltran de la Cueva, who was also a friend of the King.

He was clever, this brilliant and handsome young man. He knew how to entertain the King, how to be his witty and adventurous companion while at the same time he was the Queen's devoted and passionate lover.

There were many to laugh at the audacity of this man, some to admire it; but there were also those whom it angered and who felt themselves neglected.

Two of these were the Marquis of Villena and his uncle,

Alfonso Carillo, Archbishop of Toledo.

'This,' said Villena to his uncle, 'is a ridiculous state of affairs. If the Queen is pregnant it is certainly not with Henry's child. What shall we do? Allow an illegitimate child to be heir to the throne?'

'We must do everything to prevent it,' said the Archbishop righteously.

They were both determined to bring about the fall of Beltran de la Cueva, who was gradually ousting them from the positions of authority over the King which they had held for so long.

It was not that Beltran alone was politically ambitious, but about him, as about all favourites, there gathered the hangers-on, the seekers after power; and these, naturally enough, were in opposition to Villena and the Archbishop and desired to snatch from them the power they had held.

'If this child is born and lives,' said Villena to his uncle, 'we shall know what to do.'

'In the meantime,' added the Archbishop, 'we must make sure everyone bears in mind that the child cannot possibly be the King's, and that without a doubt Beltran de la Cueva is its father.'

Henry was delighted that at last, after eight years of marriage, the Queen had become pregnant.

He knew that there were rumours, not only of his sterility, but of his impotence. It was said that it was for this reason that unnatural and lascivious orgies had to be arranged for him. Therefore the fact of Joanna's pregnancy delighted him. It would, he hoped, quash the rumours.

Did he believe himself to have been the cause of it? He could delude himself. He had come to depend more and more on delusions.

So he gave balls and banquets in honour of the unborn child. He was seen in public more often with his Queen than hitherto. Of course Beltran de la Cueva was often their companion – dear friend of both King and Queen.

When Henry raised Beltran to the rank of Count of Ledesma, the Court raised cynical eyebrows.

'Are there now to be honours for obliging lovers who supply that which impotent husbands cannot?'

Henry cared not for the whispers, and pretended not to hear them.

As for Joanna she laughed at them, but she constantly referred to the child as hers and the King's, and in spite of the whispers there were some who believed her.

Now the Court was tense, waiting for the birth. A boy? A girl?

Would the child resemble its mother or its father?

'Let us hope,' said cynical courtiers, 'that it resembles somebody in some way which can be recognized. Mysteries that cannot be solved are so wearying.'

Change came to Arevalo on that March day, such change as Isabella would never forget, because there came with it the end of childhood.

Isabella had been living in a state of exultation since she had heard of the death of Carlos. It seemed to her then that her prayers had been answered; she had prayed that there should be a miracle to save her for Ferdinand, and behold, the man who was to have taken his place had been removed from this world.

It was her mother who brought the news, as she always did bring news of the first magnitude.

There was the wildness in her eyes once more, but Isabella was less afraid than she had been as a child. One could grow accustomed to those outbursts, which almost amounted to frenzy. On more than one occasion she had seen the physicians, holding her mother down while she laughed and cried and waved her arms frantically.

Isabella accepted the fact that her mother could not always be relied upon to show a sane front to the world. She had heard it whispered that one day the Dowager Queen would have to retire into solitude, as other members of her family had before her.

This was a great sadness to the girl, but she accepted it with resignation.

It was the will of God, she told Alfonso; and both of them must accept that and never rail against it.

It would have been comforting if she had a calm gentle mother in whom she could have confided. She could have talked to her of her love for Ferdinand – but perhaps it would have been difficult to talk to anyone of a love one felt for a person whom one had never seen.

Yet, said Isabella, to herself, I know I am for Ferdinand and he is for me. That is why I would rather die than accept another husband.

But how could one explain this feeling within her which was based, not on sound good sense, but on some indescribable intuition? It was, therefore, better not to talk of it.

And in the peace of Arevalo, Isabella had gone on dreaming.

Then came this day, and Isabella had rarely seen her mother look more wild. There was the angry light in her eyes. So Isabella knew that something alarming had happened.

Isabella and her brother Alfonso had been summoned to their mother's presence and, before they had time to perform the necessary curtsies and bows, the Dowager Queen exclaimed: 'Your brother's wife has given birth to a child.'

Isabella had risen to her feet with astonishing speed. Her mother did not notice this breach of etiquette.

'A girl ... fortunately ... but a child. You know what this means?' The Queen glared at Alfonso.

'Why, yes, Highness,' said the boy in his high-pitched voice, 'it means that she will be heir to the throne and that I must step aside.'

'We shall see,' said the Queen. 'We shall see who is going to step aside.'

Isabella noticed that a fleck of foam had appeared at the side of her mouth. That was a bad sign.

'Highness,' she began, 'perhaps the child is not strong.'

'I have heard nothing of that. A child there is ... a girl brought into the world to ... to rob us of our rights.'

'But Highness,' said Alfonso, who had not learned to keep quiet as Isabella had, 'if she is my brother's child she is heir to the throne of Castile.'

'I know. I know.' The Dowager Queen's eyes flashed briefly on Isabella. 'There is no law to prevent a woman's taking the crown. I know that. But there are rumours about this girl. You would not understand. But let us say this: Has she a right to the throne? Has she ...?'

'Holy Mother of God,' prayed Isabella. 'Calm her. Do not let the doctors have to hold her down this time.'

'Highness,' she said soothingly, 'here we have lived very happily.'

'You are not going to live here happily much longer, my daughter,' spat out the Queen. 'In fact, you are to prepare for a journey at once.'

'We are going away?'

'Ah!' cried the Queen, her voice rising on a note of hysterical laughter. 'He does not trust us here. He thinks that Arevalo will become a hot-bed of rebellion now. And he is right. They cannot foist a bastard on Castile ... a bastard who has no right to the crown. I doubt not that there will be many who will want to take Alfonso and put a crown upon his head....'

Alfonso looked alarmed.

'Highness,' said Isabella quickly, 'it would not be possible while the King my brother lives.'

The Queen surveyed her children through narrowed eyes.

'Your brother commands,' she said, 'that I, taking you two children with me, return at once to Court.'

Isabella's heart was leaping within her, and she was not sure whether it was with fear or pleasure.

She said quickly: 'Highness, give us your leave to retire and we will begin preparations. We have been here so long that there will be much for us to do.'

The Queen looked at her eleven-year-old daughter and nodded slowly.

'You may go,' she said.

Isabella seized her brother's hand and, forcing him to bow, almost dragged him from the apartment.

As she did so she heard her mother's muttering; she heard the laughter break out.

This, thought Isabella, is really the end of my childhood. At Court I shall quickly become a woman.

How would she fare at that most scandalous Court – she who had been so carefully nurtured here at Arevalo? She was a little alarmed, remembering the rumours she had heard.

Yet she was conscious of an intense elation, for she believed that she must now grow up quickly; and growing up meant marriage ... with Ferdinand.

LA BELTRANEJA

T HE March sunshine shone through the windows of the Chapel in the Palace of Madrid on to the brilliant vestments of those taking part in the most colourful ceremony Isabella had ever witnessed. She was awed by the chanting voices, by the presence of glittering and important men and women.

She was not unconscious of the tension in the atmosphere, for she was wise enough to know that the smiling faces were like the masks she had seen worn at the fêtes and tournaments which had heralded this event.

The whole Court pretended to rejoice because of the birth of Isabella's little niece, but Isabella knew that those smiling masks hid the true feelings of many people present at this christening.

There stood her half-brother Henry, looking very tall indeed and somewhat untidy, with his reddish hair straggling out beneath his crown. Beside him stood his half-brother, nine-year-old Alfonso.

Alfonso was quite handsome, thought Isabella, in his robes of state. He appeared to be solemn too, as though he knew that many people would be looking his way on this occasion. It seemed to Isabella that Alfonso was one of the most important people present – more important than the baby herself perhaps – and Isabella knew why. She could never entirely escape from that high-pitched voice of her mother's, reminding them that, should the people decide they had had enough of Henry, they would turn to Alfonso.

Isabella herself had an important part to play in the christening.

With the baby's sponsors, of whom she was one, she stood beside the font. The others were the Frenchman, Armignac, and the brilliantly clad Juan Pacheco, Marquis of Villena, and his wife. It was the Marquis who held her attention. Through eavesdropping whenever possible, she had heard his name mentioned often and she knew a great deal about him.

Echoes of conversations came back to her. 'He is the King's right hand.' 'He is the King's right eye.' 'Henry does not take a step without consulting the Marquis of Villena.' 'Ah, but have you heard that ... lately there has been a little change?' 'It cannot be ...' 'Oh, but they say it is so. Now that *is* a joke.'

It was so interesting. Far more interesting here at Court, where she could actually see the people who had figured so largely in the rumours she had overheard at Arevalo.

The Marquis was smiling now, but Isabella felt that his mask was the most deceitful of them all. She sensed the power of the man and she wondered what he would look like when he was angry. He would be very formidable, she was sure.

Now the heavy, dark brows of Alfonso Carillo, the Archbishop of Toledo, were drawn together in a frown of concentration as he performed the christening ceremony and blessed the baby girl who had been carried to him under a canopy by Count Alba de Liste.

There was another whom Isabella could not fail to notice. This was a tall man, who might be said to be the handsomest man present; his clothes were more magnificent than those of any other; his jewels glittered with a brighter lustre – perhaps because there were so many of them. His hair was so black that it held a bluish tinge, his eyes were large and dark, but he had a fine fair skin which made him look very young.

He was particularly noticeable, standing close to Henry, for he was almost as tall as the King; and, thought Isabella, if one did not know who was the real King and was asked to pick him out from all those assembled, one would pick Bel-

tran de la Cueva, who had recently been made Count of
Ledesma.

The Count was another of those people who were attract-
ing so much attention, and as he watched the baby under the
canopy, many watched him.

Unaccustomed though she was to such ceremonies, Isabella gave no sign of the excitement which she was feeling;
and, if it appeared that there was a certain watchfulness directed at those three – the King, the Queen and the new
Count of Ledesma – Alfonso and Isabella also had their
share of this attention.

The thought was in many minds on that day that, if the
rumours which were beginning to be spread through the
Court were true – and there seemed every reason why they
should be – these two children were of the utmost significance. And the fact that the boy was so handsome, and
clearly showed he was eager to do what was expected of him,
was noted. And so, also, with the decorous behaviour of the
young girl, as she stood with the other sponsors, rather tall
for her eleven years, her abundant hair – with the reddish
tinge inherited from her Plantagenet ancestors – making a
charming frame for her placid face.

In a small ante-chamber adjoining the chapel, the Archbishop of Toledo, whilst divesting himself of his ceremonial
robes, was in deep conversation with his nephew, the Marquis of Villena.

The Archbishop, a fiery man, who would have been more
suited to a military than an ecclesiastical career, was almost
shouting: 'It is an impossible situation. I never imagined
anything so fantastic, so farcical in all my life. That man ...
standing there looking on ...'

Villena, the wily statesman, had more control over his feelings than his uncle had over his. He lifted a hand and signed
towards the door.

'Why, nephew,' said the Archbishop testily, 'the whole

Court talks of it, jeers at it, and the question is asked: "How long will those who want to see justice done endure such a situation?" '

Villena sat on one of the tapestry-covered stools and sardonically contemplated the tips of his shoes. Then he said: 'The Queen is a harlot; the child is a bastard; the King is a fool; and the people in the streets cannot long be kept in ignorance of all that. Perhaps there have been wanton Queens who have foisted bastards on foolish kings before this. What I find impossible to endure is the favour shown to this man. Count of Ledesma! It is too much.'

'Henry listens to him on all occasions. Why, in the name of God and all His saints, does he behave with such stupidity?'

'Perhaps, Uncle, because he is grateful to their Beltran.'

'Grateful to his wife's lover, to the father of the child who is to be foisted on the nation as his own!'

'Grateful indeed,' said Villena. 'I fancy our Henry did not care to see himself as one who cannot beget a child. Beltran is so obliging: he serves the King in every way ... even to providing the Queen with his bastard to set upon the throne. We know Henry is incapable of begetting children. None of his mistresses has produced a child. After twelve years he was divorced from Blanche on the grounds that both were impotent. And he has been married to Joanna for eight years. It is surprising that Beltran and his mistress have taken so long.'

'We must not allow the child to be foisted on the nation.'

'We must go carefully, Uncle. There is time in plenty. If the King continues to shower honours on Beltran de la Cueva, he will turn more and more from us. Very well then, we will turn more and more from him.'

'And lose our places at Court, lose all that we have worked for?'

Villena smiled. 'Did you notice the children in chapel? What a pleasant pair!'

The Archbishop was alert. He said: 'It would never do. You could never set up young Alfonso while Henry is alive.'

'Why not ... if the people are so disgusted with him and his bastard?'

'Civil war?'

'It might be arranged more simply. But, Uncle, as I said, there is no need to act immediately. Keep your eyes on those two ... Alfonso and Isabella. They made a good impression on all who beheld them. Such pleasant manners. I declare our mad Dowager Queen has made an excellent job of their upbringing. They already have all the dignity of heirs to the throne. Depend upon it, their mother would raise no objection to our schemes. And what struck you most about them, Uncle? Was it the same as that which struck me? They were so docile, both of them, so ... malleable.'

'Nephew, this is dangerous talk.'

'Dangerous indeed! That is why we will not be hasty. Rumour is a very good ally. I am going to send for your servant now to help you dress. Listen to what I say in his hearing.'

Villena went to the door and, opening it, signed to a page.

In a few moments the Archbishop's servant entered. As he did so, Villena was saying in a whisper which could easily be heard by anyone in the room: 'It is to be hoped the child resembles her father in some way. What amusement that is going to cause throughout the Court. La Beltraneja should be beautiful, for her true father, I believe, is far more handsome than our poor deluded King; and the Queen has beauty also.'

'La Beltraneja,' mused the Archbishop, and he was smiling as the servant took his robe.

Within a few days the baby was being referred to throughout the Palace and beyond as La Beltraneja.

In the apartments of the Dowager Queen her two children stood before her, as they had been summoned. Isabella wondered whether Alfonso was as deeply aware as she was of the glazed look in their mother's eyes, of the rising note in her voice.

The christening ceremony had greatly excited her.

'My children,' she cried; then she embraced Alfonso and over his head surveyed Isabella. 'You were there. You saw the looks directed at that ... at that child ... and at yourselves. I told you ... did I not. I told you. I knew it was impossible. An heir to the throne of Castile! Let me tell you this: I have the heir of Castile here, in my arms. There is no other. There can be no other.'

'Highness,' said Isabella, 'the ceremony has been exhausting for you ... and to us. Could you not rest and talk to us of this matter later?'

Isabella trembled at her temerity, but her mother did not seem to hear her.

'Here!' she cried, raising her eyes to the ceiling as though she were addressing some celestial audience, 'here is the heir to Castile.'

Alfonso had released himself from the suffocating embrace. 'Highness,' he said, 'there may be some who listen at our door.'

'It matters little, my son. The same words are being spoken all over the Court. They are saying the child is the bastard daughter of Beltran de la Cueva. And who can doubt it? Tell me that ... tell me that, if you can! But why should you? You will be ready to accept the power and the glory when it is bestowed on you. That is the day I long for. The day I see my own Alfonso King of Castile!'

'Alfonso,' said Isabella, quietly, authoritatively, 'go and call the Queen's women. Go quickly.'

'It will not be long,' went on the Dowager Queen, who had not noticed that Isabella had spoken, nor that her son had slipped from the room. 'Soon the people will rise. Did you not sense it in the chapel? The feeling ... the anger! It would not have surprised me if the bastard had been

snatched from under her silken canopy. Nothing ... nothing
would have surprised me....'

'Holy Mother,' prayed Isabella, 'let them come quickly.
Let them take her to her apartment. Let them quieten her
before I have to see her held down by the doctors and forcibly drugged to quieten her.'

'It cannot go on,' cried the Queen. 'I shall live to see my
Alfonso crowned. Henry will do nothing. He will be powerless. His folly in showering honours on the bastard's father
will be his undoing. Did you not see the looks? Did you not
hear the comments?' The Queen had clenched her fists and
had begun beating her breast.

'Oh let them come quickly,' prayed Isabella.

When her mother had been taken away she felt exhausted.
Alfonso lingered and would have talked to her, but she was
afraid to talk to Alfonso. There were so many imminent
dangers, she felt certain, and in the great Palace one could
never be sure who was hidden away in some secret place to
listen to what was said.

It was highly dangerous, she knew very well, to discuss the
displacement of kings while they still lived; and if it were
true – which of course it was – that she and Alfonso had been
brought to Court so that their brother might be sure that they
should not be the centre of rebellion, it was certain that they
were closely watched.

She put on a cloak and went out into the gardens. Those
occasions when she could be alone were rare and, she knew,
would become more so, for she must not expect to enjoy the
same freedom here at Court as she had in the peace of Arevalo.

Still, as yet, she was regarded as but a child and she hoped
that she would continue to be so regarded for some time to
come. She did not want to be embroiled in the rebellious
schemes which tormented her mother's already overtaxed
brain.

Isabella believed firmly in law and order. Henry was King because he was the eldest son of their father, and she thought it was wrong that any other should take his place while he lived.

She stared down at the stream of the Manzanares and then across the plain to the distant mountains; and as she did so she became aware of approaching footsteps and, turning, saw a girl coming towards her.

'You wish to speak with me?' called Isabella.

'My lady Princesa, if you would be so gracious as to listen.'

This was a beautiful girl with strongly marked features; she was some four years older than Isabella and consequently seemed adult to the eleven-year-old Princess.

'But certainly,' said Isabella.

The other knelt and kissed Isabella's hand, but Isabella said: 'Please rise. Now tell me what it is you have to say to me.'

'My lady, my name is Beatriz Fernandez de Bobadilla, and it is very bold of me to make myself known to you thus unceremoniously; but I saw you walking alone here and I thought that if my mistress could behave without convention, so might I.'

'It is pleasant to escape from convention now and then,' said Isabella.

'I have news, my lady, which fills me with great joy. Shortly I am to be presented to you as your maid of honour. Since I learned this was to be I have been eagerly awaiting a glimpse of you, and when I saw you at the ceremony in the chapel I knew that I longed to serve you. When I am form-ally presented I shall murmur the appointed words which will convey nothing ... nothing of my true feelings. Princesa Isabella, I wanted you to know how I truly felt.'

Isabella stifled the disapproval which these words aroused in her. She had been brought up to believe that the etiquette of the Court was all-important; but when the girl lifted her eyes she saw there were real tears in them, and Isabella was not proof against such a display of emotion.

She realized she was lonely. She had no companion to whom she could talk of those matters which interested her. Alfonso was the nearest to being such a companion, but he was too young and not of her own sex. She had never enjoyed real companionship with her mother, and the thought of having a maid of honour who could also be a friend was very appealing.

Moreover in spite of herself, she could not help admiring the boldness of Beatriz de Bobadilla.

She heard herself say: 'You should have waited to be formally presented, but as long as no one sees us ... as long as no one is aware of what we have done ...'

This was not the way in which a Princess should behave, but Isabella was eager for this friendship which was being offered.

'I knew you would say that, Princesa,' cried Beatriz. 'That is why I dared.'

She stood up and her eyes sparkled. 'I could scarcely wait for a glimpse of you, my lady,' she went on. 'You are exactly as I imagined you. You will never have reason to regret that I was chosen to serve you. When we are married, I beg you let it make no difference. Let me continue to serve you.'

'Married?' said Isabella.

'Why yes, married. I am promised to Andres de Cabrera, even as you are promised to Prince Ferdinand of Aragon.'

Isabella flushed slightly at the mention of Ferdinand, but Beatriz hurried on: 'I follow the adventures of Prince Ferdinand with great interest, simply because he is betrothed to you.'

Isabella caught her breath and murmured: 'Could we walk a little?'

'Yes, my lady. But we should be careful not to be seen. I should be scolded for daring to approach thus, if we were.'

Isabella for once did not care if they were discovered, so

urgently did she desire to talk of Ferdinand.

'What did you mean when you said you had followed the adventures of Prince Ferdinand?'

'That I had gleaned information about him on every possible occasion, Princesa. I gathered news of the troublous state of affairs in Aragon, and the dangers which beset Ferdinand.'

'Dangers? What dangers?'

'There is civil war in Aragon, as you know, and that is a dangerous state of affairs. They say it is due to the Queen of Aragon, Ferdinand's mother, who would risk all she possesses in order to ensure the advancement of her son.'

'She must love him dearly,' said Isabella softly.

'Princesa, there is no one living who is more loved than young Ferdinand.'

'It is because he is so worthy.'

'And because he is the only son of the most ambitious woman living. It is a mercy that he has emerged alive from Gerona.'

'What is this? I have not heard of it.'

'But, Princesa, you know that the Catalans rose against Ferdinand's father on account of Carlos, Ferdinand's elder brother whom they loved so dearly. Carlos died suddenly, and there were rumours. It was said he was hastened to his death, and this had been arranged so that Ferdinand should inherit his father's dominions.'

'Ferdinand would have no hand in murder!'

'Indeed no. How could he? He is only a boy. But his mother – and his father too, for she has prevailed upon him to become so – are overweeningly ambitious for him. When his mother took Ferdinand into Catalonia, to receive the oath of allegiance, the people rose in anger. They said that the ghost of Ferdinand's half-brother, Carlos, walked the streets of Barcelona crying out that he was the victim of murder and that the people should avenge him. They say that miracles have been performed at his grave, and that he was a saint.'

'He asked for my hand in marriage,' said Isabella with a shudder. 'And shortly afterwards he died.'

'Ferdinand is intended for you.'

'Yes, Ferdinand and no other,' said Isabella firmly.

'It was necessary for the Queen of Aragon and her son Ferdinand to fly from Barcelona to Gerona; and there, with Ferdinand, she took possession of the fortress. I have heard that the fierce Catalans almost captured that fortress, and only the Queen's courage and resource saved their lives.'

'He was in such danger, and I did not know it,' murmured Isabella. 'Tell me . . . what is happening to him now?'

Beatriz shook her head. 'That I cannot say, but I have heard that the war persists in the dominions of the King of Aragon and that King John and Queen Joan will continue to be blamed for the murder of Carlos.'

'It is a terrible thing to have happened.'

'It was the only way for Ferdinand to become his father's heir.'

'He knew nothing of it,' affirmed Isabella. 'He can never be blamed.'

And to herself she said: Nor could Alfonso be if they insisted on putting him in Henry's place.

'I think,' she said aloud, 'that there are stormy days ahead for both Castile and Aragon – for Ferdinand and perhaps for me.'

'A country divided against itself provides perpetual danger,' said Beatriz solemnly; then her eyes sparkled. 'But it will not be long before Ferdinand comes to claim you. You will be married. I shall be married. And, Princesa, you said that, when we were, we should still be . . . friends.'

Isabella was astonished that she could be so touched by this offer of friendship.

She said in subdued tones: 'I think it is time that I returned to my apartments.'

Beatriz sank to her knees and Isabella swept past her. But

not before Beatriz had lifted her face and Isabella had given her a swift, almost shy smile.

From that moment Isabella had a new friend.

The Queen's little daughter lay on her silken cushions under a canopy in the state apartments, and one by one the great nobles came forward to kiss her hand and swear allegiance to her as heiress of the throne of Castile.

Beltran de la Cueva looked down at her with satisfaction. His position was unique. So many suspected that he was the baby's father, and yet, instead of this suspicion arousing the wrath of the King, it had made Henry feel more kindly towards him.

He could see a glorious future before him; he could still remain the Queen's very good friend, the King's also. And the child – now generally known as La Beltraneja – was to inherit the throne.

He fancied he had behaved with great skill in a difficult situation.

As he stood smiling with satisfaction his eyes met those of the Archbishop of Toledo, and he was quickly conscious of the smouldering anger there.

Rant as much as you like, my little Archbishop! thought Beltran. Plot with your sly nephew whose nose has been considerably put out of joint during this last year. I care not for you ... nor does the King nor the Queen, nor this baby here. There is nothing you can do to harm us.

But Beltran de la Cueva, gallant courtier though he was, so expert in the jousts, such an elegant dancer, lacked the sly cunning necessary to make of himself a statesman. He did not know that, even while they kissed the baby's hand and swore allegiance, the Archbishop and his nephew were planning to have her proclaimed illegitimate and oust her father from the throne.

The Marquis of Villena called on the King. Henry was with

his favourite mistress. There had been many since Alegre, and if she had been mentioned in his hearing it was doubtful whether he would now have remembered her name.

Henry had grown more indolent with the years. He was pleased that the royal cradle was at last occupied, and did not want to raise the question as to how this could have come about. Suffice it that there was an heir to the throne.

There were entertainments to be planned – those orgies which were growing more and more wild in an endeavour by those, whose duty it was, to tempt his jaded palate.

What new schemes, Henry was wondering, had they thought of this time? What pleasures would they show him that could give him new sensations, or could help him to recapture the old?

Then the Marquis of Villena was announced and with him, to Henry's dismay, was that villainous uncle of his, the Archbishop. Reluctantly and with a show of irritation Henry dismissed his mistress.

'We crave leave to speak to you, Highness, on a very important matter,' said Villena.

Henry yawned. Angry lights shot up in the Archbishop's eyes but Villena flashed a warning glance at him.

'I think, Highness,' said the Marquis, 'that this matter is one to which it would be well to give your close attention.'

'Well, what is it?' Henry demanded ungraciously.

'Grave suspicions have been cast on the legitimacy of the little Princess.'

Henry shrugged his shoulders. 'There are always rumours.'

'These are more than rumours, Highness.'

'What do you mean by that?'

'We fear something will have to be done. The peace of the country is threatened.'

'If people would stop meddling we should have peace.'

'The people must be assured,' said the Archbishop, 'that the heiress to the throne is the legitimate heiress.'

'The Princess is my daughter. Is not my daughter the legitimate heir to the throne?'

'Only if she *is* your daughter, Highness.'

'You are not going to say that another child was smuggled into the Queen's bed?'

'Rather, Highness,' said Villena with a snigger, 'that another *lover* was smuggled therein.'

'Gossip! Scandal!' muttered Henry. 'A plague on them. Have done. Let us accept what is. There is an heiress to the throne. The people have been crying out for an heir; now they have one let them be satisfied.'

'They'll not be satisfied with a bastard, Highness,' said the fierce Archbishop.

'What is this talk?'

'Highness,' said Villena, almost placatingly, 'you should know that throughout the Court the Princess is known by the name of La Beltraneja – after the man who, the majority are beginning to declare, is her father, Beltran de la Cueva.'

'But this is monstrous,' said the King with a mildness which exasperated the Archbishop.

'Your Highness,' went on Villena, 'puts yourself in a difficult position by showering honours on the man who is believed to have cuckolded you.'

Henry laughed. 'You are angered because honours and titles have gone to him which you believe should have found their way to you two. That is the point, is it not?'

'Your Highness surely will admit that it is unseemly to honour the man who has deceived you and attempted to foist his bastard upon you?'

'Oh, have done. Have done. Let the matter be, and let us have peace.'

'I am afraid, Highness, that is not possible. Certain of your ministers are demanding an enquiry into the birth of the child you are calling your daughter.'

'And if I forbid it?'

'Highness, that would be most unwise.'

'I am the King,' said Henry, hoping his voice sounded strong yet fearing that it was very weak.

'Highness, it is because we wish you to remain King that we beg you to give this matter your closest attention,' whispered Villena.

'Let them leave me in peace. The matter is done with. There is a Princess in the royal cradle. Leave it at that.'

'It is impossible, Highness. There is also a Prince in the Palace now, your half-brother Alfonso. There are many who say that, should the new-born child be proved a bastard, he should be named as your successor.'

'This is all very wearying,' sighed Henry. 'What can *I* do about it?'

Villena smiled at the Archbishop. 'There was a time, Highness,' he said gently, 'when I heard that question more often on your lips. Then you knew, Highness, that you could rely upon me. Now you put your faith and trust in a pretty young gentleman who makes scandals with the Queen herself. Highness, since you have asked me, this is my advice: Cease to honour Beltran de la Cueva so blatantly. Let him see that you doubt the honourable nature of his conduct. And allow a commission of churchmen – which I and the Archbishop will nominate – to enquire into the legitimacy of the child.'

Henry looked about hopelessly. The only way to rid himself of these tiresome men and to bring back his pretty mistress was to agree.

He waved his hand impatiently. 'Do as you wish ... do as you wish,' he cried. 'And leave me in peace.'

Villena and the Archbishop retired well satisfied.

It had become clear to all astute observers of the Castilian scene that the Marquis of Villena would not lightly abandon his hold upon the King, and if the King and Queen persisted in their allegiance to Beltran de la Cueva, Villena would

raise such a strong party against them that it might well lead
to civil war.

There was one who watched this state of affairs with great
satisfaction. This was the Marquis of Villena's brother, Don
Pedro Giron, a very ambitious man who was a Grand Master
of the Order of Calatrava.

The Knights of Calatrava belonged to an institution which
had been established as long ago as the twelfth century.

The Order had sprung into being because of the need to
defend Castile against Moorish conquerors. Calatrava stood
on the frontiers of Andalusia, which was occupied by the
Moors, and the town, which commanded the pass into Castile, became of paramount importance. The Knights Tem-
plar had attempted to hold it, but, unable to withstand the
constant and ferocious attacks of the Mussulmans, had aban-
doned it.

The reigning King of Castile, Sancho, the Beloved, offered the town to any knights who would defend it from the
Moors, and certain monks from a Navarrese convent immediately took possession. The situation captured the imagination of the people and many rallied to the defence of the
town, so enabling it to be held against all attacks.

The monks then founded an order which consisted of
knights, monks and soldiers; and this they named the
Knights of Calatrava; it was recognized by Pope Alexander
III as a religious Order in 1164, adopted the rules of St
Benedict and imposed strict discipline on its community.

The first and most important rule of the community was
that of celibacy. Its members were to follow the rule of silence, and to live in great austerity. They ate meat only once
a week; but they were not merely monks; they must remember that their Order had come into being through their
prowess with the sword; and it was their custom to sleep with
their swords beside them, ready to go into action against the
Moors at any moment when they might be called upon to do
so.

Don Pedro Giron, while enjoying the prestige his position in the Order brought to him, had no intention of carrying out its austere rules.

He was a man of tremendous political ambition and he did not see why, since his brother the Marquis was reckoned to be the most important man in Castile – or had been deemed so before the coming of the upstart Beltran de la Cueva – he should not bask in his brother's glory and use the influence of the Marquis to better his own position.

He was ready to obey his brother's wishes, to rouse the people to revolt if need be, to spread any rumour that his brother wished to be spread. Nor did he hesitate to follow his own life of pleasure, and he had a score of mistresses. Indeed the Grand Master of Calatrava was noted throughout Castile for his licentious habits. None dared criticize him; if he saw a flicker of disapproval on any face he would ask the offender if he knew his brother the Marquis of Villena. 'We are great friends, my brother and I. We are jealous of the family honour. His enemies are mine and mine are his.'

Consequently most people were too much in awe of the powerful Villena to continue the criticism of his somewhat disreputable brother. He was greatly amused by the scandal which the Queen of Castile had caused in the Court.

It pleased him to consider that Queens were as frail as other women, and as he was a vain man, he began to fancy himself as the lover of Joanna. She however was besottedly devoted to Beltran de la Cueva, and he himself was not an overwhelmingly handsome or attractive man.

Then one day he saw Isabella, the Dowager Queen of Castile, walking in the grounds, and he considered her.

She was still an attractive woman; he had heard rumours of her wildness and how it was sometimes necessary to lure her from her moods of hysteria by means of soothing powders and potions.

His brother the Marquis was turning more and more from King Henry and his Queen, which meant that he was turning towards the young Alfonso and Isabella. There was no doubt that the Dowager Queen, who was obviously ambitious for her children, would welcome the friendship of the Marquis of Villena.

And if she is a wise woman, mused Don Pedro, she will be eager to be on the best of terms with all our family.

So he watched her on more than one occasion, and it seemed to him that his latest mistress had little charm for him. She was a beautiful girl, but he had set his heart on sharing the bed of a Queen.

He swaggered about the Court, seeing himself as another Beltran de la Cueva.

At last he could contain his patience no longer; he found an opportunity of speaking alone to the Dowager Queen.

He had formally requested a private interview, and this was granted him.

As he dressed himself with the utmost care, as he demanded flattering compliments from his valets – who gave them slavishly, realizing that if they did not it would be the worse for them – it did not occur to him that he could fail in his plans regarding the Dowager Queen.

The Dowager Queen was with her daughter.

She had sent for Isabella, although she knew that Don Pedro Giron was on his way to visit her.

When Isabella saw her mother, she was quick to notice the suppressed excitement shining in her eyes. Yet, there was no hint of the madness. Something had made her happy, and Isabella had come to know that it was depression and frustration which brought on those attacks of madness.

'Come here, daughter,' said the Dowager Queen. 'I have sent for you because I wish you to be aware of what is going on about us.'

'Yes, Highness,' said Isabella demurely. She *was* aware, more than she had ever been. Her constant companion, Beatriz de Bobadilla, was proving to be very knowledgeable on

Court matters, and life had become full of intrigue and interest since Beatriz had formally been presented to her as her maid of honour. Now Isabella knew of the scandal concerning Queen Joanna and the birth of the baby who, many were beginning to say, was not the true heiress of Castile.

'I do not think it can be long now before your brother is proclaimed the King's successor,' said the Dowager Queen. 'There are protests from all directions. The people are not going to accept Beltran de la Cueva's daughter as their future Queen. Now, my dear Isabella, I have called you to me because I am expecting an important visit very shortly. I did not send for Alfonso because he is too young, and this concerns him too deeply. You are going to be present during the interview, although you will not be seen. You will be hidden behind the hangings there. You must stand very still, that none may know that you are present.'

Isabella caught her breath in fear. Was this a new version of that wildness? Her mother, actually arranging that she should eavesdrop!

'Very soon,' went on the Dowager Queen, 'the brother of the Marquis of Villena is to call upon me. He will come as his brother's messenger. I know the reason for his coming. It is to tell me that his brother's adherents are going to demand that Alfonso be acknowledged as Henry's heir. You will hear how calmly I accept his statements. It will be a lesson to you for the future, daughter; when you are Queen of Aragon you will have to receive ambassadors of all kinds. There may be some who bring startling news to you. You must never betray your emotions. Whatever the news ... good or bad ... you must accept it as a Queen, as you will see me do.'

'Highness,' began Isabella, 'could I not remain in your presence? Must I hide myself?'

'My dear child, do you imagine that the Grand Master of Calatrava would disclose his mission in your presence! Now ... obey me immediately. Come. This will hide you completely. Stay perfectly still, and listen to what he has to say.

And particularly note my acceptance of the news.'

Feeling that it was some mad game she was being forced to play, a game not in accord with her dignity, which had increased since her coming to Court, Isabella allowed herself to be placed behind the hangings.

After a few minutes Don Pedro was ushered into the apartments of the Dowager Queen.

'Highness,' he said, kneeling, 'it is gracious of you to receive me.'

'It gives me pleasure,' was the answer.

'I had a feeling within me, Highness, that I should cause you no offence by coming to you thus.'

'On the contrary, Don Pedro. I am ready to listen to your proposition.'

'Highness, have I your permission to sit?'

'Assuredly.'

Isabella heard the scrape of chair-legs as they sat down.

'Highness.'

'Well, Don Pedro?'

'I have long been aware of you. On those happy occasions when I have been at some ceremony which Your Highness attended I have been aware of no one else.'

There was a strange silence in the room, not lost on the hidden Isabella.

'I trust that you, Highness, have not been completely unaware of me.'

The Dowager Queen answered, and her voice showed she was bewildered: 'One would not be unaware of the brother of such a personage as the Marquis of Villena.'

'Ah, my brother. Highness, I would have you know that his interests are mine. We are as one ... in our desire to see peace in this Kingdom.'

Now the Queen felt and sounded happier. 'I had guessed that, Don Pedro.'

'Would it surprise you, Highness, if I told you that there have been occasions when my brother, the Marquis, has discussed his policies with me and listened to my advice?'

'It would not. You are Grand Master of a Holy Order. Naturally you should be able to advise your brother ... spiritually.'

'Highness, there is one thing I would work for ... body and soul ... that is the acceptance of your son the Infante Alfonso as heir to the throne of Castile. I would see the little bastard girl, now known as the heir, proclaimed for what she is. It need not be long before this happens ... if ...'

'If, Don Pedro?'

'I have made Your Highness aware of the influence I have with my brother, and you know full well the power he wields in this land. If you and I were friends, there is nothing I would not do ... not only to have the boy proclaimed heir, but to ... I must whisper this ... Come, sweet lady, let me put my lips to your ear ... to depose Henry in favour of your son Alfonso.'

'Don Pedro!'

'I said, my dearest lady, *if* we were friends.'

'I do not understand you. You speak in riddles.'

'Oh, you are not so blind as you would have me believe. You are still a beautiful woman, dear lady. Come ... come ... I hear you lived most piously at that deadly place in Arevalo ... but this is the Court. You are not old ... nor am I. I think we could bring a great deal of pleasure to each other's lives.'

'I think, Don Pedro,' said the Dowager Queen, 'that you must be suffering from a temporary madness.'

'Not I, dear lady, not I. As for yourself you would be completely well if you lived a more natural life. Come, do not be so prudish. Follow the fashion. By the saints, I swear you will never regret the day you and I become lovers.'

The Dowager Queen had leaped to her feet. Isabella heard the urgent scrape of her chair. She heard also the note of alarm in her mother's voice. Looking through the folds of brocade she saw a purple-faced man who seemed to her to symbolize all that was beastly in human nature. She saw her mother – no longer calm – afraid and shocked beyond her understanding.

Isabella knew that unless the man was dismissed her mother would begin to shout and wave her arms, and he would witness one of those wild scenes which she, Isabella, was so anxious should not be seen except by those whom she could trust.

Isabella forgot the instruction that she was to remain hidden. She stepped from her hiding-place into the room.

The purple-faced man with the evil expression stared at her as though she were a ghost. Indeed it must have seemed strange to him that she had apparently materialized from nowhere.

She drew herself to her full height and never before had she looked so much a Princess of Castile.

'Sir,' she said coldly, 'I ask you to leave ... immediately.'

Don Pedro stared at her incredulously.

'Is it necessary,' went on young Isabella, 'for me to have you forcibly removed?'

Don Pedro hesitated. Then he bowed and left them.

Isabella turned to her mother, who was trembling so much that she could not speak.

She led her to a chair and stood beside her, her arms about her protectively.

She whispered gently: 'Dearest Highness, he has gone now. He is evil ... but has left us. We will never see him again. Do not tremble so. Let me take you to your bed. There you will lie down. He has gone now, that evil man.'

The Dowager Queen stood up and allowed Isabella to take her arm.

From that moment Isabella felt that she was the one who must care for her mother, that she was the strong one who must protect her brother and her mother from this wicked Court, this whirlpool of intrigue which was threatening to drag them down to . . . what? She could not imagine.

All she knew was that she was capable of defending herself, of bridging the dangerous years through which she must pass before she was safe as the bride of Ferdinand.

The Dowager Queen sent for Isabella. She had recovered from the shock of Giron's proposals and was no longer stunned; she was very angry.

'I am sorry, my daughter,' said the Queen, 'that you should have overheard such a revolting outburst. That man shall be severely punished. He shall very soon regret the day he submitted me to such indignity. You are coming with me to the King, to bear witness of what you overheard.'

Isabella was alarmed. She fully realized that the Grand Master of the Order of Calatrava had behaved disgracefully, but she had hoped that, once the man had been dismissed from her mother's presence, his conduct might be forgotten; for remembering it could only serve to over-excite her mother.

'We are going to Henry now,' said the Dowager Queen. 'I have told him that I must see him on a matter of great importance, and he has agreed to receive us.' The Dowager Queen looked at her daughter, and tears came into her eyes. 'My dear Isabella,' she said, 'I fear you are fast leaving childhood behind you. That is inevitable, since you must live at this Court. I could wish, my dear, that you and I and your brother could return to Arevalo. I think we should be so much happier there. Come.'

Henry received them with a show of affection.

He complimented Isabella on her appearance. 'Why,' he said, 'my little sister is no longer a child. She grows every day. We are a tall family, Isabella; and you are no exception.'

He greeted his stepmother with equal warmth, although he was wondering what grievance had brought her – he felt sure it was a grievance.

'Henry,' said the Dowager Queen, 'I have a complaint to make ... a complaint of a most serious nature.'

The King put on an expression of concern, but Isabella, who was watching closely, saw that it thinly veiled one of exasperation.

'I have been insulted by Don Pedro Giron,' said the Dowager Queen dramatically.

'That is very shocking,' said Henry, 'and I am grieved to hear it.'

'The man came to my apartment and made outrageous proposals.'

'What were these proposals?'

'They were of an immoral nature. Isabella will bear witness, for she heard all that was said.'

'He made these proposals in Isabella's presence then?'

'Well ... she was there.'

'You mean he was not aware that she was there?'

'No ... he was not. I know, Henry, that you will not allow such outrageous conduct to go unpunished.'

Henry shifted his gaze from his stepmother's face. He said, 'He did not ... attack you?'

'He attacked my good name. He dared presume to make immoral suggestions to me. If Isabella had not come from her hiding-place in time ... I think it is very possible that he might have laid hands on me.'

'So Isabella was in hiding?' Henry looked sternly at his half-sister.

'I thank the saints that she was!' cried the Queen. 'No woman's virtue is safe when there are such men at Court. My dear son, you will, I know, not suffer such conduct to go unpunished.'

Henry said: 'Dear Mother, you excite yourself unnecessarily. I have no doubt that you protected your virtue from this man. You are still a beautiful woman. I cannot entirely blame him – nor must you – for being aware of that. I am sure, if you consider this matter calmly, you will come to the conclusion that the best of men sometimes forget the honour due to rank when beauty beckons.'

'This is carnal talk,' cried the Queen. 'I beg of you not to use it before my daughter.'

'Then I marvel that you should bring her to me when making such a complaint.'

'But I told you she was there.'

'She had been concealed ... by your wishes, or was it some sly prank of her own? Which was it, eh? You tell me, Isabella.'

Isabella looked at her mother; she dared not lie to the King, yet at the same time she could not betray her mother.

Henry saw her embarrassment and was sorry for her. He laid a hand on her shoulder. 'Do not fret, Isabella. Too much is being made of very little.'

'Do you mean,' screeched the Queen, 'that you will ignore the insulting behaviour of this man towards a member of the royal family?'

'Dear Mother, you must be calm. I have heard how excited you become on occasions, and it has occurred to me that it might be advisable if you left Court for some place where events which excited you were less likely to occur. As for Don Pedro Giron, he is the brother of the Marquis of Villena, and therefore not a man who can be lightly reprimanded.'

'You would allow yourself to be ruled by Villena!' cried the Queen. 'Villena is important ... more important than your father's wife! It matters not that she has been insulted. It is the brother of the great Villena who has done it, and he must not be reprimanded! I had thought Villena was of less importance nowadays. I thought there was a new sun beginning to rise, and that we must all fall down and worship it. I thought that since Beltran de la Cueva – that most obliging man – became the friend of the King ... and the Queen ... the Marquis of Villena was not the man he had once been.'

Isabella half closed her eyes with horror. Previously the

scenes had been threatening in the private apartments. What would happen if, in the presence of the King, her mother began to shout and laugh!

She longed to take her mother by the hand, to whisper urgently that they should beg permission to go; and only the rigorous training she had received prevented her from doing so.

Henry saw her distress and was as eager to put an end to this discussion as she was.

'I think,' he said gently, 'that it would be well if you considered returning to Arevalo.'

His quiet tone had its effect on the Dowager Queen. She was silent for a few seconds, then she cried out: 'Yes, it would be better if we returned to Arevalo. There I was safe from the lewdness of those whom Your Highness is pleased to honour.'

'You may leave when you wish,' said Henry. 'I only ask that my little sister and brother remain at Court.'

Those words completely subdued the Queen.

Isabella knew that they had touched her with a terrible fear. One of the worst terrors of her mother's wild imagination had always been that her children might be separated from her.

'You have leave to retire,' said Henry.

The Queen curtsied; Isabella did the same; and they returned in silence to their apartment.

MURDER AT THE CASTLE OF
ORTES

THERE were days when the château of Ortes in Béarn
seemed like a prison to Blanche, and her apartments
there took on the aspect of a condemned cell.

Within those ancient walls she felt as though assassins hid
behind the hangings, that in dark corners they waited for her.

Sometimes, after she had dismissed her servants, she
would lie in bed, tense . . . waiting.

Was that a creak of a floor-board? A soft footfall in her
room?

Should she close her eyes and wait? How would it come?
A pillow pressed over her mouth? A knife thrust into her
breast?

Yet what is my life that I should cling to it? she asked
herself. For what can I hope now?

Perhaps there was always hope. Perhaps she believed that
her family would repent; that ambition, which had dominated it for so many years and had robbed its members of
their finer feelings, would miraculously depart leaving room
only for loving kindness.

Miracles there might be, but not such miracles as that.

Here she lived, the prisoner of her sister and her sister's
husband. It was terrible to know that they planned to rid
themselves of her, that they were prepared to kill her for the
sake of acquiring Navarre. It was a rich province, and many
had cast covetous eyes on that maize and wheat-growing, that
wine-producing land. But what land was worth the disinte-
gration of a family, and the sordid criminality of its members
against each other?

It would have been better, she often thought, if her mother had never inherited Navarre from Charles III, her father.

Often she dreamed that Carlos came to her, that he warned her to flee from this grim castle. In the mornings she was never sure whether she had dreamed that she had seen him or whether he had actually been with her. It was said that his ghost walked the streets of Barcelona. Perhaps the ghosts of murdered men did walk the earth, warning those they loved who were in similar danger, perhaps seeking revenge on their murderers. But Carlos had never been one to seek revenge. He had been too gentle. If he had been less so, he could not have failed to lead the people successfully against his father and his stepmother, and would doubtless now be the heir of Aragon in place of little Ferdinand. But it was the gentle ones who were sacrificed.

Blanche shivered. Her character was not unlike that of Carlos, and it seemed to her that there were warnings all about her that her time must come, as had that of Carlos.

There were occasions when she felt that she wanted to make the journey into Aragon to reason with her father and her stepmother, or to go to her sister, Eleanor, and her husband, Gaston de Foix, and tell them what was in her mind.

To her father and stepmother she would say: 'What has your terrible crime brought to you? You have made Ferdinand heir of Aragon in place of Carlos. But what has happened to Aragon? The people murmur continually against you. They do not forget Carlos. There is continual strife. And one day, when you come near to the end of your days, you will remember the man who died at your command, and you will be filled with such remorse that you would rather have died before you committed such a crime.'

And to Eleanor and Gaston: 'You want me removed so that Navarre can pass to you. You desire your son Gaston to be the ruler of Navarre. Oh Eleanor, take warning in time. Remember what happened to Carlos. Do not, for the sake of land, for the sake of wealth, for the sake of ambition – even though this is centred in your son – stain your souls with the murder of your sister.'

One must not blame young Gaston. One must not blame young Ferdinand. It was for their sakes that their parents were ready to commit crimes, but these boys were not parties to those crimes. Yet what kind of men would they be, they who must eventually know that murder had been committed for their sakes? Would they, as their parents had, make ambition the over-ruling feature of their lives?

'I am a lonely woman,' she told herself, 'a frightened woman.'

Yes, she was frightened. She had lived with fear now for two years; each day on waking she wondered whether this would be her last, each night wondered whether she would see the morning.

When she had come into Béarn she had been frantic, looking about for means of escape.

There had seemed to be no one to help her ... until she remembered Henry, the husband who had repudiated her. It was strange that she should have thought of him; and yet was it so strange? There was about him a gentleness which others lacked. He was a lecher; he had deceitfully led her to believe that he intended to keep her in Castile even while he was planning to rid himself of her; and yet it was to him she had turned in her extremity.

She had written to him then; she had reminded him that he was not only her former husband but her cousin. Did he ever remember their happiness when she had first come to Castile? Now they were parted and she was a lonely woman, forced to exile far from her home.

Now, recalling that letter, she wept a little. She had been happy during those first days of her marriage. She had not known Henry then; she had been too young, too inexperienced to believe that any man, so gentle, so determined to please her as her husband had seemed, could be so shallow and insincere, not really feeling the deep emotion to which he had falsely given expression.

How could she have guessed in those days that tragedy was waiting for her in the years ahead? How could she have visualized those barren years, the inevitable conclusion of which had been banishment to this gloomy castle where death lurked, waiting to spring upon her at an unguarded moment?

'For two years I have been here,' she murmured. 'Two years … waiting … sensing evil … knowing that I have been brought here to end my days.'

In that last frantic letter to Henry she had renounced her claim to Navarre in favour of the husband who had repudiated her, for it had seemed to her then that if she removed the cause of envy she might be allowed to live.

Was that letter a plea to Henry? Was she telling him that she was handing him Navarre because she was in Béarn, a lonely frightened prisoner? Did she still believe that Henry was a noble knight who would come and rescue the lady in distress, even though he had ceased to love her?

'I was always a foolish woman,' mused Blanche sadly.

Henry in Castile was living his gay and voluptuous life, there surrounded by his mistresses and his wife who shared his tastes, it seemed. How foolish to imagine that he would have a thought to spare for the dangers of a woman who had ceased to concern him once he was satisfactorily – from his point of view – divorced from her and had sent her away. There was no help from Henry. She might as well never have offered him Navarre. He was too indolent to take it.

So Navarre remained – her inheritance, the coveted land, on account of which death stalked the castle of Ortes, waiting until the moment was propitious to strike.

With the coming of night her fears increased.

Her women helped her to bed. They slept in her apartment, as she felt happier with them there.

They could not be unaware of the sense of fear which

pervaded the place; she noticed how they would start at a footfall, leap to their feet when they heard voices or footsteps at the door.

A messenger arrived at Ortes with a letter from the Comtesse de Foix to her sister Blanche. It was an affectionate letter, containing news of a marriage the Comtesse was trying to arrange for her sister. Because of that unfortunate incident in Castile, Blanche must not imagine that her family would allow her to lead the life of a hermit.

I do not care if I live the life of a hermit, thought Blanche. All I care is that I live.

In one of the kitchens the messenger from the Comtesse de Foix was drinking a glass of wine.

The servant who had brought it to him lingered as he refreshed himself, and there came a moment when they were quite alone. Then the messenger ceased to smile pleasantly as he sipped his wine.

He frowned in annoyance and said to the servant: 'Why is there this delay? If it continues you will have some explaining to do.'

'Sir, it is not easy.'

'I cannot comprehend the difficulties; nor can others.'

'Sir, I have attempted . . . once or twice.'

'Then you are a bungler. We do not suffer bunglers. Can you guess what your fate may well be? Put out your tongue. Good! I see it is pink, and that I believe is a sign of health. I'll swear it's plausible too. I'll swear it has played its part in luring the maidens to your bed, eh? Ah, I know. You have paid too much attention to them and neglected your duty. Let me tell you this: that tongue could be cut out, and you'd be a sorry fellow without it. And that, my friend, is but one of the misfortunes which could befall you.'

'Sir, I need time.'

'You have wasted time. I give you another chance. It must happen within twenty-four hours after I leave. I shall stay at the inn nearby, and if the news is not brought to me within twenty-four hours ...'

'You ... you shall not be disappointed, sir.'

'That is well. Now fill my glass. And ... remember.'

The messenger had left and Blanche felt easier in her mind as she watched him ride away.

She always believed that her sister or her father would send their creatures to do their work.

She called to her women to bring her embroidery. They would work awhile, she said.

There was comfort in the stitching; she could believe she was back in the past – in her home in Aragon when her mother had been alive, before sinister schemes had rent their household – when she had been a member of a happy family; or in the early days of marriage in Castile.

And thus, during those hours which followed the departure of the messenger, her fears were less acute.

She took her dinner with her ladies, as was her custom, and it was shortly after the meal that she complained of pains and dizziness.

Her women helped her to bed and, as the pain grew more violent, Blanche understood.

So this was it. It was not a knife in the dark, nor murderous hands about her throat. Foolish again to have suspected that it would be, when this was the safe way ... the way Carlos had gone. They would say: She died of a colic, of a fever. And those who doubted that she had died a natural death would either not bother to question the verdict or not dare to.

'Let it be quick,' she prayed. 'Oh Carlos ... I am coming to you now.'

A message was taken to the inn, and when it was handed to its recipient he read it calmly and gave no sign that he was surprised or shocked by its contents.

He said to his groom: 'We shall return to the castle.' And they left at once, riding full speed towards Ortes.

When he arrived there, he summoned the servants together and addressed them.

'I am speaking in the name of the Comte and Comtesse de Foix,' he told them. 'You are to go about your business as though nothing has happened. Your mistress will be quietly interred, but news of her death is not to go beyond these walls.'

One of the women stepped forward. She said: 'I would like to say, sir, that I fear my mistress is the victim of an evil assassin. She was well when she sat down to her meal. She suffered immediately afterwards. If you please, I think some investigation should be made.'

The messenger lifted his heavy-lidded eyes to stare at the woman. There was something so cold, so menacing in his look, that she began to tremble.

'Who is this?' he demanded.

'Sir, she served Queen Blanche and was much beloved by her.'

'It would account for her derangement perhaps.' The cold implacable tone held a warning which was clear to everyone. 'Poor lady,' went on the messenger, 'if she is the victim of hallucinations we must see that she has proper attention.'

Then another of the women spoke. She said: 'Sir, she is hysterical. She knows not what she says. She had a great affection for Queen Blanche.'

'Nevertheless, she shall be cared for ... unless she recovers her balance. Now do not forget the orders of the Comte and Comtesse. This distressing news is to be a secret until orders are given to the contrary. If any should disobey these orders it will be necessary to punish them. Take care of the late Queen's poor friend. Make the wishes of the Comte and Comtesse known to her.'

It was as though a shudder ran through all those listening. They understood. A murder had been committed in their midst. Their gentle mistress, who had harmed no one and done much good to so many, had been eliminated; and they were being warned that painful death would be their reward if they raised their voices against her murderers.

ALFONSO OF PORTUGAL – A
SUITOR FOR ISABELLA

Queen Joanna let her fingers play in the dark glistening hair of her lover. He bent over her couch and, as they kissed, she knew that his thoughts were not so much with her as with the brilliant materialization of his dreams of fortune.

'Dear Beltran,' she asked, 'you are contented?'

'I think, my love, that life goes well for us.'

'What a long way you have come, my Beltran, since I looked from my window and beckoned you to my bedchamber. Well, one way to glory is through the bedchambers of Kings. Also through the Queen's, you have discovered.'

He kissed her with passion. 'To combine desire with ambition, love with power! How singularly fortunate I have been!'

'And I. You owe your good fortune to me, Beltran. I owe mine to my own good sense. So you see I may congratulate myself even more than you do yourself.'

'We are fortunate ... in each other.'

'And in the King, my husband. Poor Henry! He grows more shaggy with the years. I often think he is like a dear old dog, growing a little obese, a little blind, a little deaf – figuratively, of course – but remaining so good-tempered, never growling even when he is neglected or insulted, and always ready to give a friendly bark, or wag his tail at the least attention.'

'He realizes his good fortune in possessing such a Queen. You are incomparable.'

She laughed. 'Indeed I begin to think I am. Who else could have produced the heiress of Castile?'

'Our dearest little Joanna – how enchanting she is!'

'So enchanting that we must make sure no one snatches the crown from her head. They will try, my love. They grow insolent. Someone referred to her as La Beltraneja yesterday in my hearing.'

'And you were angry?'

'I gave evidence of my righteous anger, but inwardly I was just a little pleased, a little proud.'

'We must curb that pride and pleasure, dearest. We must plan for her sake.'

'That is what I intend to do. I visualize the day when we shall see her mount the throne. I do not feel that Henry will live to a great age. He is too indulgent in those pleasures which, while giving him such amusement, rob him of his health and strength.'

Beltran was thoughtful. 'I often wonder,' he mused, 'what his inner thoughts are when he hears our darling's nickname.'

'He does not hear. Did you not know that Henry has the most obliging ears in Castile? They are only rivalled by his eyes, which are equally eager to serve him. When he does not want to listen, he is deaf; when he does not wish to see, he is blind.'

'If only we could contrive some magic to render the ears and eyes of those about him equally accommodating!'

Joanna gave a mock shudder. 'I do not like the all-important Marquis. He has too many ideas swirling about in that haughty head of his.'

Beltran nodded slowly. 'I have seen his eyes resting with alarming speculation on the young Alfonso. Also on his sister.'

'Oh, those children! And especially Isabella. I fear the years at Arevalo, under the queer and pious guardianship of mad Mamma, have done great harm to the child's character.'

'One can almost hear her murmuring: "I will be a saint among women." '

'If that were all, Beltran, I would forgive her. I fancy the murmuring is: "I will be a saint among ... *Queens*." '

'Alfonso is of course the main danger.'

'Yes, but I would like to see those two removed from Court. The Dowager has gone. Oh, what a blessing not to have to see *her*! Long may she remain in Arevalo.'

'I heard that she has lapsed into a deep melancholy and is resigned to leaving her son and daughter at Court.'

'Let her stay there.'

'You would like to banish Alfonso and Isabella to Arevalo with her.'

'Farther away than that. I have a plan ... for Isabella.'

'My clever Queen...' murmured Beltran; and laughing, Joanna put her lips to his.

'Later,' she said softly, 'I will explain.'

Beatriz de Bobadilla regarded her mistress with a certain dismay. Isabella was sitting, quietly stitching at her embroidery, as though she were unaware of all the dangers which surrounded her.

There was about Isabella, Beatriz decided, an almost unnatural calm. Isabella believed in her destiny. She was certain that one day Ferdinand of Aragon would come to claim her; and that Ferdinand would conform exactly with that idealized picture which Isabella had made of him.

What a lot she has to learn of life! thought Beatriz.

Beatriz felt as though she were an experienced woman compared with Isabella. It was more than those four years seniority which made her feel this. Isabella was an idealist; Beatriz was a practical woman.

Let us hope, thought Beatriz, that she will not be too greatly disappointed.

Isabella said: 'I wish there were news of Ferdinand. I am growing old now. Surely our marriage cannot long be delayed?'

'You may be sure,' Beatriz soothed, 'that soon there will be plans for your marriage.'

But, wondered Beatriz, bending over her work, will it be to Ferdinand?

'I hope all is well in Aragon,' said Isabella.

'There is great trouble there since the rebellion in Catalonia.'

'But Carlos is dead now. Why cannot the people settle down and be happy?'

'They cannot forget how Carlos died.'

Isabella shivered. 'Ferdinand had no hand in that.'

'He is too young,' agreed Beatriz. 'And now Blanche is dead. Carlos ... Blanche. ... There is only Eleanor alive of King John's family by his first wife, and she will not stand in the way of Ferdinand's inheritance.'

'He is his father's heir by right now,' murmured Isabella. 'Yes, but ...'

'But what?' demanded Isabella sharply.

'How will Ferdinand feel ... how would anyone feel ... knowing that it had been necessary for one's brother to die before one could inherit the throne?'

'Carlos died of a fever ...' began Isabella. Then she stopped. 'Did he, Beatriz? Did he?'

'It would have been a most convenient fever,' said Beatriz.

'I wish I could see Ferdinand ... talk to Ferdinand ...' Isabella held her needle poised above her work. 'Why should it not be that God has chosen Ferdinand to rule Aragon, and it is for this reason that his brother died?'

'How can we know?' said Beatriz. 'I hope Ferdinand is not made unhappy by his brother's death.'

'How *would* one feel if a brother were removed so that one inherited the throne? How should I feel if Alfonso were taken like that?' Isabella shivered. 'Beatriz,' she went on solemnly, 'I should have no wish to inherit the throne of Castile unless it were mine by right. I would wish no harm to Alfonso of course, nor to Henry ... in order that I might reach the throne.'

'I know full well that you would not, for you are good. Yet

what if the well-being of Castile depended on the removal of a bad king?'

'You mean ... Henry?'

'We should not even speak of such things,' said Beatriz. 'What if we were overheard?'

Isabella said: 'No, we must not speak of them. But tell me this first. You do not know of any plan to remove ... Henry?'

'I think that Villena might make such plans.'

'But why?'

'I think he and his uncle might wish to put Alfonso in Henry's place as ruler of Castile, that they might rule Alfonso.'

'That would be highly dangerous.'

'But perhaps I am wrong. This is idle gossip.'

'I trust you *are* wrong, Beatriz. Now that my mother has gone back to Arevalo I often think how much more peaceful life has become. But perhaps I delude myself. My mother could not hide her desires, her excitement. Perhaps others desire and plan in secret. Perhaps there is as much danger in the silences of some as in the hysteria of my mother.'

'Have you heard from her since she reached Arevalo?'

'Not from her but from one of her friends. She often forgets that we are not there with her. When she remembers she is very melancholy. I hear that she lapses into moods of depression, when she expresses her fears that neither Alfonso nor I will ever wear the crown of Castile. Oh, Beatriz, I often think how happy I might have been if we were not a royal family. If I were your sister, shall I say, and Alfonso your brother, how happy we might have been. But from the time I was able to speak I was continually told: "You could be Queen of Castile." It made none of us happy. It seems to me that there has always been a reaching out for something beyond us ... for something that would be highly dangerous should we possess it. Oh, you should be happy, Beatriz. You do not know how happy.'

'Life is a battle for all of us,' murmured Beatriz. 'And you shall be happy, Isabella. I hope I shall always be there to see and perhaps, in my small way, contribute to that happiness.'

'When I marry Ferdinand and go to Aragon, you must accompany me there, Beatriz.'

Beatriz smiled a little sadly. She did not believe that she would be allowed to follow Isabella to Aragon; she herself would have to marry; her husband would be Andres de Cabrera, an officer of the King's household, and her duty would be to stay with him, not to go with Isabella – if Isabella ever went to Aragon.

She smiled fondly at her mistress. For Isabella had no doubt. Isabella saw her future with Ferdinand as clearly as she saw the piece of needlework now in her hand.

Beatriz gazed out of the window and said: 'There is your brother. He has returned from a ride.'

Isabella dropped her work and went to the window. Alfonso looked up, saw them and waved.

Isabella beckoned, and Alfonso leaped from his horse, left it with a groom and came into the Palace.

'How he grows,' said Beatriz. 'One would not believe he is only eleven.'

'He has changed a great deal since he came to Court. I think we both have. He has changed too since our mother went away.'

They were both more light-hearted now, Beatriz thought. Poor Isabella, how she must have suffered through that mother of hers! It had made her serious beyond her years. Alfonso came into the room. He was flushed and looked very healthy from his ride.

'You called me,' he said, embracing Isabella and turning to bow to Beatriz. 'Did you want to talk to me?'

'I always want to talk to you,' said Isabella. 'But there is nothing in particular.'

Alfonso looked relieved. 'I was afraid something had gone amiss.'

'You were expecting something?' she asked anxiously.

Alfonso looked at Beatriz.

'You must not mind Beatriz,' said Isabella. 'She and I discuss everything together. She is as our sister.'

'Yes, I know,' said Alfonso. 'And you ask if I am expecting something. I would say I am always expecting something. There is always something either happening or threatening to happen here. Surely all Courts are not like this one, are they?'

'In what way?' asked Beatriz.

'I do not think there could be another King like Henry in the world. Nor a Queen like Joanna ... and a situation such as that relating to the baby.'

'Such situations may have occurred before,' mused Isabella.

'There is going to be trouble. I know it,' said Alfonso.

'Someone has been talking to you.'

'It was the Archbishop.'

'You mean the Archbishop of Toledo?'

'Yes,' said Alfonso. 'He has been very gracious to me of late ... too gracious.'

Beatriz and Isabella exchanged glances of apprehension.

'He shows me a respect which I have not received before,' went on Alfonso. 'I do not think the Archbishop is very pleased with our brother.'

'It is not for an Archbishop to be displeased with a King,' Isabella reminded him.

'Oh, but it could be for this Archbishop and this King,' Alfonso corrected her.

Isabella said: 'I have heard that Henry has agreed to a match between the little Princess and Villena's son. Thus he could make sure of keeping Villena his friend.'

'The people would never agree to that,' said Beatriz.

'And,' put in Alfonso, 'there is going to be an enquiry into the legitimacy of the little Princess. If it is found that she cannot be the King's daughter, then ... they will proclaim me heir to the throne.' He looked bewildered. 'Oh, Isabella,' he went on, 'how I wish that we need not be bothered. How tiresome it is! It is as it was when our mother was with us. Do you remember – at the slightest provocation we would be told that we must take care, we must do this, we must not do that, because it was possible that we should one day inherit the crown? How tired I am of the crown! I wish I could ride and swim and do what other boys do. I wish I did not have to be regarded always as a person to be watched. I do not want the Archbishop to make a fuss of me, to tell me he is my very good friend and will always be at hand to protect me. I will choose my own friends, and they will not be Archbishops.'

'There is someone at the door,' said Beatriz.

She went towards it and opened it swiftly.

A man was standing there.

He said: 'I have a message for the Infanta Isabella.' And Beatriz stood aside for him to enter.

As he came towards her Isabella thought: How long has he been standing outside the door? What has he heard? What had they said?

Alfonso was right. There was no peace for them. Their actions were watched; everything they did was spied upon. It was one of the penalties for being a possible candidate for the throne.

'You would speak with me?' she asked.

'Yes, Infanta. I bring a message from your noble brother, the King. He wishes you to come with all speed to his presence.'

Isabella inclined her head. 'You may return to him,' she said, 'and tell him that I am coming immediately.'

As Isabella entered her brother's apartments she knew that this was an important occasion.

Henry was seated, and beside him was the Queen. Standing behind the King's chair was Beltran de la Cueva, Count of Ledesma; and the Marquis of Villena, with his uncle the Archbishop of Toledo, was also present.

Isabella knelt before the King and kissed his hand.

'Why, Isabella,' said Henry kindly, 'it gives me pleasure to see you. Does she not grow apace!' He turned to Queen Joanna, who flashed on Isabella a smile of great friendliness which seemed very false to the young girl.

'She is going to be tall, as you are, my dear,' said the Queen.

'How old are you, sister?' asked the King.

'Thirteen, Highness.'

'A young woman, no less. Time to put away childish things, and think of . . . marriage, eh?'

They were all watching her, Isabella knew, and she was angry because she was aware of the faint flush which had risen to her cheeks. Did she show the joy which she was feeling?

At last she and Ferdinand were to be united. Perhaps in a few days they would be meeting. She was a little apprehensive. Would he be as pleased with her as, she was certain, she was going to be with him?

How one's thoughts ran on. They went beyond one's control.

'We keep your welfare very close to our hearts – the Queen, myself, my friends and ministers. And, sister, we have decided on a match for you, one which will delight you by its magnificence.'

She bowed her head and waited, hoping that she would be able to curb her joy and not show unseemly delight in the fact that at last she was to be the bride of Ferdinand.

'The Queen's brother, King Alfonso V of Portugal, asks your hand in marriage. I and my advisers are delighted by this offer and we have decided that it can only bring happiness and advantage to all concerned.'

Isabella did not believe that she heard correctly. She was conscious of a rush of blood to her ears; she could hear and feel the mighty pounding of her heart. For a few seconds she believed she would faint.

'Well, sister, I see that you are overcome by the magnificence of this offer. You are a personable young woman now, you know. And you deserve a good match. It is my great pleasure to provide it for you.'

Isabella lifted her eyes and looked at the King. He was smiling, but not at her. He knew of her obsession with the idea of the Aragonese marriage. He remembered hearing how upset she was when she heard that a match had been arranged for her with the Prince of Viana. It was for this reason that he had told her in a formal manner of the proposed marriage with Portugal.

As for the Queen, she was smiling brightly. The match was entirely to her liking. She wanted to see Isabella safely out of Castile, for while she remained there she was a menace to Joanna's daughter. She would of course have preferred to remove young Alfonso, but that would have presented too many difficulties at the moment. However, the brother would now be weakened by the loss of his sister's support.

One of them will be out of the way, mused Joanna.

Isabella spoke slowly but clearly, and no one in that chamber remained unimpressed by the calm manner in which she addressed them.

'I thank Your Highness for making such efforts on my behalf, but it seems that a certain fact has been overlooked. I am already betrothed, and I and others consider that betrothal binding.'

'Betrothed!' cried Henry. 'My dear sister, you take a childish view of these things. Many husbands are suggested for Princesses, but there is nothing binding in these suggestions.'

'Nevertheless I am betrothed to Ferdinand of Aragon; and in view of this, marriage elsewhere is impossible.'

Henry looked exasperated. His sister was going to be stubborn, and he was too weary of conflict to endure it. If he had been alone with her he would have agreed with her that she was betrothed to Ferdinand, that the King of Portugal's offer must be refused; and then, as soon as she had left him, he would have gone ahead with arrangements for the marriage, leaving someone else to break the news to her.

He could not do this, of course, in the presence of the Queen and his ministers.

'Dear Isabella!' cried Joanna. 'She is but a child yet. She does not know that a great King like my brother cannot be refused when he asks her hand in marriage. You are fortunate indeed; you will be very happy in Lisbon, Isabella.'

Isabella looked from Villena to the Archbishop and then appealingly at Henry. None of them would meet her gaze.

'The King of Portugal himself,' said Henry, studying the rings on his fingers, 'is coming to Castile. He will be here within the next few days. You must be ready to receive him, sister. I would have you show your pleasure and gratitude that he has chosen you for this high honour.'

Isabella stood very still. She wanted to speak her protests but it seemed to her that her throat had closed and would not let the words escape.

In spite of that natural calm, that extraordinary dignity, standing here in the audience chamber with the eyes of all the leading ministers of Castile upon her, she looked like an animal desperately seeking a means of escape from a trap which it saw closing about it.

Isabella lay on her bed; she had the curtains drawn about it that she might be completely shut in. She had prayed for long hours on her knees, but she did not cease to pray every hour of the day.

She had talked to Beatriz; and Beatriz could only look sad and say that this was the fate of Princesses; but she had tried to comfort her. 'This is an obsession you have built up for Ferdinand,' she told her. 'How can you be sure that he is the only one for you? You have never seen him. You know nothing of him except what has come to you through hearsay. Might it not be that the King of Portugal will be a kind husband?'

'I love Ferdinand. That sounds foolish to you, but it is as though he has grown up with me. Perhaps when I first heard his name I needed comfort, perhaps I allowed myself to build an ideal – but there is something within me, Beatriz, which tells me that only with Ferdinand can I be happy.'

'If you do your duty you will be happy.'

'I do not feel that it is my duty to marry the King of Portugal.'

'It is what the King, your brother, commands.'

'I shall have to go away from Castile ... away from Alfonso ... away from you, Beatriz. I shall be the most unhappy woman in Castile, in Portugal. There must be a way. They were determined to marry me to the Prince of Viana, but he died, and that was like a miracle. Perhaps if I prayed enough there might be another miracle.'

Beatriz shook her head; she had little comfort to offer. She believed that Isabella must now leave her childish dreams behind her; she must accept reality, as so many Princesses had been obliged to do before her.

And since Beatriz could not help, Isabella wished to shut herself away, to pray, if not to be saved from this distasteful marriage, to have the courage to endure it.

There was a movement in her room and she sat up in bed, whispering: 'Who is there?'

'It is I, Isabella.'

'Alfonso!'

'I came to you quietly. I did not want anyone to disturb us. Oh ... Isabella, I am frightened.'

The bed curtains divided and there stood her brother. He looked such a child, she thought, and she forgot her own misery in her desire to comfort him.

'What is it, Alfonso?'

'There are plots and intrigues all about us, Isabella. And I

... I am the centre of them. That is what I feel. They are going to send you away so that I shall not have the comfort of your presence and advice. Isabella ... I am afraid.'

She held out her hand and he took it; then he threw himself into her arms and for a few seconds they clung together.

'They are going to make me the heir to the throne,' said Alfonso. 'They are going to say the little Princess has no right to it. I wish they would leave me alone, Isabella. Why cannot they leave us in peace ... myself to be as other boys, you to marry where you wish.'

'They will never leave us in peace, Alfonso. We are not as other boys and girls. The reason is that our half-brother is the King of Castile and that many people believe the child, who is known as his daughter, is not a child of his at all. That means that we are in the direct line of succession. There are some to support Henry and his Queen ... and there are others who will use us in their quarrel with the King and Queen.'

'Isabella ... let us run away. Let us go to Arevalo and join our mother there.'

'It would be of no use. They would not let us remain there.'

'Perhaps we could all escape into Aragon ... to Ferdinand.'

Isabella considered this, imagined herself with her hysterical mother and her young brother arriving at the Court of Ferdinand's father John. In Aragon there was a state of unrest. It might even be that John had decided to choose another bride for Ferdinand.

She shook her head slowly. 'Our feelings, our loves and hates ... they are not important, Alfonso. We must try to see ourselves ... not as people ... but as pieces in a game, to be moved this way and that ... whichever is most beneficial to our country.'

'If they would leave me alone and not try to force the King

to make me his heir, surely *that* would be beneficial to the country.'

'Terrible things are happening in Castile, Alfonso. The roads are unsafe; the people have no protection; there is much poverty. It may be that it would be beneficial if you *were* made King of Castile with a Regency to rule until you are of age.'

'I do not want it, I do not want it,' cried Alfonso. 'I want us to be together ... quietly and at peace. Oh, Isabella, what can we do? I am frightened, I tell you.'

'We must not be frightened, Alfonso. Fear is unworthy of us.'

'But we are no different from other people,' cried Alfonso passionately.

'We are. We are,' insisted Isabella. 'We make a mistake if we do not recognize this. It is not for us to harbour dreams of a quiet happiness. We have to face the fact that we are different.'

'Isabella, people who are in the way of others with a wish to ascend the throne often die. Carlos, Prince of Viana, died. I have heard that was to make way for his young brother, Ferdinand.'

Isabella said slowly: 'Ferdinand played no part in that murder ... if murder there was.'

'It was murder,' said Alfonso. He crossed his hands on his chest. 'Something within me tells me it was murder. Isabella, if they made me heir ... if they made me King ...' He looked over his shoulder furtively; and Isabella thought of Carlos, the prisoner of his own father, feeling as Alfonso was now, looking over his shoulder as Alfonso looked, furtively, afraid of the greed and lust of men for power. 'There was Queen Blanche too,' went on Alfonso. 'I wonder what she felt on her last day on Earth. I wonder what it felt like to be shut up in a castle, knowing that you have that which others want and only your death can give it to them.'

'This is foolish talk,' said Isabella.

'But they are marrying you into Portugal. You will not be here to see what happens. I know they are making plans concerning me, Isabella. Oh ... how I wish that I were not the son of a King. Have you ever thought, Isabella, how wonderful it must be to be the child of a simple peasant?'

'To suffer hunger? To have to work hard for a cruel master?'

'There is nothing so much to be feared in your life,' said Alfonso, 'as the knowledge that men are planning to take it from you. I think if you could ask poor Queen Blanche to confirm this, she would do so. I know, you see, Isabella. Because ... I have read the thoughts in men's eyes as they look at me. I know. They are sending you away because they fear you. I shall be left without a friend. For, Isabella, although the Archbishop tells me he loves me – and so does the Marquis of Villena – I do not trust them. You are the only one I can be sure of.'

Isabella was deeply moved.

'Little brother,' she said, and she seemed to draw strength and determination from Alfonso's melancholy words. 'I will *not* go to Portugal. I will find some means of avoiding this marriage.'

Alfonso, looking up at her and seeing the resolve in her face, began to believe that when Isabella made up her mind she could not be defeated.

It was when Alfonso had left her that inspiration came to Isabella.

She needed advice. She should discover whether she must inevitably accept this marriage with Portugal, or whether there was some way out of the situation.

She herself was a young girl, with little knowledge of the laws of the country, but did suspect that the King and his adherents were endeavouring to rush her into this marriage and if this were so that they might have an ulterior reason for this haste.

She still believed that happiness for her lay in a marriage which had caught her childhood's imagination when she had made an ideal of Ferdinand; but common sense told her that a marriage between Castile and Aragon could bring the greatest good to Spain. During the revolt in Catalonia there had been strife between Castile and Aragon; and Isabella had begun to realize that one of the reasons why the Moors still governed a great part of Spain was because of the quarrels among Spaniards.

United they might defeat the Infidel. Warring among themselves they became weakened. How much more satisfactory it would be if Spaniards united and fought the Moors instead of each other.

A marriage between Castile and Aragon then must be of the greatest advantage to Spain; and Isabella believed that if she and Ferdinand were united that would be the first step towards driving the Moors from the country. Therefore their marriage must be the one to take place.

She was certain that the Prince of Viana had met his death by Divine interference. Perhaps that had come about by way of poisoned broth or wine. But who dared question the designs of Providence? God had decided that Aragon was for Ferdinand. Had He also decided that Isabella was for Ferdinand?

God was more inclined to consider those who sought to help themselves, they being more worthy of His support than those who idly accepted whatever fate was thrust upon them.

Isabella accordingly made up her mind that she would work with all her might to evade this marriage with Alfonso V of Portugal.

She had more than her own desires to consider. Her brother Alfonso needed her. To some he might appear as the heir to the throne; to Isabella he was her frightened little brother. His father was dead; his poor unbalanced mother was shut away from the world. Who was there to care for little Alfonso but his sister Isabella?

But they were children in a Court in which conflict raged. In such a Court, thought Isabella, the difficulty is to know who are your friends, who your enemies. Whom could she trust except Beatriz? It seemed that greater wisdom came to her and she understood that the only way to be sure whose side people were on was to consider their interests and motives.

She knew that the King and Queen wished to see her leave the country. The reason was plain. They had realized that differences of opinion concerning the rights of the Queen's baby daughter to the throne could bring the country to civil war. Therefore they wanted the little Princess's rivals out of the way. They could not remove Alfonso yet; that would be too drastic a step. But how easy it was to marry off Isabella and so remove her in a seemly way from the sphere of action.

The Marquis of Villena was against Isabella's marriage with Ferdinand for very strong personal reasons. A great deal of the property which he now held had once belonged to the House of Aragon, and he guessed that if Ferdinand attained influence in Castile, some means would be found of removing that property from the Marquisate of Villena and bringing it into the possession of its original owners.

There was, however, one person in Castile who Isabella believed would welcome the marriage between herself and Ferdinand. This was Don Frederick Henriquez, who was Admiral of Castile and father of the ambitious Joan Henriquez, Ferdinand's own mother.

The Admiral would naturally support the marriage between his grandson and one who was only separated from the throne of Castile by a few short steps.

There could be no doubt then where the Admiral's sympathies would lie; and, if anyone in Castile could help her now, this was the man.

Isabella had learned her first lesson in statecraft.

She would send for Frederick Henriquez, Admiral of Castile, a man of great experience; he would be able to tell her exactly how she stood in regard to the suggested marriage with Alfonso of Portugal.

In the great apartment lighted by a hundred torches which threw shadows on the tapestried walls, Isabella came to pay her respects to the visiting King of Portugal.

She held her head high as she walked towards the dais where the two Kings sat; and even though she felt that her wildly beating heart would leap into her throat and suffocate her, she yet managed to retain a certain serenity.

'I am for Ferdinand and Ferdinand is for me,' she told herself even at this moment, as she had been telling herself while her women had prepared her for the interview.

Henry took her into his arms and she was held against his scented and jewel-decorated robes of state. He called her 'our dearest sister'; and he was smiling with what most people would believe to be real affection.

Queen Joanna looked glitteringly beautiful; and of course Beltran de la Cueva was in attendance behind the chairs of the King and Queen, darkly handsome, dazzlingly clad, and ... triumphant.

Now she saw the man whom they were eager to make her husband, and she shivered.

He seemed very old and repulsively ugly to the thirteen-year-old girl.

I will not, I will not, she told herself. If they force me, I will take a knife and kill myself rather than submit.

In spite of these wild thoughts her hand did not tremble as it was taken by the King of Portugal.

His eyes were a little glazed as they rested on her – this young virgin, with innocence shining in her eyes. A delectable morsel, thought the King of Portugal, and one who could conceivably bring a crown with her.

There was trouble in Castile. Wicked Joanna! What had she been about? He could guess. And this Beltran de la Cueva was such a handsome fellow that one could hardly blame Joanna. She should have arranged it, though, so that there were no suspicions. Yet why should he regret that! It was very possible that this delicious young girl would one day be the heiress of Castile. There was a young brother, but he might be killed in battle; for there would certainly be battles in Castile before long. And the baby Joanna? Oh, Isabella's chances were fair enough.

Isabella's eyes met his and she flinched. His lips were a little wet as though his mouth was watering at the sight of her.

Isabella's whole being called out in protest, but she respectfully returned the smiles of her brother, his Queen, and the Queen's brother, who so clearly was not averse to taking her as wife.

Henry said: 'Our Isabella is overcome with joy at the prospect which awaits her.'

'She has scarcely slept for excitement since we made her aware of her great good fortune,' put in the Queen.

'She is conscious of the great honour done to her,' went on Henry, 'and now that she has seen you I know she will be doubly eager for the match. That is so, is it not, sister?'

'Highness,' said Isabella earnestly, 'would you not consider it indecorous of a young woman to discuss her marriage before she was betrothed?'

Henry laughed. 'Isabella has been very carefully nurtured. She lived the life of a nun before she joined us here at Court.'

'I know of no better upbringing,' said Alfonso V of Portugal. His eyes continued to wander over Isabella, so that she felt he was already picturing her in many different situations of intimacy which she could only vaguely imagine.

'My dear Isabella,' said the Queen, 'your brother and I will not be as strict with you as your mother was at Arevalo. We shall allow you to dance with the King of Portugal. You shall become friends before he takes you back with him to Lisbon.'

Isabella forced herself to speak then. She said in a loud, clear voice, which could be heard by those courtiers who were in the room but some little distance from the royal group: 'We cannot be sure yet that the betrothal will be agreed upon.'

Henry looked surprised, the Queen angry, and the King of Portugal nonplussed.

But Isabella boldly resumed: 'I know you have not forgotten that, as a Princess of Castile, my betrothal could not take place without the consent of the Cortes.'

'The King gives his consent,' said Joanna quickly.

'That is true,' said Isabella, 'but, as you are aware, it is essential that the Cortes also give consent.'

'The King of Portugal is my brother,' retorted Joanna haughtily. 'Therefore we can dispense with the usual formality.'

'I could not allow myself to be betrothed without the consent of the Cortes,' Isabella affirmed.

It was the weariness in Henry's face, rather than the anger and astonishment in those of the Queen and the King of Portugal, which told Isabella how right the old Admiral had been when he assured her that the only way in which the King and Queen dare marry her off would be to do so at great speed, before the Cortes had time to remind them that they must have a say in the matter.

And, the Admiral had added, it was hardly likely that the Cortes would give their consent to Isabella's marriage with the Queen's brother. The people had little love for the Queen; they had always considered her levity most unbecoming, and now with the scandal concerning the parentage of her little daughter about to break, they would blame her more than ever.

The Cortes would never consent to a marriage repugnant to their Princess Isabella, and so desired by their weak and lascivious King and his less weak but hardly less lascivious wife.

When Isabella left the audience chamber she knew that she had planted dismay in the hearts of two Kings and a Queen.

How right the Admiral of Castile had been! She had learned a valuable lesson, and once again she thanked God for saving her for Ferdinand.

OUTSIDE THE WALLS OF AVILA

A BRILLIANT cavalcade was riding northwards to the shores of the River Bidassoa, the boundary between Castile and France, and a meeting-place close to the town of Bayonne.

In the centre of this procession rode Henry, King of Castile, his person glittering with jewels, and his Moorish Guard dazzling in their colourful uniforms.

His courtiers had done their utmost to rival the splendour of their King, although none, with the exception of Beltran de la Cueva, had been able to do so. Still, it was a splendid concourse that gathered to meet King Louis XI of France, his courtiers and his ministers.

This meeting had been arranged by the Marquis of Villena and the Archbishop of Toledo, the purpose of it being to settle the differences between the Kings of Castile and Aragon.

When John of Aragon had come into conflict with Catalonia over his treatment of his eldest son Carlos, Prince of Viana, Henry of Castile had thrown in certain men and arms to help the Catalans. Now, Villena had decided that there should be peace and that the King of France should be the mediator in a reconciliation.

Villena and the Archbishop had their own reasons for arranging this meeting between the Kings. Louis wished it and the two statesmen, having a profound respect for Louis' talents, had accepted certain favours from him in return for which they must not be unmindful of his wishes when at their master's Court.

Louis was a man who was eager to have a say in the affairs

of Europe. He was determined to make France the centre of Continental politics, the most powerful of countries, and he deemed it necessary therefore to lose no opportunity of meddling in his neighbours' affairs if he could do so to the advantage of France.

He was interested in the affairs of Aragon, for he had lent the King of that Province three hundred and fifty thousand crowns, taking as security for the loan the provinces of Roussillon and Cerdagne. If there were to be peace between Castile and Aragon he was anxious that it should be brought about with no disadvantage to France. It was for this reason that he had his 'pensioners' – such as Villena and the Archbishop of Toledo – in every country in which he could place them.

Louis was in his prime, for it was but some three years since he had ascended the throne at the age of thirty-eight, and he was already making good the ravages of the Hundred Years War. He knew Henry for a weak King growing more and more foolish as the years passed, and he could not but believe that, in conference, he would get the better of him, particularly as this King of Castile's two chief advisers were ready to accept bribes from himself, the King of France.

When Louis and Henry met there arose an immediate hostility between their followers.

Henry, magnificently attired, his company glittering in gold brocade and with the dazzle of their jewels, made a strange contrast to the sombrely-clad French King.

Louis had made no concession to the occasion and wore the clothes he was accustomed to wear at home. He delighted in making himself the least conspicuous of Frenchmen, and consequently favoured a short worsted coat with fustian doublet. His hat had clearly served him as well and as long as any of his followers; in it he wore a small image of the Virgin – not in glittering diamonds or rubies as might have been expected, but of lead.

French eyes smiled at the garments of the Castilians; there

were suppressed guffaws and murmurs of 'Fops! Popinjays!'

The Castilians showed their disgust of the French; and asked each other whether there had been a mistake, and it was the king of the beggars not the King of the French who had come to greet their King.

Tempers were hot and there was many a fracas.

Meanwhile the Kings themselves took each other's measure and were not greatly impressed.

Louis stated his terms for the peace, and these were not entirely favourable to Castile. Henry however, always eager to take that line which demanded the least exertion on his part, was eager for one thing only: to have done with the conference and return to Castile.

There was a great deal of grumbling among his followers.

'Why,' they asked each other, 'was our King ever allowed to make this journey? It is almost as though he must pay homage to the King of France and accept his judgement. Who is this King of France? He is a moneylender – and a seedy-looking one at that.'

'Who arranged this conference? What a question! Who arranges everything at Court? The Marquis of Villena, of course, with that rascal, his uncle, the Archbishop of Toledo.'

During the journey back to Castile Henry's adviser, the Bishop of Cuenca, and the Marquis of Santillana, who was head of the powerful Mendoza family, came to the King and implored him to re-consider before he allowed himself to enter into such humiliating negotiations again.

'Humiliating!' protested Henry. 'But I should not consider my meeting with the King of France humiliating.'

'Highness, the King of France treats you as a vassal,' said Santillana. 'It is unwise to have too many dealings with him; he is a wily old fox; and, as you will agree, the conference has brought little good to Castile. Highness, there is another matter which you should not ignore: Those who arranged this conference serve the King of France whilst feigning to serve Your Highness.'

'That is a serious and dangerous accusation.'

'It is a dangerous situation, Highness. We are certain that the Marquis and the Archbishop are in league with the King of France. Conversations between them have been overheard.'

'It is difficult for me to believe this.'

'Did they not arrange this conference?' asked Cuenca. 'And what advantage has it brought to Castile?'

Henry looked bewildered. 'Are you suggesting that I bring them before me and confront them with their villainies?'

'They would deny the accusation, Highness,' Santillana put in. 'That does not mean that they would speak the truth. We can bring you witnesses, Highness. We are assured that we are not mistaken.'

Henry looked from his old teacher, the Bishop of Cuenca, to the Marquis of Santillana. They were trustworthy men, both of them.

'I will ponder this matter,' he said.

They looked dismayed, and he added: 'It is of great importance, and I believe that, if you are right, I should not continue to give these men my confidence.'

The Archbishop of Toledo stormed into the apartments of his nephew.

'Have you heard what I have?' he demanded.

'I understand from your expression, Uncle, that you refer to our dismissal.'

'Our dismissal! It is preposterous. What will he do without us?'

'Cuenca and Santillana have persuaded him that they will prove adequate substitutes.'

'But why ... why ...?'

'He objects to our friendship with Louis.'

'Fool! Why should we not listen to Louis and give Henry our advice?'

Villena smiled at his fiery uncle. 'It is a common failing

among kings,' he murmured, 'and perhaps not only kings. They insist that those who serve them should serve no other.'

'And does he think that we are going to lie down meekly under this ... this insult?'

'If he does, he is more of a fool than we thought him.'

'Your plans, nephew?'

'To call together a confederacy, to proclaim La Beltraneja illegitimate, to set up Alfonso as the heir to the throne ... or ...'

'Yes, nephew, or ... what?'

'I do not know yet. It depends how far the King will proceed in this intransigent attitude of his. I can visualize circumstances in which it might be necessary to set up a new King in his place. Then, of course, we should put little Alfonso on the throne of Castile.'

The Archbishop nodded, smiling. As a man of action he was impatient to go ahead with the scheme.

Villena smiled at him.

'All in good time, Uncle,' he warned. 'This is a delicate matter. Henry will have his supporters. We must act with care; but never fear, since Henry listens to others, he shall go. But the displacement of one King by another is always a dangerous operation. Out of such situations civil wars have grown. First we will test Henry. We will see if we can bring him to reason, before we depose him.'

Queen Joanna paced angrily up and down the King's apartments.

'What are they doing, these ex-ministers of yours?' she demanded. 'Oh, it was time they were dismissed from their posts. They are against us ... do you not see? They are trying to push you aside and set up Alfonso in your place. Oh, it was folly not to force Isabella to go to Portugal. There she would at least have been out of the way. How do we know what she says to that brother of hers? You can be assured that she repeats the doctrines of her mad mother. She is priming Alfonso, telling him that he should be the heir to the throne.'

'They cannot do this ... they cannot do this,' wailed Henry. 'Have I not my own child!'

'Indeed you have your own child. I gave you that child. And there were not many women in Castile who could have managed that. Look at your trials and failures with your first wife. Now you have your child. Our little Joanna will remain heiress to the throne. We will not have Alfonso.'

'No,' said the King. 'There is little Joanna. She is my heir. There is no law in Castile to prevent one of the female sex taking the crown.'

'Then we must be firm. One of these days Villena will march to the executioner's knife, and he'll take that villainous old Archbishop with him. In the meantime we must be firm.'

'We will be firm,' echoed Henry uncertainly.

'And not forget those who are ready to stand firmly beside us.'

'Oh yes, I wish there were more to stand firmly with us. I wish there need not be this strife.'

'We shall be strong. But let us make sure of the strength of our loyal supporters. Let us give them our grateful thanks. You *are* grateful, are you not, Henry?'

'Yes, I am grateful.'

'Then you must show your gratitude.'

'Do I not?'

'Not sufficiently.'

Henry looked surprised.

'There is Beltran,' the Queen went on. 'What honours has he had? The Count of Ledesma! What is that for one who has worked with us ... for us ... unflinchingly and devotedly? One to whom we should be for ever grateful. You must honour him further.'

'My dear, what do you suggest?'

'That he be made Master of Santiago.'

'Master of Santiago! But that is the greatest of honours. He would be endowed with vast estates and revenues. Why, he would have the largest armed force in the Kingdom put into his hands.'

'And it is too much, you think?'

'*I* think, my dear? It is the people who will think it is too much.'

'Your enemies?'

'It is necessary to placate our enemies.'

'Coward! Coward! You have always been a coward! You fret over your enemies and forget your friends.'

'I am willing to honour him, my dear. But to make him Master of Santiago . . . !'

'It is too much . . . too much for your friend! You would rather give it to your enemies!'

The Queen put her hands on her hips and laughed at him.

Now she was ready to begin pacing the apartment again. She was going to start once more on that diatribe which he had heard many times before. He was a coward; he deserved his imminent fate; when he was thrust from his throne he would remember that he had spurned her advice; he placated his enemies, and those who served him with every means at their disposal – like Beltran de la Cueva – were forgotten.

Henry lifted his hands as though to ward off this spate of accusation.

'That is enough,' he said. 'Let him have it. Let us bestow on Beltran the Mastership of Santiago.'

Now the new party was in revolt. It was humiliating enough, they said, to be forced to suspect the legitimacy of the heiress to the throne, but to see the King so far forget his dignity as to heap honours on the man who was generally accepted as her father was intolerable.

Castile trembled on the edge of civil war.

Valladolid was entered by the rebels and several of Villena's party of confederates declared that they were holding

the city against the King. However, the citizens of Valladolid, while deploring the weakness of the King, were not
ready to ally themselves with Villena; and they expelled the
intruders. But when Henry, travelling to Segovia, very nar-
rowly escaped being kidnapped by the confederates, he was
thoroughly alarmed. He, who had worked hard at nothing
except avoiding trouble, now found himself in the midst of
it.

Villena wrote to him. He was grieved, he said, that enemies had come between them. If the King would see him and
the heads of his party he would do his utmost to put an end
to the strife which trembled so near to civil war.

The King had deplored the loss of Villena's counsel. Villena had been the strong man Beltran could never be. Beltran
was charming, and his company pleasant; but Henry needed
the strength of Villena to lean on; and when he received this
communication he was anxious to meet his ex-minister.

Villena, delighted at the turn of events, met Henry. With
Villena came his uncle, the Archbishop, also the Count
Benavente.

'Highness,' Villena addressed Henry when they were gathered together, 'the Commission, which has been set up to test
the legitimacy of the Princess Joanna, has grave doubts that
she is your daughter. In view of this we deem it wise that
your half-brother Alfonso be proclaimed as your heir. You
yourself must abandon your Moorish Guard and live a more
Christian life. Beltran de la Cueva is to be deprived of the
Mastership of Santiago. And finally your half-brother Alfonso is to be delivered into my hands that I may be his
guardian.'

'You ask too much,' Henry told him sadly. 'Too much.'

'Highness,' urged Villena, 'it would be wise for you to
accept our terms.'

'The alternative?' asked Henry.

'Civil war, I greatly fear, Highness.'

Henry hesitated. It was so easy to agree, but he had later

to face an enraged Joanna, who was determined that her daughter should have the crown. Then Henry slyly thought of a way of pleasing both Joanna and Villena.

'I agree,' he said, 'that Beltran de la Cueva shall be deprived of the Mastership of Santiago and that you shall become the guardian of Alfonso. He shall be proclaimed heir to the throne, but there is a condition.'

'What condition is this?' asked Villena.

'That he shall, in due course, marry the Princess Joanna.'

Villena was startled. The heir to the throne marry the King's illegitimate daughter! Well, on consideration it was not a bad suggestion. There would always be some to declare that La Beltraneja had been falsely so called; there would also be others who, seeking a cause for which to make trouble, would choose hers. Moreover, it would be some years before La Beltraneja was of an age to marry. By that time, if necessary, other arrangements could be made.

'I do not see,' said Villena, 'why this should not be.'

Henry felt pleased with his little effort of diplomacy. He could now more easily face the Queen.

Alfonso sat at his sister's feet, watching her as she worked at her embroidery. Beatriz de Bobadilla was with her.

Alfonso had lately made a habit of spending a great deal of time in his sister's apartments.

Poor Alfonso, mused Isabella; he is old enough to understand the intrigues which split the Court in two; and he knows that he – even more than I – is at their very core.

'Alfonso,' she said. 'You must not brood. It does no good.'

'But I have a feeling that I shall not be allowed to stay here much longer.'

'Why should they take you away?' asked Beatriz. 'They know you are safe here.'

'Perhaps they do not greatly care for my safety.'

'You are wrong in that,' said Isabella. 'You are very important to them.'

'I wish,' said Alfonso, 'that we were a more normal family. Why could not we all have been the children of our father's first wife! Then I think Henry would have loved us as you and I love each other. Why could not Henry have taken a wife who was more like a Queen, and had many sons about whose parentage there would have been no question!'

'You want everyone to be perfect in a perfect world,' murmured Beatriz with a smile.

'No, not perfect ... merely normal,' said Alfonso sadly. 'Do you know that the heads of the confederacy are meeting the King this day?'

'Yes,' said Isabella.

'I wonder what they will decide.'

'We shall soon know,' said Beatriz.

'These confederates,' went on Alfonso, 'they have chosen me ... me ... as their figurehead. I do not want to be part of the confederacy. All I want is to stay here and enjoy my life. I want to go riding; I want to fence and play games. I want to sit with you two and talk now and then, not about unpleasant things ... but about comfortable, cosy things.'

'Well, let us do that,' said Isabella. 'Let us now be cosy ... comfortable.'

'How can we,' demanded Alfonso passionately, 'when we can never be sure what is going to happen next?'

There was silence.

What a pity, thought Isabella, it is that princes and princesses cannot always be children. What a pity that they have to grow up and that people often fight over them.

'Do the people hate Henry so much?' asked Alfonso.

'Some of them are displeased,' Beatriz answered him.

'They have reason to be,' Isabella spoke with some vehemence. 'I have heard that it is unsafe to travel through the countryside without an armed escort. This is terrible. It is an indication of the corrupt state into which our country is falling. I have heard that travellers are captured and held to ransom, and that even noble families have taken up this evil trade and ply it shamelessly.'

'There is the Hermandad, which has been set up to restore law and order,' said Beatriz. 'Let us hope it will do its work well.'

'It does what it can,' Isabella pointed out. 'But it is a small force as yet; and everywhere in our country villainies persist. Oh, Alfonso, what a lesson this is to us. If ever we should be called upon to rule we must employ absolute justice. We must never install favourites; we must set good examples and never be extravagant in our personal demands; we must always please our people while helping them to become good Christians.'

A page had come into the room.

He bowed before Isabella and said that the Marquis de Villena with the Archbishop of Toledo were below; they were asking to be received by the Infante Alfonso.

Alfonso looked sharply at his sister. His eyes appealed. He wanted to say that he could not be seen; for these were the two men whom he feared more than any others, and the fact that they had come to see him filled him with dread.

'You should receive them,' said Isabella.

'Then I will do so here,' said Alfonso almost defiantly. 'Bring them to me.'

The page bowed and retired, and Alfonso turned in panic to his sister.

'What do they want of me?'

'I know no more than you do.'

'They have come from their audience with the King.'

'Alfonso,' said Isabella earnestly, 'be careful. We do not know what they are going to suggest. But remember this: You cannot be King while Henry lives. Henry is the true King of Castile; it would be wrong for you to put yourself at the head of a faction which is trying to replace him. That would mean war, and you would be on the wrong side.'

'Isabella...' Tears filled his eyes, but he dared not shed

them. 'Oh, why will they not let us alone! Why do they torment us so?'

She could have answered him. She could have said: Because in their eyes we are not human beings. We are lay figures placed at certain distances from the throne. They want power and they seek to obtain it through us.

Poor, poor Alfonso, even more vulnerable than she was herself.

The page was ushering in the Marquis of Villena and the Archbishop of Toledo, who seemed astonished to find Isabella and Beatriz there; but Alfonso immediately put on the air of an Infante and said: 'You may tell me your business. These ladies share my confidence.'

The Marquis and the Archbishop smiled almost obsequiously, but their respect could only disturb the others.

'We come from the King,' said the Archbishop.

'And you have a message from His Highness for me?' Alfonso enquired.

'Yes, you are to prepare to leave your apartments here for new ones.'

'Which apartments are these?'

'They are mine,' said the Marquis.

'But I do not understand.'

For answer the Marquis came forward, knelt and took Alfonso's hand.

'Principe, you are to be proclaimed heir to the throne of Castile.'

A faint colour crept into Alfonso's cheeks.

'That is preposterous. How can I be? My brother will beget children yet. Moreover he has a daughter.'

The Archbishop gave his short rasping laugh. He deplored wasting time.

'Your brother will never beget children,' he said, 'and a commission, set up to study the matter, has grave doubts that the young Joanna *is* his daughter. In view of this we have insisted that you be proclaimed the heir, and my nephew here has permission to take you under his guardianship that you may be trained in all the duties which, as King, will be yours.'

There was a short silence, and when Alfonso spoke, his tone was bleak. 'So,' he said, 'I am to settle under your wing.'

'It shall be my greatest pleasure to serve Your Highness.'

Then Alfonso smiled in momentary hopefulness. 'I am capable of looking after myself, and I am very happy here in my apartments next to my sister's.'

'Oh,' laughed the Marquis, 'there will not be much change. We shall merely look after you and see that you are prepared for your role. You will see much of your sister. There will be no attempt to curtail your pleasures.'

'How can you know that?'

'Dear Highness, we will make sure of it.'

'What if my pleasure is to stay as I am and not come under your guardianship?'

'Your Highness is pleased to joke. Could you leave at once?'

'No. I wish to be with my sister a little longer. We were talking together when you interrupted us.'

'We crave Your Highness's pardon,' said Villena in false concern. 'We will leave you to finish your conversation with your sister, and we will await your pleasure in the ante-room. You should bring your most trusted servant with you. I have already given him instructions to prepare for your departure.'

'But you ... *you* gave instructions!'

'In matters like this one must act with speed,' said the Archbishop.

Alfonso appeared resigned. He watched the two schemers retire, but when he turned to Isabella and Beatriz, they were both struck by the look of despair in his face.

'Oh, Isabella, Isabella,' he cried, and she put her arms about him and held him close.

'You see,' he went on, 'it has come. I know what they will

try to do. They will make me King. And I do not want to be King, Isabella. I am afraid of them. I shall have forced upon me that which is greatly coveted. All Kings should be wary, but none so much as those who are forced to wear the crown before it is theirs by right. Isabella, perhaps one day someone will do to me what was done to Carlos . . . to Blanche . . .'

'These are morbid fancies,' Isabella chided him.

'I do not know,' said Alfonso. 'Isabella, I am afraid because I do not know.'

Joanna stormed into her husband's apartments.

'So you have allowed them to dictate to you!' she cried. 'You have allowed them to bring about the disinheritance of our daughter, and put up that sly young Alfonso in her place.'

'But do you not see,' cried Henry piteously, 'that I have insisted on his betrothal to Joanna?'

The Queen laughed bitterly. 'And you think they will allow that? Henry, are you a fool. Do you not see that, once you have proclaimed Alfonso your heir, you will have no say in deciding whom he shall marry? And the very fact that you allow him to be proclaimed your heir can only be because you accept these vile slanders against me and your daughter.'

'It was the only way,' murmured Henry. 'It was either that or civil war.'

He was thinking sadly of Blanche, who had been so meek and affectionate. Physically she had not excited him, but what a peaceful companion she had been. Poor Blanche! She had left this stormy life; she had been sacrificed to her family's ambition. One could almost say, Most fortunate Blanche, for there was no doubt that she would find a place in Heaven.

If I had never divorced her, he thought now, she might be alive at this time. And should I have been worse off? It is true there is a child now – but is she mine, and what a storm of controversy she is arousing!

'You are a coward,' cried the Queen. 'And what of Beltran? What will he think of this? He deserves to be Master of Santiago, and now you have agreed to deprive him of the title.'

Henry spread his hands helplessly. 'Joanna, would you see Castile torn in two by civil war?'

'Would it be if it had a King at its head instead of a lily-livered poltroon!'

'You go too far, my dear,' said Henry mildly.

'At least I will not be dictated to by these men. As for Beltran, unless you wish to offend him mortally, there is only one thing you can do.'

'What is that?'

'You have taken from him with one hand; therefore you must give with the other. You have sworn to deprive him of the Mastership of Santiago, therefore you should make him Duke of Albuquerque.'

'Oh but ... that would be tantamount to ... to ...'

'To opposing your enemies! Indeed it would. And if you are wise there is one other thing you will do. You will prevent your enemies from plotting your downfall. For, depend upon it, their scheme is not merely to set up an heir of their choosing in place of your own daughter, but to oust you from the throne.'

'You may well be right.'

'And what will you do about it? Sit on your throne ... waiting for disaster?'

'What can I do? What would happen if we were plunged into civil war?'

'We should fight, and we should win. But at least you are the King. You could act quickly now. These people are not popular. Most hate the Marquis of Villena. Look what happened when he and his friends tried to seize Valladolid. You are not unpopular with the people, and you are the rightful King. Have these ringleaders of revolt quickly and quietly seized. When their leaders are in prison the people will not be so ready to rebel against their King.'

The King gazed at his fiery wife. 'My dear,' he said, slowly, 'I think perhaps you may be right.'

The Marquis of Villena was alone when the man was shown into his presence.

The visitor was wrapped in a concealing cloak and, when he removed it, revealed himself as one of the King's Guards.

'Forgive the unceremonious intrusion, my lord,' he said, 'but the matter is urgent.'

He then repeated the conversation which he had overheard between the King and Queen.

Villena nodded. 'You have done your work well,' he said. 'I trust you were not recognized on your way here. Go back to your post and keep us informed. We shall find means to prevent these arrests which the King now plans.'

He dismissed his spy and immediately called on the Archbishop.

'We are leaving at once,' he said, 'for Avila. There is not a moment to lose. I, with Alfonso, will meet you there. We shall take immediate action. De la Cueva is to be created Duke of Albuquerque in compensation for the loss of the Mastership of Santiago. This is the way the King observes his pledges!'

'And when we reach Avila with the heir to the throne, what then?'

'Alfonso will no longer be the heir to the throne. He will ascend it. At Avila we will proclaim Alfonso King of Castile.'

Alfonso was pale, not with the strain of the journey, but with a fear of the future. He had spent long hours on his knees praying for guidance. He felt so young; it was a pitiable situation for a boy of eleven years to have to face.

There was no one whose advice he could ask. He could not reach those whom he loved. His mother's mind was becoming more and more deranged and sunk in oblivion, and, even if he were allowed to see her, it would be doubtful whether he would be able to explain to her his need. And when he thought of his childhood, his mother's voice seemed to come echoing down to him: 'Do not forget that one day you could be King of Castile.' So even if he could make her understand what was about to happen she would doubtless express great pleasure. Was this not what she had always longed for?

But Isabella – his dear, good sister – she would advise. Isabella was anxious to do what was right, and he had a feeling that Isabella would say: 'It is not right for you to be crowned King, Alfonso, while our brother Henry lives, for Henry is undoubtedly the son of our father and is therefore the rightful heir to Castile. No good can come of a usurpation of the crown, for, if God had willed that you should be King, He would have taken Henry as He took Carlos that Ferdinand might be his father's heir.'

'No good can come of it,' murmured Alfonso. 'No good ... no good.'

This city enclosed in its long grey walls depressed him. He looked out on the woods of oak and maple and those hardy trees which had been able to withstand the cruel winter.

Avila seemed to him a cruel city, a city of granite fortresses, set high above the plains, to receive the full force of the summer sun and the biting winds of a winter which was notoriously long and rigorous.

Alfonso was afraid, as he had never been afraid in his life.

'No good can come of this,' he repeated.

The June sun was hot. From where he stood surrounded by some of the most important nobles of Castile, Alfonso could see the yellowish grey walls of Avila.

Here on the arid plain within sight of the city a strange spectacle was about to be enacted and he, young Alfonso, was to play an important part in it.

He experienced a strange feeling as he stood there. That

clear air seemed to intoxicate him. When he looked at the city above the plain he felt an exultation.

Mine, he thought. That city will be mine. The whole of Castile will be mine.

He looked at those men who surrounded him. Strong men, all men who were eager for power; and they would come to him and take his hand, and when they took it they would offer him allegiance, for they intended to make him their King.

To be King of Castile! To save Castile from the anarchy into which it was falling! To make it great; perhaps to lead it to great victories!

Who knew, perhaps one day he might lead a campaign against the Moors. Perhaps in the years to come people would link his name with that of the Cid.

And as he stood there on the plain outside Avila, Alfonso found that his fear was replaced by ambition, and that he was now no unwilling participator in the strange ceremony which was about to take place.

Crowds had gathered on the plain. They had watched the cavalcade leave the gates of the city; at its head had been the Marquis of Villena and beside him was the young Alfonso.

On the plain there had been set up scaffolding and on this a throne had been placed. Seated on the throne was a life-sized dummy, representing a man, clad in a black robe; and on the head had been put a crown, in its hand a sceptre. A great sword of state was placed before it.

Alfonso had been led to a spot some distance from the scaffolding whilst certain noblemen, who had formed the procession which had been led by Villena and Alfonso, mounted the scaffolding and knelt before the crowned dummy, treating is as though is were the King.

Then one of the noblemen stepped to the front of the platform, and there was a tense silence among the multitude as he began to read a list of the crimes which had been committed by King Henry of Castile. The chaos and anarchy which persisted in the land were attributed to the King's evil rule.

The people continued to listen in silence.

'Henry of Castile,' cried the nobleman, turning to the figure on the throne, 'you are unworthy to wear the crown of Castile. You are unworthy to be given royal dignity.'

Then the Archbishop of Toledo stepped on to the platform and snatched the crown from the head of the figure.

'You are unworthy, Henry of Castile, to administer the laws of Castile,' went on the voice.

The Count of Plascencia then took his place on the platform and removed the sword of state.

'The people of Castile will no longer allow you to rule.'

The Count of Benavente took the sceptre from the dummy's hand.

'The honour due to the King of Castile shall no longer be yours, and the throne shall pass from you.'

Diego Lopez de Zuñiga picked up the dummy and threw it down on to the scaffolding, setting his foot upon it.

The people then were caught up in the hysteria which such words and such a spectacle aroused in them.

Someone in the crowd shouted: 'A curse on Henry of Castile!' And the rest took up the cry.

Now the great moment had come for Alfonso to take his place on the platform. He felt very small, there under that blue sky. The town looked unreal with its granite ramparts, squat posterns and belfries.

The Archbishop lifted the boy in his arms as though he would show him to the people.

Alfonso appeared beautiful in the eyes of those watching crowds; this innocent boy appealed to them and tears came to the eyes of many assembled there because of his youth and the great burden which was about to be placed upon him.

The Archbishop announced that it had been decided to deprive the people of their feeble, criminal King, but in his place they were to be given this handsome, noble boy whom, now that they saw him, they would, he knew, be willing to serve with all their hearts.

And there on the plains before Avila there went up a shout from thousands of throats.

'Castile! Castile for the King, Don Alfonso!'

Alfonso was set upon the throne on which, shortly before, the dummy had been.

The sword of state was set before him, the sceptre placed in his hand, and the crown upon his head. And one by one those powerful nobles who had now openly declared their intention to make him King of Castile, came forward to swear allegiance as they kissed his hand.

The words echoed in Alfonso's brain.

'Castile for the King, Don Alfonso!'

DON PEDRO GIRON

ISABELLA was distraught. She was torn between her love for her brother Alfonso and her loyalty towards her half-brother Henry.

She was in her sixteenth year, and the problems which faced her seemed too complex for a girl of her limited experience to solve.

She could trust few people. She knew that she was watched by many, that her smallest gestures were noticed, and that even in her intimate circle she was spied upon.

There was one whom she could trust, but Beatriz herself had been a little absent-minded lately. It was understandable; she had been married to Andres de Cabrera, and it was inevitable that the preoccupation of Beatriz with her new status should somewhat modify the devotion she was ready to give to her mistress.

I must be patient, thought Isabella; and she continued to dream of her own marriage, which surely could not be long delayed.

But this was not the time, when Alfonso had been placed in such a dangerous position, to think of her own selfish hopes.

There was civil strife in Castile, as there must be when two Kings claimed the throne. Sides must be taken, it seemed, by everybody; and although there were many in the kingdom who disapproved of Henry's rule, the theatrical ceremony outside the walls of Avila seemed to many to be revolutionary conduct in the worst taste. Henry was the King, and Alfonso was an impostor, declared many of the great nobles of Castile. At the same time there were many more who, not having been favourites of the King and

Queen, were ready to seek their fortunes under a new monarch who must have a regency to help him govern.

Henry was almost hysterical with grief. He hated bloodshed and was determined to avoid it if possible.

'A firm hand is needed, Highness,' his old tutor, the Bishop of Cuenca, warned him.

Henry turned on him with unusual anger. 'How like a priest,' he declared, 'not being called upon to engage in the fight, to be very liberal with the blood of others!'

'Highness, you owe it to your honour. If you do not stand firm and fight your enemies, you will be the most humiliated and degraded monarch in the history of Spain.'

'I believe that it is always wiser to settle difficulties by negotiation,' Henry retorted.

News was brought to him of the unrest throughout the country. In the pulpits and market squares the position was discussed. Was not a subject entitled to examine the conduct of his King? If the land was being drained of all its riches, if a state of anarchy had replaced that of law and order, had not the subject a right to protest?

From Seville and Cordova, from Burgos and Toledo, came the news that the people deplored the conduct of King Henry and were rallying to the support of King Alfonso and a regency.

Henry wept in his despair.

'Naked came I from my mother's womb,' he cried. 'And naked must I go down to the grave.'

But he deplored war and let it be known that he would be very happy to negotiate a settlement.

There was at least one other who was not very happy about the turn of events, although he had been largely responsible for it. This was the Marquis of Villena.

He had believed that the youthful Alfonso would be his creature, and that he himself would be virtually ruler of Castile.

But this was not so. Don Diego Lopez de Zuñiga, the Counts of Benavente and Plascencia – those noblemen who had played a leading part in the charade which had been acted outside the walls of Avila – were also seeking power.

The Marquis wondered whether it might not be a good idea to seek some secret communication with Henry and thus, by some quick *volte-face*, score an advantage over his old allies who were fast becoming his new rivals.

He was brooding on this when his brother, Don Pedro Giron, came to him.

Don Pedro was still smarting under the rebuff which had been given him some time before by Isabella's mother. Grand Master of the Order of Calatrava though he was, he enjoyed the company of many mistresses; but there was not one who could make him forget the slight he had received at the hands of the Dowager Queen, nor could they collectively.

Don Pedro was a vindictive man; he was also a very vain man. The Dowager Queen had rejected his advances, and he often asked himself what he could do to anger her as much as she had angered him.

Poor mad thing, he said to himself. She did not know what was good for her.

It did soothe his vanity a little to remind himself that her madness was responsible for her rejection of him. It did please him a little to think of her living in retirement at Arevalo, sometimes, so he had heard, unaware of who she was and what was going on in the world.

He would like to get even with the girl too, that sedate little creature who had been hiding somewhere when he had made the proposals to her mother.

It was true that his brother, the great Marquis, sometimes talked to him of his plans.

'All is not going well, brother?' he asked on this occasion.

The Marquis frowned. 'There are too many powerful men seeking more power. I found Henry easier to deal with.'

'I have heard, brother, that Henry would give a great deal to have your friendship. He would be happy if you turned from Alfonso and his adherents back to him. Poor Henry, I have heard that he is ready to do a great deal for you if you would be his friend once more.'

'Henry is a weak fool,' said the Marquis.

'Alfonso is but a boy.'

'That's true.'

'Marquis, it is a pity that you cannot bind yourself more closely to Henry. Now, if you were not married already you might ask for the hand of Isabella in marriage. Such a connection would please the King, I am sure, and I do believe he would be ready to promise you anything to ensure your return.'

The Marquis was silent for a while. He continued to study his brother through half-closed eyes.

The Queen and the Duke of Albuquerque were with the King. One on either side of him they explained to Henry what he must do.

'For,' said the Queen, 'you wish to end this strife. If you do not, there may be defeat for you. Alfonso is becoming more beloved of the people every day; which, my dear husband, is more than can be said for you.'

'I know, I know,' wailed Henry. 'I am a most unhappy man, the most unhappy King that Spain has ever known.'

'There must be an end to this strife, Highness,' said the Duke.

'It *can* be brought about,' the Queen added.

'Explain to me how. I would be ready to reward richly anyone who could put an end to our troubles.'

The Queen smiled at her lover over the bowed head of her husband.

'Henry,' she said, 'there are two men who made the revolt, who lead the revolt. If they could be weaned from the traitors and brought to our side, the revolt would collapse. Alfonso would find himself without his supporters. Then our troubles would be over.'

'You refer of course to the Marquis of Villena and the Archbishop,' sighed Henry. 'Once they were my friends ... my very good friends. But enemies came between us.'

'Yes, yes,' said Joanna impatiently. 'They must be brought back. They *can* be brought back.'

'How so?'

'By making a bond, between our family and theirs, which is so strong that nothing can untie or break it.'

'I repeat, how so?'

'Highness,' said Beltran almost nervously, 'you may not like what we are about to suggest.'

'The King will like whatever is going to end his troubles,' said the Queen scornfully.

'I pray you acquaint me with what you have in your minds,' pleaded Henry.

'It is this,' said the Queen. 'The Archbishop and the Marquis are uncle and nephew. Therefore of one family. Let us unite the royal family of Castile with theirs ... then both Archbishop and Marquis will be your most faithful adherents for ever.'

'I do not understand.'

'Marriage,' hissed the Queen. 'Marriage is the answer.'

'But what marriage ... with whom?'

'We have Isabella.'

'My sister! And whom could she marry? Villena is married, and the Archbishop is a man of the Church.'

'Villena has a brother.'

'You mean Don Pedro?'

'Why not?'

'Don Pedro to marry a Princess of Castile!'

'The times are dangerous.'

'Her mother would go completely mad.'

'Let her. She is half way there already.'

'And ... the man ... is a Grand Master of the Order of

Calatrava, and sworn to celibacy.'

'Bah! A dispensation from Rome would soon settle that.'

'I could not agree to it. Isabella ... that innocent child and that lecherous ...'

'You do well to talk of *his* lechery!' The Queen laughed on a high note of scorn. 'Isabella is grown up. She must know of the existence of lechers. After all, has she not been at Court for some time?'

'Isabella ... marry that man!'

'Henry, you are as usual foolish. Here is an opportunity to right our troubles. Isabella must marry to save Castile from bloodshed and war. She must marry to save the throne for its rightful King.'

Henry covered his face with his hands. Hideous pictures kept forming in his mind. Isabella, sedate and somewhat prim Isabella, whose upbringing had been so sternly pious ... at the mercy of that coarse man, that notorious lecher!

'No,' murmured Henry. 'No. I'll not agree.'

But the Queen smiled at her lover, and both knew that Henry could always be persuaded.

Isabella stood before her brother. The Queen was present and her eyes glittered – perhaps with malice.

'My dearest sister,' said Henry, 'you are no longer a child and it is time you married.'

'Yes, Highness.'

Isabella waited expectantly while Joanna watched her with amusement. The girl had heard fine stories of handsome Ferdinand, the young heir to Aragon. Ferdinand was a little hero and a handsome one at that. And Isabella believed that she was to have the pretty boy.

This, thought Joanna, will teach her to reject my brother, the King of Portugal! When she has had a taste of married life with Don Pedro she will wish she had not been so haughty, nor so foolish, as to reject the crown my brother offered her. Perhaps now she would wish to change her mind.

'I have decided,' said Henry, 'that you shall marry Don Pedro Giron, who is eager to become your husband. It is a match of which I ... and the Queen ... approve; and as you are of a marriageable age, we see no reason why there should be any delay.'

Isabella had grown pale. Joanna was amused to see that the sedate dignity, for which she was now noted, had deserted her.

'I – I do not think I can have heard you correctly, Highness. You said that I was to marry...'

Henry's eyes were softened with pity. Not this innocent young girl to that coarse creature! He would not allow it.

But he said: 'To Don Pedro Giron.'

Don Pedro Giron! She remembered that scene in her mother's apartments: Don Pedro making obscene suggestions, her mother's indignation and horror – and her own. This was a nightmare surely. She could not really be in her half-brother's apartments. She must be dreaming.

There was a cold sweat on her forehead; her heart was beating uncertainly. Her voice was playing tricks and would not shout the protests which her brain dictated.

The Queen spoke then. 'It is a good match and, my dear Isabella, you have rejected so many. We cannot allow you to reject another. Why, my dear, if you do that you will end with no husband at all.'

'That would be preferable to ... to...' stammered Isabella.

'Come, you were not meant to die a virgin.' The Queen spoke gaily.

'But ... Don Pedro...' began Isabella. 'I think your Highnesses have forgotten that I am betrothed to Ferdinand, the heir of Aragon.'

'The heir of Aragon!' laughed the Queen. 'There will be little left for the heir of Aragon if the unhappy state of that country continues.'

'And, Isabella,' said Henry, 'we, here in Castile, are not too happy, not too secure. The Marquis of Villena and the Archbishop of Toledo will be our friends when you are affianced to the brother of one and the nephew of the other. You see, my dear, Princesses must always serve their countries.'

'I do not think any happy purpose could be served by such a . . . such a cruel and preposterous union.'

'You are too young, Isabella, to understand.'

'I am not too young to know that I would prefer death to marriage with that man.'

'I think,' said the Queen, 'that you forget the respect due to the King and myself. We give you leave to retire. But before you go, let me say this: Suitors have been suggested to you and you have refused them. You should know that the King and I will allow no more refusals. You will prepare yourself for marriage, for in a few short weeks you are to be the bride of Don Pedro Giron.'

Isabella curtsied and retired.

She still felt as though she were in a dream. That was her only comfort. This terrible suggestion could not be of this world.

It was too humiliating, too degrading, too heart-breaking to contemplate.

In her own apartment Isabella sat staring before her.

Beatriz, who drew authority from the fact that she was not only Isabella's maid of honour but her friend, dismissed everyone except Mencia de la Torre whom, next to herself, Isabella loved better than anyone in her circle.

'What can have happened?' whispered Mencia.

Beatriz shook her head. 'Something has shocked her deeply.'

'I have never seen her like this before.'

'She has never been like this before.' Beatriz knelt and took Isabella's hand. 'Dearest mistress,' she implored, 'would it not be easier if you talked to those who are ready to share your sorrows?'

Isabella's lips trembled, but still she did not speak.

Mencia also knelt; she buried her face in Isabella's skirts, for she could not bear to see that look of despair on the face of her beloved mistress.

Beatriz rose and poured out a little wine. She held this to Isabella's lips. 'Please, dearest. It will revive you. It will bring back your power of speech. Let us share your trouble. Who knows, there may be something we can do to banish it.'

Isabella allowed the wine to moisten her lips; and as Beatriz put an arm about her, she turned and buried her face against her friend's breast.

'Death,' she muttered, 'would I believe, be preferable.'

Beatriz knew that what she had feared had now happened. The match with Ferdinand must have been broken off and a new suitor proposed.

'There must be some way of preventing this,' said Beatriz.

Mencia raised her face and said passionately: 'We will do anything ... anything ... to help, will we not, Beatriz?'

'Anything,' Beatriz agreed.

Then Isabella spoke: 'There is nothing you can do. This time they meant it. I saw it in the Queen's face. This time there will be no escaping it. Moreover, it is the wish of Villena, and that will decide it.'

'It is a match for you?'

'Yes,' said Isabella. 'The most degrading match I could make. I think it has been chosen for me by the Queen as a deliberate revenge for having refused her brother and won the approval and sanction of the Cortes to do so. But this time ...'

'Highness,' whispered Mencia, 'who?'

Isabella shuddered. 'You will scarcely be able to believe it when I tell you. I cannot bear to say his name. I hate him. I despise him. I would rather be dead.' She looked desperately from one to the other. 'You see, I was trying to avoid saying his name, for even to speak of him fills me with such dread and disgust that I truly believe I shall die before the marriage ceremony can take place. But you will hear ... if I do not tell you. The whole Court may be talking of it now. It is the brother of the Marquis of Villena – Don Pedro Giron.'

Neither of her women could speak. Beatriz had turned pale with horror; Mencia rocked on her heels, forgetful of everything but this overwhelmingly distasteful news. The thought of her mistress, in the coarse hands of the man whose reputation was one of the most unsavoury in Castile, made Mencia put her hands over her face to prevent herself betraying the full force of her horror.

'I know what you are thinking,' said Isabella. 'Oh, Beatriz ... Mencia ... what shall I do? What *can* I do?'

'There must be some way out of this,' Beatriz tried to soothe.

'They are determined. The Marquis naturally will do everything in his power to bring about the marriage. The Archbishop of Toledo will do the same. After all, this ... this monster is his nephew. You see, my dear friends, they have taken Alfonso; they have forced him to call himself King of Castile while the King still lives. How do we know what that will cost him? And for myself I am to be the victim of the Queen's revenge, of Villena's and the Archbishop's ambition, and ... the lust of this man.'

Beatriz stood up; her face was hard and she, who Isabella had always known was possessed of a strong character, had never before looked so determined.

'There must be a way,' she said, 'and we will find it.' Then suddenly her expression lightened. 'But how can this marriage take place?' she demanded. 'This man is a Grand Master of a religious Order and sworn to celibacy. Marriage is not for him.'

Mencia clasped her hands together and looked eagerly at

Isabella. 'It's true, Highness, it's true,' she cried.

'But of course it's true,' insisted Beatriz. 'He cannot marry. So that's an end to it. Depend upon it, this is merely a spiteful gesture of the Queen's. Nothing will come of it. And when you consider, how could it? It is too fantastic ... too preposterous.'

Isabella smiled at them wanly. She found a faint pleasure in the fact that they could comfort themselves thus, for they were two dear good friends who would suffer with her. She even allowed herself to be cheered a little. She must do something to lift herself from the blank despair into which she had fallen.

All through the night she had scarcely slept. She would awake from a doze, and the terrible knowledge would be there like a jailer sitting by her bed.

She dreamed of him; she saw him laying hands on her mother, making his obscene suggestions; and in her dream she ceased to be a looker-on, but the central figure in the repulsive scene.

She was pale when her women came to her. She asked that only Beatriz and Mencia should wait upon her. It would be unbearable to face any others, to see their pitying glances, for surely everyone would pity her.

Beatriz and Mencia were anxious. They talked together in her presence, because often when they addressed her she did not answer, for she did not hear.

'We shall hear no more of this,' said Beatriz. 'Of course Pedro Giron cannot marry.'

'Of course he cannot!'

They did not tell Isabella that the news was spreading through the Court that the marriage was not to be long delayed, because it was going to be the means of luring Villena and the Archbishop from the side of the rebels. 'Once the marriage is announced, the rebels will become of less importance. Once it is fact, Villena and the Archbishop will stand firmly with the King, who will be their kinsman.'

They were glad that Isabella remained in her apartments; they did not wish her to hear what was being said.

The Queen came to see Isabella, and she was looking well pleased.

Isabella was lying on her bed when she entered. Beatriz and Mencia curtsied to the floor.

'What is wrong with the Infanta?' asked Joanna.

'She has been a little indisposed this day,' Beatriz told her. 'I fear she is too sick to receive Your Highness.'

'That is sad,' said Joanna. 'She should be rejoicing at the prospect before her.'

Beatriz and Mencia lowered their eyes; and the Queen went past them to the bed.

'Why, Isabella,' she said, 'I am sorry to see you sick. What is wrong? Is it something you have eaten?'

'It is nothing I have eaten,' said Isabella.

'Well, I have good news for you. Perhaps you were a little anxious, eh? My dear sister, there is no need for further anxiety. I have come to tell you that a dispensation has arrived from Rome. Don Pedro is released from his vows. There is now no impediment to the marriage.'

Isabella said nothing. She had known that there would be no difficulty in Don Pedro's obtaining his dispensation, because his powerful brother desired it.

'Well,' coaxed Joanna, 'does that not make you feel ready to leave your bed and dance with joy?'

Isabella raised herself on her elbow and looked stonily at Joanna.

'I shall not marry Don Pedro,' she said. 'I shall do everything in my power to prevent such an unworthy marriage for a Princess of Castile.'

'Stubborn little virgin,' said the Queen lightly. She put her face close to Isabella's and whispered: 'There is nothing to fear, my dear, in marriage. Believe me, like so many of us, you will find much to delight you. Now, leave your bed and come down to the banquet which your brother is giving to celebrate this event.'

'As I have nothing to celebrate, I shall stay here,' Isabella replied.

'Oh come ... come, you are being somewhat foolish.'

'If my brother wishes me to come to his banquet, he will have to take me there by force. I warn you that should he do so, I shall then announce that this marriage is not only against my wishes but that the very thought of it fills me with dismay.'

The Queen tried to hide her discomfiture and anger.

'You are sick,' she said. 'You must stay in your bed. Take care, Isabella. You must not over-excite yourself. Remember how your mother was affected. Your brother and I wish to please you in every possible way.'

'Then perhaps you will leave me now.'

The Queen inclined her head.

'Good day to you, Isabella. You need have no fear of marriage. You take these things too seriously.'

With that she turned and left the apartment; and when Isabella called Beatriz and Mencia to her bedside she saw from the blank expression on their faces that they had heard all, and that now even they had lost all hope.

Preparations for the wedding were going on at great speed.

Villena and the Archbishop had brought their tremendous energy to the event. Henry was as eager. Once the marriage had taken place, the leaders of his enemies would become his friends.

Henry had always said that gifts should be bestowed on one's enemies to turn them into friends; he was following that policy now, for there was not a greater gift he could bestow, and on a more dangerous enemy, than the hand of his half-sister on Don Pedro.

There was murmuring in certain quarters. Some said that now Villena and his uncle would be more powerful than ever,

and that was scarcely desirable; a few even deplored the fact
that an innocent young girl was being given to a voluptuary
of such evil reputation. But many declared that this was a
way to put an end to civil war, and that such conflicts could
only bring disaster to Castile.

Once the marriage had taken place and Villena and his
uncle had transferred their allegiance from the rebels to the
King's party, the revolt would collapse; Alfonso would be
relegated to his position of heir to the throne, and there
would no longer be this dangerous situation of two Kings
'reigning' at the same time.

As for Isabella, she felt numb with grief and fear as the
days passed. She had lost a great deal of weight, for she
could eat little. She had grown pale and drawn because she
could not sleep.

She spent the days in her own apartments, lying on her
bed, scarcely speaking; she prayed for long periods.

'Let me die,' she implored, 'rather than suffer this fate.
Holy Mother of God, kill one of us ... either him or myself.
Save me from this impending dishonour and kill me that I
may not be tempted to kill myself.'

Somewhere in Spain was Ferdinand; had he heard of the
fate which was about to fall upon her? Did he care? What
had Ferdinand been thinking, all these years, of their betrothal? Perhaps he had not seen their possible union as she
had, and to him she had been merely a match which would
be advantageous to him. If he heard that he had lost her, perhaps he would shrug his shoulders, and look about him for
another bride.

Ferdinand, fighting side by side with his father in his own
turbulent Aragon, would have other matters with which to
occupy himself.

She liked to imagine that he might come to save her from
this terrible marriage. That was because she was a fanciful
girl who had dreamed romantic dreams. She could not in her
more reasonable moments hope that Ferdinand – a year

younger than herself and as powerless as she was – could do anything to help her.

Her great comfort during these days of terror was Beatriz, who never left her. At night Beatriz would lie at the foot of her bed and, during the early hours of morning when sleep was quite impossible, they would talk together and Beatriz would make the wildest plans, such as flight from the Palace. This was impossible, they both knew, but there was a little comfort to be derived from such talk – or at least so it seemed in the dreary hours before dawn.

Beatriz would say: 'It shall not be. We will find some means of preventing it. I swear it! I swear it!'

Her deep vibrating voice would shake the bed and, such was the power of her personality, she made Isabella almost believe her.

There was great strength in Beatriz; she had not the same love of law and order which was Isabella's main characteristic. There had been times in the past when Isabella had warned Beatriz against her rebellious attitude to life; now she was glad of it, glad of any mite of comfort which could come her way.

With the coming of each day, Isabella felt her load of misery growing.

'No escape,' she murmured to herself. 'No escape. And each day it comes nearer.'

Andres de Cabrera came to visit his wife. He had scarcely seen her since Isabella had heard that she was to marry Don Pedro.

'I cannot leave her,' Beatriz had told him, 'no ... not even for you. I must be with her all through the night, for I fear she might be tempted to do herself some injury.'

Isabella received Andres with as much pleasure as she could show to anyone. He was very shocked to see the change in her. Gone was the serene Isabella. He felt saddened to see such a change; and he was doubly alarmed to see that Beatriz was almost equally affected.

'You cannot go on in this way,' he remonstrated. 'Highness, you must accept your fate. It is an evil one, I know, but you are a Princess of Castile. You will be able to extract obedience from this man.'

'You can talk like that!' stormed Beatriz. 'You can tell us to accept this fate! Look at her ... look at my Isabella, and think of him ... that ... that ... But I will not speak his name. Is it not enough that we are aware of him every hour of the day and night!'

Andres put his arm about his wife's shoulders. 'Beatriz, my dearest, you must be reasonable.'

'He tells me to be reasonable!' cried Beatriz 'It seems, Andres, that you do not know me if you can imagine I am going to stand aside and be reasonable while my beloved mistress is handed over to that coarse brute.'

'Beatriz ... Beatriz....' He drew her to him and was aware of something hard in the bodice of her gown.

She laughed suddenly. Then she put her hand into her bodice and drew out a dagger.

'What is this?' cried Andres growing pale as her flashing eyes rested upon him.

'I will tell you,' said Beatriz. 'I have made a vow, husband. I have promised Isabella that she shall never fall into the hands of that crude monster. That is why I carry this dagger with me day and night.'

'Beatriz, have you gone mad?'

'I am sane, Andres. I think I am the sanest person in this Palace. As soon as the Grand Master of Calatrava approaches my mistress, I shall be there between them. I shall take my dagger and plunge it into his heart.'

'My dearest ... what are you saying! What madness is this?'

'You do not understand. Someone must protect her. You do not know my Isabella. She, so proud, so ... so pure ... I think that she will kill herself rather than suffer this degradation. I shall save her by killing him before he has a chance to besmirch her with his foulness.'

'Give me that dagger, Beatriz.'

'No,' said Beatriz, slipping it into the bodice of her dress.

'I demand that you give it to me.'

'I am sorry, Andres,' she answered calmly. 'There are two people in this world for whom I would give my life if necessary. You are one. She is the other. I have sworn this solemn vow. There shall be no consummation of this barbarous marriage. That is the vow I have sworn. So it is no use your asking me for this dagger. It is for him, Andres.'

'Beatriz, I implore you ... think of *our* life together. Think of our future!'

'There could be no happiness for me if I did not do this thing for her.'

'I cannot allow you to do it, Beatriz.'

'What will you do, Andres? Inform on me? I shall die doubtless. Perhaps they will torture me first; perhaps they will say, This is a plot to assassinate Isabella's bridegroom. So, Andres, you will inform against your wife?'

He was silent.

'Andres, you will do no such thing. You must leave this to me. I have sworn he shall not deflower her. It is a sacred vow.'

Her eyes were brilliant and her cheeks were scarlet; she looked very beautiful; and as powerful as a young goddess – tall, handsome and full of fire.

And he loved her dearly. He knew her well enough to understand that this was no wild talk. She was bold and completely courageous. He had no doubt that she would keep her word and, when the moment came, she would lift her hand and plunge the dagger into the heart of Isabella's bridegroom.

And when he murmured: 'It must not be, Beatriz!' she answered: 'It cannot be otherwise.'

In his house at Almagro Don Pedro Giron was making preparations for his wedding. He had lost no time since the arrival of the dispensation from Rome.

He strolled about his apartment while his servants made ready his baggage. He put on the rich garments in which he would be married, and strutted before them.

'Look!' he cried to his servants. 'Here you see the husband of a Princess of Castile. How does he look, eh?'

'My lord,' was the answer, 'there could not be a more worthy husband of a Princess of Castile.'

'Ah!' laughed Don Pedro. 'She will find me a worthy husband, I'll promise you.'

And he continued to laugh, thinking of her – the prim young girl who had been in hiding when he had made certain proposals to her mother. He remembered her standing before them, her blue eyes scornful. He would teach her to be scornful!

He gave himself up to pleasant contemplation of his wedding night. Afterwards, he promised himself, she should be a different woman. She would never again dare show her scorn of him. Princess of Castile though she was he would show her who was her master.

He gave himself up to his sensual dreaming, to the contemplation of an orgy which would be all the more enticing because it would be shared by a prim and – oh, so sedate – Princess.

'Come on,' he cried. 'You sluggards, work harder. It is time we left. It is a long journey to Madrid.'

'Yes, my lord. Yes, my lord.'

How docile they were, how eager to please! They knew it would be the worse for them if they were not. She would soon learn also.

What a blessing it was to be the brother of a powerful man. But people must not forget that Don Pedro himself was also powerful – powerful in his own right.

One of the self-appointed tasks of Don Pedro was to assure those about him that, although he drew some of his power from his brother's high office, he was himself a man to be reckoned with.

He scowled at his servants. He was impatient to leave. He longed for the journey to be over; he longed for the wedding celebrations to begin.

With great pomp Don Pedro set out on the journey to Madrid. All along the road people came out to greet him; graciously he accepted their homage. Never had he been so pleased with himself. Why, he reckoned, he had come farther even than his brother, the Marquis. Had the Marquis ever aspired to the hand of a Princess? What glorious good fortune that he had joined the Order of the Calatrava and thus had escaped the web of matrimony. How disconcerting it would have been if this opportunity had come along and he had been unable to take advantage of it because of a previous entanglement. But no, a little dispensation from Rome had been all that was needed.

They would stay the first night at Villarubia, a little hamlet not far from Ciudad Real. Here members of the King's Court had come to greet him. He noticed with delight their obsequious manners. Already he had ceased to be merely the brother of the Marquis of Villena.

He had the innkeeper brought before him.

'Now, my man,' he shouted, as he swaggered in his dazzling garments, 'I doubt you have ever entertained royalty before. Now's your chance to show us what you can do. And it had better be good. If it is not, you will be a most unhappy man.'

'Yes, my lord ... yes, Highness,' stuttered the man. 'We have been warned of your coming and have been working all day for your pleasure.'

'It is what I expect,' cried Don Pedro.

He was a little haughty with the officers of the King's Guard who had come to escort him on his way to Madrid. They must understand that in a few days' time he would be a member of the royal family.

The innkeeper's feast was good enough to satisfy even him; he gorged himself on the delicious meats and drank deep of the innkeeper's wine.

Furtive eyes watched him, and there were many at the table to think sadly of the Princess Isabella.

Don Pedro was helped to his bed by his servants. He was very drunk and sleepy, and incoherently he told them what a great man he was and how he would subdue his chaste and royal bride.

It was during the night that he awoke startled. His body was covered with a cold sweat and he realized that it was a gripping pain which had awakened him.

He struggled up in his bed and shouted to his servant.

Andres Cabrera came to Isabella's apartments and was greeted by his wife.

'Isabella?' he asked.

'She lies in her bed. She grows more and more listless.'

'Then she has not heard the news. So I am the first to bring it to her.'

Beatriz gripped her husband's arm and her eyes dilated. 'What news?'

'Give me the dagger,' he said. 'You'll not need it now.'

'You mean...?'

'He was taken ill at Villarubia four days ago. The news has just been brought to me that he is dead. Soon all Madrid will know.'

'Andres!' cried Beatriz, and there was a question in her eyes.

'Suffice it,' he said, 'that there will be no need for you to use your dagger.'

Beatriz swayed a little, and for a few seconds Andres thought that the excess of emotion which she was undergoing would cause her to faint.

But she recovered herself. She gazed at him, and there was

pride and gratitude in her eyes – and an infinite love for him.

'It is an act of God,' she cried.

Andres answered: 'We can call it that.'

Beatriz took his hand and kissed it; then she laughed aloud and ran into Isabella's bedchamber.

She stood by the bed, looking down on her mistress. Andres had come to stand beside her.

'Great news!' cried Beatriz. 'The best news that you could hear. There will be no marriage. Our prayers have been answered; he is dead.'

Isabella sat up in bed and looked from Beatriz to Andres.

'Dead! Is it possible? But ... but how?'

'At Villarubia,' said Beatriz. 'He was taken ill four days ago. I told you, did I not, that our prayers would be answered. Dearest Isabella, you see our fears were all for something which cannot happen.'

'I cannot believe it,' whispered Isabella. 'It is miraculous. He was so strong ... it seems impossible that he could ... die. And you say he was taken ill. Of what ...? And ... how?'

'Let us say,' Beatriz answered, 'that it was an Act of God. That is the happiest way of looking at this. We prayed for a miracle, Princesa; and our prayers have been granted.'

Isabella rose from her bed and went to her *prie-Dieu*.

She knelt and gave thanks for her deliverance; and behind her stood Beatriz and Andres.

ALFONSO AT CARDENOSA

THE Archbishop of Toledo and his nephew the Marquis of Villena were closeted together, it was said, deep in mourning for Don Pedro.

The chief emotion of these ambitious men was however not sorrow but anger.

'There are spies among us,' cried the militant Archbishop. 'Worse than spies ... assassins!'

'It is deplorable,' agreed Villena sarcastically, 'that they should have their spies and assassins, and that they should be as effective as our own.'

'The whole of Castile is laughing at us,' declared the Archbishop. 'They are jeering because we presumed to ally our family with the royal one.'

'And to think that we have been foiled in this!'

'I would have his servants seized, tortured. I would discover who had formulated this plot against us.'

'Useless, Uncle. Servants under torture will tell any tale. And do we need to be led to the murderers of my brother? Do we not know that they are – our enemies? The trail would doubtless lead us to the royal Palace. That could be awkward.'

'Nephew, are you suggesting that we should meekly accept this ... this murder?'

'Meekly, no. But we should say to ourselves: Pedro, who could have linked our family with the royal one, has been murdered; therefore that little plan has failed. Well, we will show our enemies that it is dangerous to interfere with our plans. The marriage was accepted by Henry as an alternative to civil war. Very well, he has declined one, let him have the other.'

The Archbishop's eyes were gleaming. He was ready now to play the part for which he had always longed.

He said: 'Young Alfonso shall ride into battle by my side.'

'It is the only way,' said Villena. 'We offered them peace and they retaliated by the murder of my brother. Very well, they have chosen. Now they shall have war.'

On the plains of Almedo the rival forces were waiting.

The Archbishop, clad in armour, wore a scarlet cloak on which had been embroidered the white cross of the Church. He looked a magnificent figure, and his squadrons were ready to follow him into battle.

Alfonso, who was not quite fourteen years old at this time, could not help but be thrilled by the enthusiasm of the Archbishop. The boy Alfonso was dressed in glittering mail, and this would be his first taste of battle.

The Archbishop called Alfonso to him while they waited in the grey dawn light.

'My son,' he said, 'my Prince, this could be the most important day of your life. On these plains our enemies are gathered. What happens this day may decide your future, my future and, what is more important, the future of Castile. It may well be that after this day there will be *one* King of Castile, and that King will be yourself. Castile must become great. There must be an end to the anarchy which is spreading over our land. Remember that, when we go into battle. Come, let us pray for victory.'

Alfonso pressed the palms of his hands together; he lowered his eyes; and with the Archbishop, in that camp on the plains of Almedo, he prayed for victory over his half-brother Henry.

In the opposing camp Henry waited with his men.

'How long the day seems in coming,' said the Duke of Albuquerque.

Henry shivered; it seemed to him that the day came all too quickly.

Henry looked at this man who had played such a big part in his life. Beltran seemed as eager for the battle as he was for the revelries of the Court. Henry could not help feeling a great admiration for this man, who had all the bearing of a King and could contemplate going into battle without a trace of fear, although he must know that he would be considered one of the greatest prizes that could fall into the enemy's hands.

It was small wonder that Joanna had loved him.

Henry wished that there was some means of preventing the battle from taking place. He would be ready to listen to their terms; he would be ready to meet them. It seemed so senseless to fight and make terms afterwards. What could war mean but misery for those who took part in it?

'Have no fear, Highness,' said Beltran, 'we shall put them to flight.'

'Ah, I wish I could be sure of that.'

While he spoke information was brought to him that a messenger had arrived from the opposing camp.

'Give him safe conduct and send him in,' said Henry.

The messenger was brought into the royal presence.

'It is a message I have from the Archbishop of Toledo for the Duke of Albuquerque, Highness.'

'Then hand it to me,' said Beltran.

Henry watched the Duke while he read the message and burst into loud laughter.

'Wait awhile,' he said, 'and I will give you an answer for the Archbishop.'

'What message is this?' asked Henry hopefully. Could it be some offer of truce? But why should it be sent to the Duke, not the King? Surely the Archbishop knew that any offer of peace would be more eagerly accepted by the King than anyone else.

Beltran said: 'It is a warning from the Archbishop, Highness. He tells me that I shall be foolish to venture on to the field this day. He says that no less than forty of his men have sworn to kill me. My chances of surviving the battle, he assures me, are very poor.'

'My dear Beltran, you must not ride into battle today. There should be no battle. What good will it do any of us? Bloodshed of my subjects ... that will be the result of this day's work.'

'Highness, it is too late for such talk.'

'It is never too late for peace.'

'The Archbishop would not accept your peace offer except under the most degrading conditions. Nay, Highness. Today we go to do battle with our enemies. Have I permission to answer this note?'

Henry nodded gloomily, and the Duke smiled as he prepared his answer.

'What have you written?' he asked.

Beltran answered: 'I have given him a description of my attire, so that those who have sworn to kill me shall have no difficulty in seeking me out.'

Henry waited some miles from the battlefield. He had taken the first opportunity to retire when he had heard that the battle was going against his side.

For what good would it be, he reasoned with himself, to endanger the life of the King?

And he covered his face with his hands and wept for the folly of men determined to go to war.

Meanwhile the young Alfonso rode into battle side by side with the warlike Archbishop.

It was long, and the slaughter was great. Nor was it effective in forcing a decision. The courage of the Archbishop of Toledo was only matched by that of the Duke of Albuquerque, and after three hours of carnage such as had rarely been known before in Castile, the forces led by the Archbishop and Alfonso were forced to leave the battlefield in the possession of the King's men.

But Henry was not eager to take advantage of the fact that his army had not been routed; and Beltran, brave soldier that he was, was no strategist; and thus that which could have been called a victory was treated as a defeat.

Now Castile was a country divided. Each King ruled in that territory over which he held sway.

And following the advantage they had won on account of the King's refusal to regard the battle of Almedo as his victory, the Archbishop and the Marquis, with Alfonso as their figurehead, decided to march on Segovia.

Isabella, with Beatriz and Mencia, was eager for every item of news of Alfonso's progress.

'What is happening to our country?' she said one day as she sat with her friends. 'In every town of Castile men of the same blood are fighting one another.'

'What can be expected when our country is plunged in civil war!' Beatriz added.

'I dream of peace for Castile,' murmured Isabella. 'Here we sit stitching at our needlework, but, Beatriz, do you not think that if we were called upon to rule this land we could do it better than those in whose hands its government now rests?'

'Think!' cried Beatriz. 'I am sure of it.'

'If Castile could be ruled by you, Infanta, with Beatriz as your first minister,' declared Mencia, 'then I verily believe all our troubles would quickly be brought to an end.'

'I shudder,' said Isabella, 'to think of my brother. It is long since I saw him. Do you remember the day the Archbishop called and told him he would be put under his care? I wonder ... has all that has happened to him changed Alfonso?'

'It is hard to conjecture,' Beatriz murmured. 'In these last months he has become King.'

'There can only be one King of Castile,' Isabella reminded her. 'And that is my half-brother Henry. Oh, how I wish that there was not this strife. Alfonso should be *heir* to the throne, because there is no doubt that the Queen's daughter is not the King's, but he should never have been proclaimed King. And to ride into battle against Henry . . . ! Oh, how I wish he had not done that.'

'It was no fault of his,' said Mencia.

'No,' Beatriz agreed. 'He is but a boy. He is only fourteen. How can he be blamed because they have caught him up in their fight for power!'

'Poor Alfonso. I tremble for him,' murmured Isabella.

'All will be well,' Beatriz soothed her. 'Dearest Princesa, remember how on other occasions we have despaired, and how all has come right.'

'Yes,' said Isabella. 'I was saved from a terrible fate. But is it not alarming to consider how a man . . . or a woman . . . can be alive and well one day and dead the next?'

'It has always been so,' said the practical Beatriz. And she added significantly: 'And sometimes it has proved a blessing.'

'Listen!' cried Mencia. 'I hear shouts from below. What can it be?'

'Go and see,' said Beatriz.

Mencia got up to go, but before she had reached the door one of the men-at-arms rushed into the room.

'Princesa, ladies, the rebels are marching on the castle.'

There was little resistance, for how could Isabella demand that resistance be shown against those at whose head rode her own brother.

As they stormed into the castle, she heard Alfonso's voice; it had changed since she had last heard it and grown deep, authoritative.

'Have a care. Remember, my sister, the Princess Isabella, is in the castle.'

And then the door was flung open and there stood Alfonso – her little brother, seeming little no longer – not a boy but a soldier, a King, even though she would maintain he had no right to wear the crown.

'Isabella!' he cried; and he was young again. His face seemed to pucker childishly, and it was as though he were begging for her approval as he used to when he took his first tottering steps about the nursery.

'Brother ... little brother!' Isabella was in his arms and for some seconds they clung together.

Then she took his face in her hands. 'You are well, Alfonso, you are well?'

'Indeed yes. And you, dearest sister?'

'Yes ... and so glad to see you once more, brother. Oh, Alfonso ... Alfonso!'

'Isabella, we are together now. Let us stay together. I have rescued you from Henry. Henceforth it shall be you and I ... brother and sister ... together.'

'Yes,' she cried. 'Yes...' And she lost her calm and was laughing in his arms.

And so she stayed with him, and on several occasions travelled with him through that territory which now considered him its King.

But she was perturbed. Her love of justice would not allow her to blind herself to the fact that he had usurped the throne, however unwillingly.

During those troublous months news came to Isabella of the disturbances which were rife throughout Castile. Old quarrels between certain noble families were renewed; nowhere was it safe for men or women to journey unescorted. Even men of the highest nobility took advantage of the situation to rob and pillage, and the Hermandad found itself almost useless against this tide of anarchy.

Alfonso's headquarters were at Avila, which had remained loyal to him since the occasion of that strange 'coronation' outside its walls. On the Archbishop and Villena, to whom he owed his position, he bestowed the honours and favours they demanded.

Isabella remonstrated with him.

'While Henry lives you cannot be King of Castile, Alfonso,' she told him, 'for Henry is our father's eldest son and the only true King of Castile.'

Alfonso had changed since those days when he had been afraid because he knew himself to be the tool of ambitious men. Alfonso had tasted the pleasures of kingship, and he was by no means prepared to relinquish them.

'But, Isabella,' he pointed out, 'a King rules by the will of his people. If he fails to please his people then he has no right to the crown.'

'There are many in Castile who are still pleased to call Henry King,' Isabella answered.

'Dear Isabella,' replied her brother, 'you are so good and so just. Henry has not been kind to you; he has tried to force you to a distasteful marriage – yet you would seem to support him.'

'But it is not a question of kindness, brother. It is a matter of what is right. And Henry is King of Castile. It is you who are the impostor.'

Alfonso smiled at her. 'We must agree to differ,' he said. 'I am glad that, although you consider me an impostor, you still love me.'

'You are my brother. Nothing can alter that. But one day I hope there will be a settlement and that you will be proclaimed heir to the throne. That is what I wish.'

'The nobles would never agree.'

'It is because they are seeking power rather than what is just and right, and they still use us, Alfonso, as puppets in their schemes. In supporting you they support that which they believe to be best for themselves, and those who support Henry do so for selfish reasons. It is only through what is just that good can come.'

'Well, Isabella, although you would appear to be on the side of my enemies ...'

'Never that! I am always for you, Alfonso. But your cause must be the just one, and you are now justly heir to the throne, but not the King.'

'I would say, Isabella, that I would never force you to make a marriage which was distasteful to you. I would put nothing in the way of your match with Ferdinand of Aragon.'

'Dear Alfonso, you wish me to be happy, as I wish you to be. For the moment let us rejoice in the fact that we are together.'

'Shortly I leave for Avila, Isabella, and you must come with us.'

'I would wish to do so,' said Isabella.

'It is wonderful to have you with me. I like to ask your advice. And you know, Isabella, I take it often. It is merely this one great matter on which we disagree. Sister, let me tell you this: I do not wish to be unjust. If I were a little older I would tell these nobles that I would lay no claim to the crown until my half-brother dies or it is agreed by all that he should relinquish it. I would. Indeed, I would, Isabella. But you see, I am not old enough and I must obey these men. Isabella, what would become of me if I refused to do so?'

'Who shall say?'

'For you see, Isabella, I should be neither the friend of these men nor of my brother Henry. I should be in that waste land between them – the friend of neither, the enemy of both.'

It was at such times that Isabella saw the frightened boy looking out from the eyes of Alfonso, the usurping King of Castile.

Isabella remained in Avila while Alfonso and his men went on to the little village of Cardeñosa, some two leagues away; for she had felt the need to linger awhile at the Convent of

Santa Clara, where the nuns received her with Beatriz and Mencia.

Isabella had wanted to shut herself away, to meditate and pray. She did not ask that her marriage with Ferdinand might become a fact, because when she visualized leaving Castile for Aragon she reminded herself that that would mean leaving her brother.

'He needs me at this time,' she told Beatriz. 'Oh, when he is with his men, when he is conducting affairs of state, none would believe that he is little more than a child. But I know he is often a bewildered boy. I believe that, if it could be arranged that this wretched state of conflict could come to an end, none would be happier than Alfonso.'

'There is some magic in a crown,' mused Beatriz, 'which makes those who feel it on their heads very reluctant to cast it aside.'

'Yet Alfonso, in his heart, knows that he has no right to wear it yet.'

'You know it, Princesa, and I verily believe that were it placed on your head before you felt it to be yours by right you would not accept it. But you are a woman in a million, dearest mistress. Have I not told you that you are good ... as few are good?'

'You do not know me, Beatriz. Did I not rejoice at the deaths of Carlos and of Don Pedro? How can anyone be good who rejoices at the misfortune of others?'

'Bah!' said Beatriz, forgetting the deference due to a Princess. 'You would have been inhuman not to rejoice on those occasions.'

'A saint would not have rejoiced, so I pray you, Beatriz, do not endow me with saintliness, or you will be sadly disappointed. I would pray now for peace in our country, not because I am good, but because I know that the country's peace will make us all so much happier – myself, Henry and Alfonso.'

There were special prayers in the Convent of Santa Clara,

and these were for peace. Isabella had asked that these should be offered. She found life in the convent inspiring. She was ready to embrace its austerity; she was pleased to be able to give herself up to prayer and contemplation.

Isabella was to remember those days she spent in the convent as the end of a certain period of her life, but she could not know, as she walked the stone corridors, as she listened to the bells which called her to the chapel, and the chanting voices there, that events were taking shape which would force her to play a prominent part in the conflict which raged about her.

It was Beatriz who brought her the news.

They had asked Beatriz to do this because no other dared to do so.

And Beatriz came to her, her face blotched with the tears she had shed, for once unable to find words for what she had to say.

'What has happened, Beatriz?' asked Isabella, and her heart grew heavy with alarm.

When Beatriz shook her head and began to weep, Isabella went on: 'Is it Alfonso?'

Beatriz nodded.

'He is ill?'

Beatriz looked at her with a tragic stare, and Isabella whispered: 'Dead?'

Beatriz suddenly found words. 'He retired to his room after supper. When his servants went to wake him they could not arouse him; he had died in his sleep.'

'Poison...' murmured Isabella. She turned away and whispered: 'So ... it has happened to Alfonso.'

She stared from the window. She did not see the black figures of the nuns hurrying to the chapel. She did not hear the tolling bell. In her mind's eye she saw Alfonso waking suddenly in the night, with the knowledge upon him. Perhaps he had called for his sister; for he would naturally call for her if he were in trouble.

And so ... it had happened to Alfonso.

She did not weep. She felt too numb, too drained of feeling. She turned to Beatriz and said: 'Where did it happen?'

'At Cardeñosa.'

'And the news was brought ...?'

'A few minutes ago. Someone came to the convent from the town. They say that the whole of Avila knows of it, and that the town is plunged into mourning.'

'We will go to Cardeñosa, Beatriz,' said Isabella. 'We will go at once and say our last farewells to Alfonso!'

Beatriz came to her mistress and put her arm about her. She shook her head sadly and her voice was poignant with emotion.

'No, Princesa, you can do no good. You can only add to your suffering.'

'I wish to see Alfonso for the last time,' stated Isabella blankly.

'You scourge yourself.'

'He would wish me to be there. Come, Beatriz, we are leaving at once for Cardeñosa.'

Isabella rode out from Avila, and as she did so the people in the streets turned their faces away from her. She was grateful to them for such understanding of her sorrow.

She had not yet begun to consider what the death of Alfonso would mean to her position; she had forgotten that those ambitious men, who had so ruthlessly terminated Alfonso's childhood to make him into a King, would now turn their attention to her. There was no room in her heart for more than this one overwhelming fact: Alfonso, little brother and companion of her early years, was dead.

She was surprised, when she rode into the little village of Cardeñosa, that there was no sign of mourning. She saw a group of soldiers cheerfully calling to each other; their laughter rang in her ears and it sounded inhuman.

When they noticed her they stopped their chatter, and

saluted her, but she received their homage as though she were unaware of them. Was this all they cared for Alfonso?

Beatriz, in sudden anger, called out: 'Is this the way you show respect for your King?'

The soldiers looked bewildered. One opened his mouth as though to speak, but Isabella with her little entourage had ridden on.

The grooms who took their horses wore the same cheerful looks as the soldiers they had seen in the streets.

Beatriz said impulsively: 'You do not mourn in Cardeñosa as they do in Avila. Why not?'

'Mourn, my lady? Why should we mourn?'

Beatriz had to use great restraint to prevent herself giving the groom a slap across his face. 'So you had no love for your King then?'

There was the same bewildered look on the groom's face as there had been on those soldiers in the village.

Then a voice from inside the inn which Alfonso had made his headquarters called: 'What is this? Has the Princess Isabella tired of convent life then, and come to join her brother?'

Beatriz saw Isabella turn pale; and she put out her arm to catch her, for she thought her mistress was about to faint. Could that have been the voice of a ghost? Could there be another who spoke with the voice of Alfonso?

But there was Alfonso, full of health and vigour, running across the courtyard calling: 'Isabella! So this is no lie. You are here then, sister.'

Isabella slid from her horse and ran to her brother; she seized him in her arms and kissed him; then taking his face in her hands she stared into it.

'So it is you, Alfonso. It is really you. You are not a ghost. This is my brother ... my little brother ...'

'Well I know of no one else it could be,' said Alfonso, laughing.

'But I heard.... How ... how could such wicked stories be spread abroad! Oh Alfonso ... I am so happy.'

And there, before the wondering eyes of grooms and soldiers, Isabella began to weep, not violently, but quietly; and they were tears of happiness.

Alfonso himself dried her eyes and, putting his arm about her, led her into the inn.

Beatriz walked beside them.

'It was an evil rumour,' she said. 'Avila is mourning your death. We heard that you had died in the night.'

'These rumours!' said Alfonso. 'How do they start? But let us not worry about that now. It is good to have you with me, Isabella. Now you will stay awhile? Tonight we shall have a special feast ... as near a banquet as we can muster in this place.' He called to his men: 'My sister, the Princess Isabella, is here. Have them prepare a banquet worthy of her.'

Alfonso was deeply moved by his sister's emotion. The fact that Isabella was usually so restrained made him aware of the depth of her feeling for him, and he was afraid he too would break down. He had to remind himself constantly that he was a King, and not a young boy any more.

He called to the innkeeper.

'A special banquet,' he cried, 'in honour of my sister's arrival! What can you put before us?'

'Highness, I have some chickens ... very good, very tender; and there are some trout. ...'

'Do your best, and let there be a banquet such as you have never served before, because my sister is come, and that is a very important matter to me.'

Then he turned to Isabella and once more they embraced.

'Isabella,' whispered Alfonso, 'how glad I am that we are once more together. Let it be so as often as we can arrange it. Sister, I need you with me. Without you ... I am still a little unsure.'

'Yes, yes, Alfonso,' she answered in the same quiet and tense tone, 'we must be together. We need each other. In future ... we must not be apart.'

* * *

It was a merry supper that was served that night in the Cardeñosa inn.

The trout was delicious. Alfonso commented on its excellence and took a second helping.

Everyone was merry. It was pleasant, they said, to have been joined by the ladies, and they had heard that the Princess Isabella intended in future to accompany her brother on his journeys through his domain.

When they retired, Isabella and Beatriz talked about the day's doings and marvelled that they could have left Avila in such distress and have found such joy, the very same day, in Cardeñosa.

Beatriz, combing her mistress's hair, said: 'Yet it surprises me how such rumours could be started.'

'It is not difficult to understand, Beatriz. So many people in high places die suddenly that the story of another death is readily believed.'

'That is so,' agreed Beatriz and did not pursue the subject, for, she reasoned with herself, why spoil the day's pleasure?

Yet she was a little uneasy. Avila was only two leagues from Cardeñosa, and the rumour had a good hold on the former. How could it have happened . . . so close?

But she was not going to brood on that terrible moment, when the news had been brought to her and she realized it was her duty to break it to Isabella.

Isabella awoke early and for a few moments could not remember where she was. Then the events of the day before came back to her mind. That strange day which had begun in such sorrow and had ended in joy.

She was of course in the Cardeñosa inn.

She lay thinking of that moment when Alfonso had come out of the inn and for a few seconds she had thought she had seen his ghost. Now, she thought, I shall always be with him. I shall make it my duty to care for him, for after all he is but a boy and my own brother.

Perhaps she would be able to influence him, to persuade him that he could be no true King while Henry lived. If he were declared heir to the throne, she would be perfectly content; for she believed without doubt that the little Joanna had no right to that title. From now on, she told herself, Alfonso and I will be together.

There was a knocking at her door and she called to whoever was there to enter.

Beatriz came in. She was pale and she looked distraught.

'Highness,' she said, 'will you come to Alfonso's bed-chamber?'

Isabella started up in dismay. 'What has happened?'

'I have been asked to take you to him.'

'He is ill!'

All the fears of yesterday were back with her.

'They cannot awaken him,' said Beatriz. 'They do not understand what can have happened.'

Beatriz flung a robe about Isabella's shoulders and they went to Alfonso's chamber.

He lay in his bed, strangely unlike himself.

Isabella bent over him. 'Alfonso ... Alfonso, brother. It is Isabella. Wake up. What ails you?'

There was no response. The room was dark, for it had but one small window.

'I cannot see him clearly,' said Isabella touching his forehead. Its coldness startled her. She took his hand; and it dropped lifelessly back to lie on the counterpane.

Isabella turned in horror to Beatriz who stood behind her.

Beatriz moved closer to the figure on the bed. She put her hand to the boy's heart and kept it there for some seconds while she wondered how she was going to say what she knew she must.

She turned to Isabella.

'No,' cried Isabella. '*No!*'

Beatriz did not answer. But Isabella knew that there was no way of turning from the truth.

'But how ... how?' she cried. 'But why ...?'

Beatriz put an arm about her. 'We will send for the doctors,' she said. She turned angrily on his page. 'Why did you not send for the doctors before this?'

'My lady, I came to wake him and he did not answer, and I was afraid; so I came for you. It is but a matter of ten minutes since I came into his room and found him lying thus. I came to you at once, knowing you would say how I should act.'

'Fetch the doctors,' Beatriz commanded.

The page went, and Isabella looked at her friend with heavy eyes.

'You know there is nothing the doctors can do, Beatriz?'

'Dearest, I fear it is so.'

'So ...' said Isabella, 'I have lost him then. I have lost him after all.'

Beatriz embraced her and for a little while Isabella remained passive.

The doctors came into the room. Isabella watched them listlessly as they stood about the bed, and they exchanged significant glances with each other.

Beatriz felt her control was snapping. 'Well, say something!' she cried. 'He is dead ... dead ... is he not?'

'We fear so, my lady.'

'And ... nothing can be done?'

'It is too late, my lady.'

'Too late,' whispered Isabella to herself. 'How foolish I was to think I could help him, to think I could save him. How could I save him except by keeping him by my side day and night, by tasting every morsel of food before it touched his lips?'

Beatriz was crying: 'But ... how ... *how* ...?'

That was a question they could not answer.

Isabella understood why she had heard the rumours in Avila. The planners had not been working in unison; something may have gone wrong at the inn while the carriers of the news went on and announced it in accordance with some preconceived plot.

Thus the news of Alfonso's death had been circulated *before* it happened.

How could Alfonso have died so suddenly unless someone had deliberately cut short his life? A few hours ago he had been full of life and health; and now he was dead.

Dear Alfonso, dear innocent Alfonso, this was what he had feared in those early days when he had talked so much of the fate of others. And it had come to him ... even as he had feared it would.

She trusted that he had not suffered much. It was incredible that she should have been close by, and that he should have awakened in his need while she was sleeping peacefully unaware.

She saw Beatriz's smouldering eyes upon her. Beatriz would want to find those who had done this. She would want revenge.

But what would be the use? That would not bring Alfonso back to her.

THE HEIRESS TO THE THRONE

IN the Convent of Santa Clara Isabella gave herself up to mourning.

She would sit thinking of the past when she and her mother had retired to Arevalo with little Alfonso. Now her mother lived, but could one call that existence living? And she, Isabella, was left to face a turbulent world.

There were times when she envied the young nuns who were about to take the veil and shut themselves off for ever from the world.

'I wish,' she told Beatriz, 'that I could so resign myself.'

But Beatriz, who was always outspoken, shook her head. 'No, my Infanta, you do not wish this. You know that a great future awaits you, and you would never turn your back on your destiny. Not for you the life of the cloistered nun. One day you will be a Queen. Your name will be honoured and remembered in the generations to come.'

'Who can say?' murmured Isabella. 'Might you not have made the same prophecy for my poor Alfonso?'

She had not been long at the convent when she had a visitor. The Archbishop of Toledo himself, representing the confederacy which was in revolt against the King, had travelled to the convent to see her. She received him with reserve and he was unusually humble.

'Condolences, Highness,' said the Archbishop. 'I know how you suffer through our great loss. I and my friends mourn with you.'

'Yet,' said Isabella, 'had Alfonso never been acclaimed King of Castile he might be alive at this hour.'

'It is true that he would not have been in Cardeñosa, and

perhaps would not have contracted the plague.'

'Or eaten trout!' said Isabella.

'Ah, these are dangerous times,' murmured the Archbishop. 'That is why we need a firm government, a royal leader of integrity.'

'The times must be dangerous in a country where two rulers are set up. I think that my brother might not have died if he had had God's blessing on his enterprise.'

'But if, as you hint, Highness, his death was due to trout, that is the result of the criminality of man surely, not the justice of God,'

'It may be,' said Isabella, 'that if God had looked with favour on Alfonso's accession, he would have prevented his death.'

'Who shall say,' said the Archbishop. 'I come to remind Your Highness of the evil state of Castile and of the need for reform.'

'There is no need to remind me of that,' said Isabella, 'for I have heard reports of the state of our country which fill me with such dismay that I could not forget them if I tried.'

The Archbishop bowed his head. 'Highness,' he said, 'we desire to proclaim you Queen of Castile and Leon.'

'I thank you,' said Isabella, 'but while my brother Henry lives no one else has a right to wear the crown. Too long has there been conflict in Castile, which was largely due to the fact that it has two sovereigns.'

'Highness, you cannot mean that you refuse to be proclaimed Queen!'

'That is exactly what I mean.'

'But ... this is incredible.'

'I know it to be right.'

'Why, Highness, were you Queen you could immediately begin to set right all that is wrong in Castile. My nephew and myself would be beside you. It could be the beginning of a new era for Castile.'

Isabella was silent. She visualized all that she longed to do for her country. She had often planned how she would strengthen the Hermandad; how she would attempt to bring her people back to a more religious life, how she would establish a Court which would be in direct opposition to that of her brother.

'Our present Queen,' murmured the Archbishop, 'is becoming notorious on account of the lecherous life she leads. There was a time when she was content with one lover; now there must be many. Do you not see, Highness, what a bad example this sets our people?'

'Indeed I see,' said Isabella.

'Then why do you hesitate?'

'Because, however good one's intentions, they will fail unless built on a foundation which is just. Were I to take what you offer me, I know I should be doing what is wrong. Therefore, I reject your offer.'

The Archbishop was stunned; he had not believed in the true piety of Isabella, and he did not think she would be proof against this offer of the crown.

'What would please me,' she went on, 'would be to achieve reconciliation with my half-brother. It is the strife between two warring factions which is responsible for our troubles. Let us have peace and, since you believe the Queen's daughter to be illegitimate, I am next in the order of succession.'

The Archbishop lifted his head.

'You agree with this?' she asked.

'Indeed I agree, Highness. It is at the root of all our troubles.'

'Then, since you are assured of the Queen's adultery, I should be proclaimed heiress to the throne. Then there would be an end to this war, and matters would stand as it is proper that they should.'

'But Highness, it is the throne itself that we are offering you.'

'I shall never take it,' Isabella told him firmly, 'while my half-brother Henry lives.'

And the astonished Archbishop was at length made to realize that she meant what she said.

His sister wanted to see him, mused Henry. Well, she had changed from the quiet little girl whose sedate manners had put a barrier of reserve between them.

She was an important person now. Villena and the Archbishop wanted to make her Queen – and it seemed that only Isabella's firm resolve that this should not be had prevented their crowning her as they had Alfonso.

Isabella had declared that she wanted peace.

Peace! thought Henry. None could want that more than I do.

He was ready to barter any of his possessions, ready to agree to whatever was suggested, for the sweet sake of peace.

He wanted Villena to be his friend again; he had great faith in Villena. The Cardinal Mendoza, who, from the time of that ceremony outside the walls of Avila, had supported Henry's cause with all the vigour of a strong nature, was not his friend as Villena had once been; he stood in awe of the Cardinal. As for Beltran de la Cueva, Duke of Albuquerque, he was more Joanna's friend than Henry's; they supported each other, those two; and often Henry felt they were not with him.

Now Villena and the Archbishop of Toledo, with Isabella replacing Alfonso as their figurehead, were asking for a meeting; and a meeting there should be.

He was surprised to receive a visit from Villena on the eve of the meeting. As soon as he was shown into Henry's presence, Villena begged to be left alone with the King.

Henry was only too willing to agree. The occasion reminded him of so many in the past.

'Highness,' said Villena, kneeling before Henry, 'I have great hopes that all may soon be as it once was between us.'

Ready tears came to Henry's eyes. 'Rise, my friend,' he

said. 'Tell me what is in your mind.'

'You are going to be asked to agree to certain proposals at Toros de Guisando. Highness, it may be difficult for you to agree to these proposals.'

Villena had stood up and was smiling at the King as he used to in the days of their friendship.

A flicker of weariness crossed Henry's face.

'But,' went on Villena, 'would you take my advice?'

'Gladly I would consider it,' said Henry.

'Highness, if there should be some condition which seems to you impossible, do not allow it to cause you too much concern.'

'You mean?'

'That it is necessary to make peace now. If at a later date you feel that the conditions which were imposed upon you were unfair . . .' Villena lifted his shoulders.

Henry smiled. He was delighted to have Villena on his side again. Villena was a man who would take over the direction of state affairs completely, a man who struck fear into all who came into contact with him; it would be greatly desirable to place everything in his capable hands once more.

'It is desirable, Highness, that we should have peace at this time.'

'Greatly desirable,' agreed Henry.

'Then you will agree to these terms; and afterwards, if we decide they are untenable, we shall re-examine them.'

'You mean . . . you and I will do so?' asked the King.

'If your Highness would graciously listen to my advice, how gladly would I give it.'

Weak tears were in Henry's eyes. The long quarrel was over. The wily Villena had left the opposite camp and was his man once more.

The meeting took place at an inn which was known as the Venta de los Toros de Guisando. Toros de Guisando took its name from the stone figures of bulls which had been left on this spot by the invading armies of Julius Caesar, as their Latin inscriptions indicated.

Here Henry embraced Isabella with great warmth and was delighted to see that she was not unmoved by their meeting.

'Isabella,' he said, 'we meet in sorrow. The saints know I bore no resentment against Alfonso. It was not he who put the crown on his own head; others did that. Like you, I long for peace. Is it impossible for us to achieve that for which we so fervently long?'

'No, brother,' said Isabella, 'it shall not be impossible.'

'I have heard, my dear,' said Henry, 'that you have refused to allow yourself to be proclaimed Queen of Castile. You are both wise and good.'

'Brother,' answered Isabella, 'there could be only one monarch of Castile at this time, and you are by right that monarch.'

'Isabella, I see that we shall come to terms.'

This was very touching, thought the Archbishop, but it was time to discuss practical details.

'The first and most important item on our declaration is that the Princess Isabella be proclaimed heir to the crowns of Castile and Leon,' he said.

'I agree to that,' said Henry.

Isabella was astonished by his alacrity, for it could only mean that he accepted the fact that his wife's little daughter was not his.

'It would be necessary,' went on the Archbishop, 'that a free pardon be given to all who had taken part in the struggle.'

'Gladly I give it,' cried Henry.

'It grieves me to say this,' went on the Archbishop, 'but the conduct of the Queen is not that which can commend itself to her people.'

The King shook his head sadly. Since Beltran had become so immersed in politics, it was true that Joanna had looked for lovers who had been more willing to make her the first consideration in their lives – and found them.

'We should require,' went on the Archbishop, 'that there be a divorce and the Queen sent back to Portugal.'

Henry hesitated. He was wondering how he was going to face an enraged Joanna after agreeing to this. But he trusted in his ability to shift that responsibility on to other shoulders. After all, Joanna could find lovers in Portugal as readily as she did in Castile. He would assure her that it was none of his doing – if he had to tell her of the discussion.

He met Villena's gaze and a look of understanding passed between them.

'I . . . give my consent,' said Henry.

'A Cortes should be invoked for the purpose of giving the Princess Isabella the title of heiress to the crowns of Castile and Leon.'

'It shall be done,' said Henry.

'And,' went on the Archbishop, 'the Princess Isabella shall not be forced to marry against her wishes; nor must she do so without the consent of yourself.'

'I agree,' said Henry.

'Then,' cried the Archbishop, 'is the Princess Isabella the heir to the crowns of Castile and Leon.'

Beatriz could rejoice that her mistress had now been acclaimed as heiress to the crowns.

This was the surest way to soothe her grief, for Isabella was now suppressing her emotions in order that she might dedicate herself to the enormous task which, should she reach maturity, would almost certainly be hers.

Isabella was determined that under her rule Castile should become great.

She gave herself up to meditation and prayer; she was studying the history of her country and others. This dedication was, said Beatriz to Mencia, like a raft to a drowning creature.

Only thus could she grow away from the terrible shock of Alfonso's death, which had seemed doubly hard to bear because, after she had heard of his death, she had had the great joy of seeing him alive, only to lose him a few hours later.

Beatriz was determined to watch over her mistress. There would be many, she believed, ready to bring tasty trout to *her* table. There were the adherents of Queen Joanna and her daughter, who could wish for nothing which would serve them better than the death of Isabella.

But Isabella was not going to die. Beatriz had determined on that, and Beatriz was a very determined woman.

Isabella, heiress to the crowns of Castile and Leon, was not now merely the sister of the self-appointed King Alfonso. Now there were many to seek her hand in marriage.

Ambassadors from England arrived in Spain. They were seeking a bride for Richard of Gloucester, the brother of their King Edward IV, who himself, before his marriage to Elizabeth Grey, had considered Isabella as a possible Queen. Isabella would suit Richard very well.

'Why,' said Beatriz, 'if you made this match, it is possible that one day you might be Queen of England.'

'But how could I serve Castile if I were England's Queen?' demanded Isabella.

There was a suitor from France. This was the Duke of Guienne, the brother of Louis XI; and he, since at this time Louis was without heirs, was next in succession to the throne of France.

'You would be Queen of France,' said Beatriz.

But Isabella only shook her head and smiled.

'You still think of Ferdinand?'

'I have always considered myself betrothed to Ferdinand.'

'You have made an image of him,' Beatriz told her anxiously. 'What if it should be a false one?'

'I do not believe that can be so.'

'But, Princesa, how can you be sure? There are so many disappointments in life.'

'Listen to me, Beatriz,' said Isabella fervently. 'Marriage with Ferdinand is the only marriage for me. By it we shall unite Castile and Aragon; do you not realize what that will mean for Spain? Sometimes I believe that it is part of a great design – a Divine design. You see how every obstacle in Ferdinand's progress to the throne of Aragon is being cleared away. And so, it would seem, is my way to the throne of Castile. Can that be a mere coincidence? I do not think so.'

'You think then that you and Ferdinand are the elect of God.'

Isabella clasped her hands together and lifted her eyes, and Beatriz caught her breath at the rapt expression she saw on her mistress's face.

Then Isabella said: 'I believe it is God's will to make an all-Christian Spain. I believe that He wishes that to be a strong Spain. I believe that Ferdinand and I, when we are united, will do His Will and that we shall drive from this land all who do not belong to the Holy Catholic Church.'

'You mean that together you and Ferdinand will convert or drive out every Jew and Moor from this country; that you will bring to the Christian Faith all those who follow other religions? What a mighty task! For centuries there have been Arabs in Spain.'

'That is no reason why they should continue to remain here.'

Beatriz was doubtful. Isabella, seeming so strong, was yet vulnerable. What if her Ferdinand were not the man she believed him to be? What if he were as lecherous as Don Pedro, as weak as her half-brother Henry?

'You will be strong. You will be capable of this, I know,' said Beatriz. 'But your partner must be equally strong and devoted to the Faith. How can we know that he is?'

'You doubt Ferdinand?'

'I know little of Ferdinand. Isabella, face the truth. What do *you* know of him?'

'I know this: that he is my betrothed husband and I will take no other.'

Beatriz was silent awhile. Then she said: 'Why do you not

send a man to Aragon ... that he may meet Ferdinand and tell you what you wish to know of him. Let him go there and let him go to France. Let him see the Duke of Guienne and discover what manner of man he is – and let him see Ferdinand and report on him. You could send your chaplain, Alonso de Coca. You could trust him.'

Isabella's eyes sparkled.

'I will send him, Beatriz,' she said. 'But not because I need reassurance. I will send him that *you* may be assured that Ferdinand is the husband – and the only husband – for me.'

The Marquis of Villena called on his uncle, the Archbishop of Toledo. Villena was a little uneasy, because he was unsure of his uncle's reaction to the turn in events.

Villena was a sly statesman; the Archbishop was a brave fighter and a man who, while seeking self-advancement, must believe in his cause. He was not the man – as his nephew was – to change his loyalties merely because they suited the immediate purpose.

Villena therefore began cautiously: 'Isabella would never be the puppet that Alfonso was.'

'It's true,' said the Archbishop. 'We have a real Queen here. One whom it will be our pleasure to serve. My only regret is that she refused to allow herself to be proclaimed Queen. She was right, of course, morally right. But I cannot help thinking that it would have been advantageous for our country if Isabella wore the crown which now is set so unbecomingly on Henry's head.'

Villena remained silent. His uncle rejoiced in that quality of Isabella's which he deplored. Villena did not want a woman of purpose to rule Castile. He wanted a puppet whom he could direct. It was not easy to explain this to his fiery uncle.

'I do not think,' went on the Archbishop, 'that Alfonso's death is such a great calamity after all. I think that in Alfonso's sister we have our Queen. I give my allegiance to her and I believe she is beginning to understand that I wish to serve her.' The Archbishop laughed. 'She is inclined to distrust me. Was I not on the side of the rebels? And Isabella is so loyal to the crown, so determined to uphold its dignity, that she deplores rebels.'

'Why, Uncle,' said Villena, 'you have allowed the young woman to bewitch you.'

'I admit she impresses me deeply. I feel delighted to serve her.'

'But, Uncle, what can a girl know of the governing of a country?'

'Depend upon it, nephew, she will never attempt to do that which is beyond her power. And I do assure you that the governing of the country is something she will quickly learn. Why, Isabella is dedicated to her task – and that is how all Kings and Queens should approach their duties.'

'H'm,' said Villena. 'You have become mild, Uncle.'

'Mild! Never! But I stand firmly beside our future Queen. And if any attack her, you will not have to complain of the mildness of Alfonso Carillo.'

'Well, well, you are happy with this turn of events then.'

'I feel more confident of the future of Castile than I ever did before.'

Villena quickly took his leave of his uncle.

He had nothing to say to him; he knew they had arrived at a great divergence of opinion.

They would no longer work together; they were on opposite sides.

When Villena left the Archbishop, he made his way to Henry's apartments.

Henry received him eagerly. He could not show his gratitude sufficiently, so delighted was he to have Villena back in his camp.

Joanna the Queen had left him now. She had been so furious that he had agreed to divorce her that she had gone to Madrid, where she now lived scandalously, taking lover after lover as though in defiance of the verdict which had been passed on her at Toros de Guisando. It had been no use Henry's explaining to Joanna that he had no intention of keeping his word in regard to what had been laid down at the meeting with Isabella; Joanna was so furious, because he could even have *pretended* to agree to divorce her, that she had gone off in a rage.

That was of no great matter, for she had long brought him more uneasiness than pleasure; he was happy enough with his own mistresses, and he took care to choose those who would not dabble in politics.

And now here was his dear friend Villena, returned to be his friend and adviser, and so happily take charge of everything and instruct him as to what had to be done.

Villena explained that he had left his uncle and that the Archbishop had given his allegiance to Isabella, as he Villena had to Alfonso.

'He is a single-minded man,' said Villena. 'He can blind himself to his own advantages at times. After all, he is a man of the Church and he needs to have faith in something. He has now put that faith in Isabella. She has managed to appeal to his sense of righteousness. It is regrettable, Highness, for we have lost a useful ally.'

'My dear Villena, I believe you will do very well without him.'

'That may be. But I am a little disturbed about our Isabella. I was hoping a marriage with England or France would attract her. It would be comforting to know that she was no longer in Castile.'

Henry nodded.

'It would be so very simple, if she were not here,' went on Villena, 'to proclaim the little Joanna heiress to the throne.'

'So much easier,' admitted Henry.

'Well, she declines England; she is preparing to decline

France. You know why. She has set her heart on Ferdinand.'
Villena's face hardened. Not on any account was he going to
allow the match with Aragon to become an accomplished
fact. That would be the end of his ambitions, he knew. Isabella and Ferdinand together would be formidable opponents
of his plans. Villena knew exactly what he wanted. A puppet
King, a puppet heir, and himself the most powerful man in
Castile. Where could he find a more suitable puppet King
than Henry, where a more pliable puppet heiress than La
Beltraneja? It was awkward to have to switch loyalties in
this way, but he saw no help for it. Isabella had clearly
shown that she would not be his puppet. Therefore Isabella
must go.

'We cannot have meddlesome Ferdinand here. He would
be ruling Castile in no time. That is why I propose to send
an embassy into Portugal. Alfonso, I have reason to believe,
will be ready to renew his suit.'

'It is an excellent plan,' said Henry. 'If Isabella married
him she would be Queen of Portugal.'

'And that would take her finally from the Castilian scene,'
added Villena.

'Then let us send an embassy to Portugal.'

'Highness, I have already forestalled your command. The
embassy has left for Portugal.'

'You always do exactly what I would do myself,' said
Henry.

'It is my greatest pleasure, Highness. And I have further
news. Many powerful noblemen, including the Mendozas,
disagree with the treaty of Toros de Guisando. They declare
that the Infanta Joanna has not been proved illegitimate and
that she, not Isabella, is the true heir to the throne.'

'Oh?' said Henry mildly.

'I think,' went on Villena slyly, 'that when our Isabella has
left for Portugal we shall have no difficulty in proclaiming
your little daughter heir to the throne.'

'It is what I would wish,' said Henry. 'Then, with Isabella

in Portugal and Joanna proclaimed heiress of the throne of Castile, there would be no more strife. We should have peace.'

Beatriz came hurrying to her mistress's apartment in the Castle at Ocaña, in which Isabella was resident.

'Highness, Alonso de Coca has returned.'

'Then bring him to me at once,' said Isabella.

The chaplain was brought to her presence and Isabella received him with affection.

'It seems long since you went away,' she told him.

'Highness, it was only the desire to obey your command which kept me, so great was my longing for Castile.'

Beatriz was chafing with impatience.

'Come, sit down,' said Isabella, 'and you shall tell me what you saw in the Courts of France and Aragon.'

Alonso de Coca then began to tell his mistress of the manners of the French Court, and how the shabby King was so parsimonious that even his own courtiers were ashamed of him.

Beatriz cried. 'And what of the Duke of Guienne?'

Alonso de Coca shook his head. 'Why, Infanta, he is a feeble man, more like a woman than a man in manner. Moreover, his legs are weak so that he cannot dance, and he seems almost deformed. His eyes are weak also; they water continually, which gives the impression that he is always in tears.'

'I do not think I should care much for such a husband,' said Isabella looking demurely at Beatriz. 'And what of your stay at the Court of Aragon? Did you set eyes on Ferdinand?'

'I did, Highness.'

'Well, well,' said the impatient Beatriz, 'what of Ferdinand? Do his eyes water? Is he weak on his legs?'

Alonso de Coca laughed. 'Ah, my Princesa, ah, my lady, Ferdinand bears no resemblance to the Duke of Guienne. His figure is all that the figure of a young Prince should be. His eyes flash; they do not water. His legs are so strong that he can do more than dance; he can fight beside his father and win the admiration of all by his bravery. He is fair of face and high of spirit. He is that Prince who could be most worthy of a young, beautiful and spirited Princess.'

Isabella was looking in triumph at Beatriz, who grimaced and murmured: 'Well, I rejoice. I rejoice with all my heart. It is not as I feared. I say now: "Long life and happiness to Isabella and Ferdinand." '

One of the pages came hurrying to the apartment of Beatriz, where she was chatting with Mencia de la Torre.

The page was white and trembling, and Beatriz was alarmed. She knew that, when anything disturbing happened, the servants always wished her to break the news to Isabella.

'What now?' she asked.

'My lady, a paper was nailed to the gates last night.'

'What paper was this?'

'Shall I have it brought to you, my lady?'

'With all speed.'

The page went out, and Beatriz turned to Mencia. 'What now?' she murmured. 'Oh, I fear that our Princess is far from the arms of her Ferdinand.'

'She should send for him,' said Mencia. 'He would surely come.'

'You forget that at Toros de Guisando she promised that she would not marry without the consent of the King, as he in turn promised that she should not be forced into marriage against her will. Do you not see that it could quite well be that Isabella will never marry at all, for such conditions, it seems, could produce a deadlock. It is for this reason that she does not communicate with Aragon. Isabella would keep her promise. But I wonder what has happened, and what paper this is.'

The page returned and handed it to Beatriz.

She read it quickly and said to Mencia: 'This is the work of her enemies. They declare that the proceedings at Toros de Guisando were not valid, that the Princess Joanna has not been proved illegitimate and is therefore heiress to the throne. They do not accept Isabella.'

Beatriz screwed up the paper in her hands.

She murmured: 'I see stormy days ahead for Isabella ... and Ferdinand.'

It was an angry Marquis of Villena who rode to Ocaña to visit Isabella.

He was determined to show her that she must obey the King's wishes – which were his own – and that she had offended deeply by her refusal of the King of Portugal.

She had received the Archbishop of Lisbon in her castle at Ocaña and, when he had put forward the proposals of his master, she had told him quite firmly that she had no intention of marrying the King of Portugal. The Archbishop of Lisbon had retired to his lodgings in Ocaña in great pique, declaring that this was a direct insult to his master.

It was for this reason that Villena came to Isabella.

She received him with dignity, yet she did not seek to hide the fact that she considered it impertinent of Henry, who at the meeting at Toros de Guisando had agreed that she should not be forced to marry without her consent, to send Villena to her thus.

'Princesa,' said Villena when he was shown into her presence. His manner was almost curt, which was doubtless his way of telling her that he did not consider her to be heiress to the throne. 'The King wishes you to know that he deeply deplores your attitude towards Alfonso, King of Portugal.'

'I do not understand why he should,' said Isabella. 'I have explained with courtesy that I decline his suit. I could do no more nor less than that.'

'You decline his suit! On what grounds?'

'That the marriage would not be one of my choosing.'

'It is the wish of the King that you should marry the King of Portugal.'

'I am sorry that I cannot fall in with the King's wishes in this respect.'

'It is the King's *command* that you marry the King of Portugal.'

'The King cannot so command me and expect me to obey. Has he forgotten our agreement at Toros de Guisando?'

'Your agreement at Toros de Guisando! That, my dear Princesa, is not taken very seriously in Castile.'

'*I* take it seriously.'

'That will avail you little, if no one else does. The King insists that you marry the King of Portugal.'

'And I refuse.'

'I am sorry, Infanta, but if you do not agree I may be forced to make you my prisoner. The King would have you remain in the royal fortress at Madrid until you obey his command.'

Isabella's heart beat fast with alarm. They would make her a prisoner. She knew what could happen to prisoners whom they wanted out of the way. She looked calmly at Villena, but her outward appearance belied the fear within her.

She said: 'You must give me a little time to consider this.'

'I will leave you and return tomorrow,' said Villena. 'But then you must tell me that you consent to this marriage. If not...' He lifted his shoulders. 'It would grieve me to make you my prisoner, but I am the King's servant and I must obey his commands.'

With that he bowed and left her.

When he had gone she sent for Beatriz and told her all that had taken place.

'You see,' she said, 'they are determined to be rid of me. And they will be rid of me in one way or another. I have been offered a choice. I may go to Portugal as the bride of Alfonso, or I must go to Madrid as the King's prisoner.

Beatriz, I have a feeling that, if I go to Madrid, one day my servants will come to me and find me as we found Alfonso.'

'That shall not be!' declared Beatriz hotly.

'And the alternative ... marriage with Alfonso? I swear I would prefer the Madrid prison.'

'We have delayed too long,' said Beatriz.

'Yes,' said Isabella, and her eyes began to sparkle, 'we have delayed too long.'

'The King,' went on Beatriz, 'no longer carries out the vows he made at Toros de Guisando.'

'So why should I?' demanded Isabella.

'Why indeed! A messenger could be sent into Aragon. It is time you were betrothed. I will go to the Archbishop of Toledo and Ferdinand's grandfather, Don Frederick Henriquez, and tell them you wish to see them urgently.'

'That is right,' said Isabella. 'I will send an embassy into Aragon.'

'This is no time,' Beatriz declared, 'for feminine modesty. This is a marriage of great importance to the state. Ferdinand's father has asked for your hand, has he not?'

'Yes, he has, and I shall send my embassy to tell him that I am now ready for marriage.'

'It is time Ferdinand came to Castile. But, Isabella, Villena is here, and he is a determined man. It may well be that, before we have news from Ferdinand, he will have carried out his threat and you will be in that Madrid prison.' Beatriz shuddered. 'They will have to take me with you. I will taste everything before it touches your lips.'

'Much good would that do!' cried Isabella. 'If they were attempting to poison me, they would poison you. What should I do without you? No. We will *not* fall into their hands. We will stay out of their Madrid prison. And I think I know how.'

'Then pray tell me, Highness, for I am in dreadful suspense.'

'Villena would have to take me out of Ocaña, and the

people of Ocaña love me ... not the King. If we let it be known that I am threatened, they would rally to me and make it impossible for Villena to take me away.'

'That is the answer,' Beatriz agreed. 'You may leave this to me. I shall see that it is known throughout the town that Villena is here to force you into a marriage which is distasteful to you, and that you have sworn to take as husband none other than handsome Ferdinand of Aragon.'

The streets of Ocaña were crowded. People stood outside the castle and cheered themselves hoarse.

'Isabella for Castile!' they cried. 'Ferdinand for Isabella!'

The children formed into bands; they made banners which they carried high. On some of these they had drawn grotesque figures to represent the middle-aged King of Portugal, and on others the young and handsome Ferdinand.

Sly songs were sung, extolling the beauty and bravery of Ferdinand, and jeering at the decrepit and lustful old man of Portugal.

And the purposes of these processions and their songs were: 'We support Isabella, heiress to the crowns of Castile and Leon. And where Isabella wishes to marry, there shall she marry; and we will rise in a body against any who seek to deter her.'

The Marquis of Villena, watching the processions from a window of his lodgings, ground his teeth in anger.

She had foiled him ... as yet, for how could he convey her through those rebellious crowds – his prisoner? They would tear him to pieces rather than allow him to do so.

The Archbishop of Toledo and Don Frederick Henriquez were with Isabella.

The Archbishop had declared himself to be completely in favour of the Aragonese match.

For, as he explained, this would be the means of uniting Castile and Aragon, and unity was needed throughout Spain.

Isabella's dream of an all-Catholic Spain had become the Archbishop's dream. He brought all his fire and fanaticism and laid them at her feet.

'The embassy,' he said, 'must be despatched into Aragon with all speed. Depend upon it, our enemies are growing restive. They will do all in their power to further the Portuguese match; and that, Highness, would be disastrous, as would any marriage which necessitated your leaving Castile.'

'I am in entire agreement with you,' said Isabella.

'Then,' cried Don Frederick Henriquez, 'why do we hesitate? Let the embassy set out at once, and I'll warrant that, in a very short time, my grandson will be riding into Castile to claim his bride.'

Thus it was that when Villena and the Portuguese envoys rode disconsolately out of Ocaña, Isabella's embassy was riding with all speed to Aragon – and Ferdinand.

FERDINAND IN CASTILE

A GREAT sorrow had descended on the King of Aragon. His beloved wife was dying and he could not help but be aware of this.

Nor was Joan Henriquez ignorant of the fact. She had for several years fought against the internal disease which she knew to be a fatal one, and only her rare and intrepid spirit had kept her alive so long.

But there came a time when she could not ignore the warnings that she had but a few hours to live.

The King sat at her bedside, her hand in his. Ferdinand sat with them, and it was when the Queen's eyes fell on her son that mingling emotions moved across her face.

There he was, her Ferdinand, this handsome boy of sixteen, with his fair hair and strong features, in her eyes as beautiful as a god. For him she had become the woman she was, and even on her death-bed she could regret nothing.

She, the strong woman, was responsible for the existing state of affairs in Aragon. She had taken her place by the side of her son and husband in the fight to quell rebellion. She was wise enough to know that they were fortunate because Aragon was still theirs. She had risked a great deal for Ferdinand.

The Catalans would never forget what they called the murder of Carlos. They had refused to admit any member of the Aragonese Cortes into Barcelona; they had elected, in place of John of Aragon, Rene le Bon of Anjou to rule over them, in spite of the fact that he was an ageing man and could not fight, as he would have to, to hold what they had bestowed upon him.

But he had a son, John, Duke of Calabria and Lorraine, a bold adventurer who, with the secret help of sly Louis XI, came to do battle against the King of Aragon. King John of Aragon was no longer young. To help him there was his energetic wife and his brave son Ferdinand; but there were times when John felt that the ghost of his murdered son, Carlos, stood between him and final victory.

For some years John's eyesight had been failing him, and he lived in daily terror of going completely blind.

Now, beside his wife's bed, he could say to himself: 'She will be taken from me, even as my eyesight. But the loss of her will mean more than the loss of my sight.'

Was ever a man so broken? And he believed he knew why good fortune had forsaken him. The ghost of Carlos knew the answer too.

And so he sat by his wife's bed. He could not see her clearly, yet he remembered every detail of that well-loved face. He could not see the handsome boy kneeling there, yet the memory of that eager young face would never leave him.

'John,' said Joan, and her fingers tightened on his, 'it cannot be long now.'

For answer he pressed her hand. He knew it was useless to deny the truth.

'I shall go,' went on Joan, 'with many sins on my conscience.'

John kissed her hand. 'You are the bravest and best woman who has ever lived in Aragon ... or anywhere else.'

'The most ambitious wife and mother,' murmured Joan. 'I lived for you two. All I did was for you. I remember that now. Perhaps because of that I may in some measure be forgiven.'

'There will be no need of forgiveness.'

'John ... I sense a presence here. It is not you. It is not Ferdinand. It is another.'

'There is no one here but ourselves, Mother,' Ferdinand reassured her.

'Is there not? Then my mind wanders. I thought I saw Carlos at the foot of my bed.'

'It could not be, my dearest,' whispered John, 'for he is long since dead.'

'Dead ... but perhaps not resting in his tomb.'

Ferdinand raised his eyes and looked at his dying mother, at his aged and blind father. He thought: The end of the old life is near. She is going, and he will not live long after her.

It was as though Joan sensed his thoughts, as though she saw her beloved Ferdinand still but a boy. He was sixteen. It was not old enough to wage a war against Lorraine, against sly Louis. John must not die. If she had committed crimes – which she would commit again for Ferdinand – they must not have been committed in vain.

'John,' she said, 'are you there, John?'

'Yes, my dearest.'

'Your eyes, John. Your eyes ... You cannot see, can you?'

'Each day they grow more dim.'

'There is a Hebrew doctor in Lerida. I have heard he can perform miracles. He has, it is said, restored sight to blind men. He must do that for you, John.'

'My eyes are too far gone for that, my love. Do not think of me. Are you comfortable? Is there anything we can do to make you happier?'

'You must allow this man to perform the operation, John. It is necessary. Ferdinand ...'

'I am here, my mother.'

'Ah, Ferdinand, my son, my own son. I was speaking to your father. I would not forget that, though you be brave as a lion, you are young yet. You must be there, John, until he is a little older. You must not be blind. You must see this Jew. Promise me.'

'I promise, my dearest.'

She seemed contented now. She lay back on her pillows.

'Ferdinand,' she whispered, 'you will be King of Aragon.

It is what I always intended for you, my darling.'

'Yes, Mother.'

'You will be a great King, Ferdinand. You will always remember what obstacles were in the way of your greatness and how I and your father removed them . . . one by one.'

'I will remember, Mother.'

'Oh Ferdinand, my son . . . Oh, John my husband, we are not alone, are we?'

'Yes, Mother, we are alone.'

'Only the three of us here together, my love,' whispered John.

'You are wrong,' said Joan; 'there is another. There is a presence here. Can you not see him? No, you cannot. It is because of your eyes. You must see that Jew, husband. You have promised. It is a sacred promise given on my death-bed. Ferdinand, you cannot see either for you are too young to see. But there is another here. He stares at me from the end of the bed. It is my stepson, Carlos. He comes to remind me. He is here that I may not forget my sins.'

'She rambles,' said Ferdinand. 'Father, should I call the priests?'

'Yes, my son, call the priests. There is little time left, I fear.'

'Ferdinand, you are leaving me.'

'I will be back soon, Mother.'

'Ferdinand, come close to me. Ferdinand, my son, my life, never forget me. I loved you, Ferdinand, as few are loved. Oh my son, how dear you have cost your mother.'

'It is time to call the priests,' said the King. 'Ferdinand, delay no longer. There is so little time left. There is only time for repentance and departure.'

So Ferdinand left the King and Queen of Aragon together, and the King bent over the bed and kissed the dying lips of the woman for love of whom he had murdered his first-born son.

* * *

King John of Aragon lay on his couch while the Jew performed the operation on his eye. The Jew had been reluctant. He was ready enough to try his skill on men of lesser rank, but he feared what would be his fate if an operation on the King should fail.

John lay still, scarcely feeling the pain, indeed being almost glad of it.

He had lost his wife and he no longer cared to live. For so long Joan had been everything to him. He saw her as the perfect wife, so handsome, so brave, so determined. He would not face the fact that it was due to her ambition for her own son that Aragon had suffered a long and bloody civil war. He had loved her with all the devotion of which he was capable; and now that she was gone, he could only find pleasure in carrying out her wishes.

That was why he now lay on this couch placing his life in the hands of the Hebrew doctor. If it were possible to save his eyes, this man would do it, he knew. There were no doctors in Spain to compare with the Jewish doctors, who had advanced far beyond the Spaniards in medical skill; and this man would know that his fortune would be made if he saved the eyes of the King.

And when I have the sight of one eye, thought John, I shall dedicate myself, as she would have wished, to making secure Ferdinand's succession to the throne of Aragon.

The operation was successful, and John had recovered the sight of one eye. He sent for the doctor and said: 'Now you must perform the same operation on the other eye.'

The man was afraid. He had done it once, but could he repeat it? Such operations were by no means always successful.

'Highness,' he said, 'I could not attempt to work on your second eye. The stars are against success.'

'A plague on the stars!' cried John. 'You will forget them and give my other eye its sight.'

Everyone at Court trembled when they heard what was about to take place. They believed that, since the stars were against the performing of the operation, it could not succeed.

The doctor was in great fear, but he thought it more expedient to obey the King than the stars, and the operation was performed.

Thus John of Aragon, now almost eighty years of age, was cured of his blindness and, in obedience to the wishes of his dead wife, prepared himself to hold the crown of Aragon for Ferdinand.

With the return of his sight, John of Aragon regained a great deal of that energy which had been his chief characteristic in the past. John was shrewd and clever; his vulnerable spot had been his love for Joan Henriquez, and that in itself had been the stronger because of the strength of his character. His love for his wife had forced him to give to her son all the affection he had for his children, which meant robbing those by his first wife. John knew that the war, which had lasted so many years and had impoverished him and Aragon, was entirely due to his treatment of Carlos. Joan had demanded the sacrifice of Carlos, that her son Ferdinand might be his father's heir; and willingly had John given her all that she asked, because he found it impossible to deny her anything.

Now he did not regret what he had done. He was as determined as Joan had been that Ferdinand should rule Aragon.

The greatest pleasure left to him was to contemplate this handsome, virile youth, who had, under his mother's tuition, been trained for the great role which was being won for him.

If, thought John, before I was a father I had imagined a son who could be all that I looked for, he would have been exactly like Ferdinand.

Ferdinand was lusty; he was brave; he cherished what he had, because he had been fully aware that it had been won with blood and anguish, and he was as determined to hold it as his parents had been to give it to him.

How blessed am I in Ferdinand, his father often said.

And so to the Court of Aragon came the embassy led by Isabella's faithful servants, Gutierre de Cardenas and Alonso de Palencia.

John received them with great pleasure, for he knew their mission; his great regret was that Joan was not alive to share this triumph. He went to his son's apartment, and when they were alone together, he told him of the arrival of the embassy from Isabella.

'It is the best possible news,' he said. 'I could not imagine a match which would have given your mother greater pleasure.'

'Isabella,' mused Ferdinand. 'I hear she is comely, though a little older than myself.'

'A year! What is a year at your age?'

'It is not much perhaps. But I hear that she has a will of her own.'

John laughed. 'It will be for you to make your will hers. She is very ready to love you. Of that we are certain. She has refused many suitors, and on all these occasions has affirmed that she was betrothed to you.'

'She will be faithful then,' said Ferdinand.

'There are conditions,' went on John. 'It would seem that Castilians believe they are greatly honouring us in bestowing the hand of their future Queen upon us.'

'Honouring us!' cried Ferdinand hotly. 'We must make them understand that we are Aragon!'

'Ah, Aragon. In sorry state is Aragon at this time. By the saints, son, I wonder how we are going to fit you out for your wedding. Now, let us look at this matter calmly. Let us not quarrel with Castile. Let them believe for the present that they greatly honour us. We must get you married quickly, and then you will show your Isabella that you are lord and master.'

'I will do that,' said Ferdinand. 'I hear she is handsome,

yet haughty. She is a little prim.' He smiled. 'I shall teach her to cast aside her primness.'

'You will remember that she is not a tavern girl.'

'Yes, but tavern girls perhaps are not so very different from Queens in some respects.'

'I would not have such remarks overheard and reported to Isabella. So have a care. Now listen. This Isabella is clearly a determined young woman. She has a year's advantage of you. You have been in battle, and have led to some extent a soldier's life, for all your tender years. She has lived a cloistered life but, make no mistake about it, she has been brought up to be a Queen. These are the conditions of the marriage agreement: You must live in Castile and not leave it without the consent of Isabella.'

'What!' interrupted Ferdinand. 'I should be as her slave.'

'Hush, my son. Think of the richness of Castile and Leon; then think of poor Aragon. You will be the master – in time. At first it may be necessary to be a little more humble than you would wish to be.'

'Well,' said Ferdinand, 'what next?'

'You are not to take property to yourself which belongs to the crown, nor make appointments without her consent. You shall jointly make decrees of a public nature; but she, personally, will nominate ecclesiastical benefices.'

Ferdinand grimaced.

His father went on: 'You will help her in every way to make war on the Moors.'

'That I will do with all my heart and all my strength.'

'You must respect the present King, and not ask for the return of that property in Castile which formerly belonged to us.'

'She makes a hard bargain, this Isabella.'

'But she comes with a handsome dowry. Moreover, she brings you Castile. Oh, my son, it cost your mother and myself a great deal to give you Aragon. Now comes Isabella to offer you Castile.'

'Then, Father, shall we accept these conditions?'

'With great delight, my son. Come, you are not looking as pleased as you should.'

'It would seem we must humble ourselves rather more than I like.'

John put his arm about his son's shoulders.

'Come, come, my boy. I doubt not you will very soon have your own way. You are a handsome man, and Isabella – she may be the future Queen of Castile, but remember, she is also a woman.'

Ferdinand laughed aloud.

He was completely confident of his power to rule both Aragon and Castile – and Isabella.

Isabella knew that her situation was dangerous and that the Marquis of Villena would sooner or later learn that she had sent an embassy to Aragon; she knew also that if it were discovered that she had gone as far as signing an agreement with Aragon, Villena would stop at nothing to prevent her marriage with Ferdinand.

Villena with Henry had gone to South Castile to deal with the last stronghold of the rebels; and Isabella, taking advantage of their absence, slipped quietly out of Ocaña to Madrigal.

Here she was received by the Bishop of Burgos; but she was somewhat alarmed, for he was the nephew of Villena and it occurred to her that he was probably more devoted to the Marquis than to that other relative, the Archbishop of Toledo.

She was right. The Bishop lost no time in sending a message to his uncle Villena telling him of Isabella's arrival.

Villena's reply came: 'Have her watched. Bribe her servants, and if you should discover that she has been in touch with Aragon, lose no time in informing me.'

The Bishop was eager to serve his powerful uncle, and in a very short time many servants in Isabella's entourage had been offered bribes to report Isabella's actions; and many letters which she wrote passed through the hands of the Bishop of Burgos before being sent on to their destination.

It was therefore not long before the Bishop discovered how far matters had gone between Isabella and Ferdinand.

Villena was furious. He raged against Isabella.

'This,' he cried to Henry, 'is your pious sister. She vows that she will not marry without your consent, but as soon as our backs are turned she is in communication with Aragon.'

'We did break our part of the bargain,' suggested Henry timidly.

Villena snapped his fingers. 'There is one thing we can do now: make her our prisoner. We were foolish not to do so before.'

'But we tried,' said Henry. 'And the people of Ocaña would not have it. I am afraid that Isabella, like young Alfonso, has that quality in her which arouses the loyalty of the people.'

'The loyalty of the people!' snapped Villena. 'We will put her where she cannot appeal to that – and where the gallant Ferdinand cannot reach her. We shall give orders at once for the Archbishop of Seville to go to Madrigal and take with him a strong enough force to seize and make her our prisoner.'

'And what of the people of Madrigal? Will they allow her to be made a prisoner, any more than those of Ocaña did?'

'We shall make them aware of our displeasure, should they help her to resist arrest. We will strike such fear into them that they will not dare.'

Henry looked worried. 'She is, after all, my sister.'

'Highness, are you prepared to leave this matter in my hands?'

'As ever, my dear friend.'

Isabella was told that the leading citizen of Madrigal was

asking to be admitted to her presence.

She received him at once.

'Highness,' he said, 'I come on behalf of my fellow citizens. We are in great peril, and so are you. We have received word from the King that you are about to be placed under arrest and that, should we attempt to help you, we shall suffer greatly. I have come to warn you to escape, for, in view of these threats, we of Madrigal dare do nothing to help you.'

Isabella graciously thanked him for his warning and sent for two of her servants, both of whom she knew she could completely trust.

'I want you to take two messages for me – one to the Archbishop of Toledo and the other to Admiral Henriquez,' she said. 'This is a matter of the utmost urgency. There is not a second to lose. You will go at once, and with all speed.'

As soon as they had gone she sent her page to summon Beatriz and Mencia to her presence, and when the women arrived she said calmly : 'We are leaving Madrigal. I want you to go ahead of me. Go to Coca . . . it is not far; and wait for me there.'

Beatriz was about to protest, but there were times when Isabella reminded her that she was the mistress, and Beatriz was always quick to appreciate her meaning.

A little hurt, the two women retired, and Isabella was uneasy until they had left. She knew that if the Bishop of Seville arrived to arrest her, he would take prisoner her confidential women also, and she wished to save Beatriz and Mencia even if she could not save herself.

They would be safe in Coca. She would not be. She needed to be under the safe protection of strong men.

Now began the anxious vigil when Isabella waited at her window. Soon she would hear the sound of advancing cavalry and shouts from below, and her future might depend upon this day's events. She did not know what would happen to her if she fell into the hands of the Bishop of Seville. She would be the King's prisoner – or more accurately, Villena's

– and she did not think she would easily regain her freedom.

Then what would the future hold for her? An enforced marriage? With Alfonso of Portugal? With Richard of Gloucester? They would rid themselves of her in some way. They would wish to banish her either to Portugal or England. And if she refused?

Would it be the old familiar pattern? Would her servants find her one morning as Alfonso's had found him?

And Ferdinand? What of him? Eagerly he had accepted the marriage agreement. He understood, she was sure, even as she did, the glory that could come from the union of Castile and Aragon. But once she fell into the hands of the Archbishop of Seville, once Villena became the master of her fate, that would be the end of all their dreams and hopes.

And so she waited.

At length she heard what she listened for, and then ... she saw him, the fiery, militant Archbishop of Toledo, now her loyal servant, ready to snatch her from under the very nose of the Bishop of Burgos who had meant to offer her up to his uncle, Villena.

She heard that resounding voice.

'Conduct me to the Princess Isabella.'

He stood before her.

'Highness, there is little time to lose. I have soldiers below. Enough to ensure our safe departure from this place, but it would be better if we left before Seville arrives with his troop. Come with all speed.'

And so Isabella rode away from Madrigal only a little while before the Archbishop of Seville arrived to find the prize was gone.

'On!' cried Alfonso Carillo, Archbishop of Toledo, from now on Isabella's most firm supporter. 'On to Valladolid, where we can be sure of a loyal welcome for the future Queen of Castile.'

What joy it was to be received with acclaim by the citizens of

Valladolid, and to know that they looked upon her as their future Queen.

But when the triumphant parade was over the Archbishop came to Isabella and reminded her – as she knew already – that this was no time for delay.

'I know my nephew, the Marquis of Villena,' said the Archbishop. 'He is a man of great resource, and he is as sly as a fox. I would meet him happily enough on the field of battle, but I would not care to have to match myself against his devious diplomacy. There is one thing we must do and that with all speed: hasten the marriage.'

'I am willing that we should proceed with all haste,' Isabella assured him.

'Then, Highness, I will despatch envoys at once to Saragossa, and this time we will inform Ferdinand that it is imperative that he set out for Castile with all speed.'

'Let it be done,' said Isabella.

When Villena heard that Isabella had escaped him he was furious.

'And to think,' he said, 'that it was due to my own uncle.' Then he laughed, and there was a note of pride in his laughter. 'Trust the old man to get there before that fool, Seville.' And it amused him that members of his family should be deciding the fate of Castile even though they were now on opposite sides.

He went to the King.

'I know my uncle, and I'll swear that his first action will be to bring Ferdinand into Castile. He will marry him to Isabella, and thus we shall have not only Isabella's adherents but Aragon against us. Moreover, once Isabella is married we cannot hope to rid ourselves of her. It is imperative that Ferdinand and Isabella never meet.'

'But how shall we prevent this?'

'By taking Ferdinand prisoner as soon as he sets foot in Castile.'

'You can do this? But how?'

'Highness, we must do it. Let us make our plans. He will come through the frontier town of Osma. There he will receive the aid of Medina Celi. So he believes. We must make sure that Medina Celi is our man ... not Isabella's.'

'That will not be easy,' said the King.

'But we will make sure of it,' answered Villena. His eyes narrowed. 'I will threaten our little Duke of Medina Celi with the direst penalties if he should aid Ferdinand. I assure Your Highness that Medina Celi will watch on our behalf, and the moment Ferdinand arrives we shall be informed. The King and Queen of Aragon went to great lengths to make him the heir to their crown. We will go to as great lengths to make sure he never touches that of Castile. Of course I have Your Highness's permission to deal with Medina Celi?'

'You must do as you wish, but how glad I shall be when all this strife is at an end.'

'Leave this matter to me, Highness. Once we have curbed our haughty Isabella ... once she is safely despatched to Portugal or ... elsewhere ... then, I promise you, there shall be peace in this land.'

'I pray the saints it will be soon,' sighed Henry.

When the embassy arrived at Saragossa, John of Aragon found himself in a quandary.

He sent for Ferdinand.

'Here is a pretty state of affairs,' he said. 'I hear from the Archbishop of Toledo that Villena is trying to prevent the match; and the Archbishop fears he will succeed unless the marriage takes place immediately. He suggests that you set out at once for Valladolid.'

'Well, Father, I am ready.'

John of Aragon groaned. 'My son, how can you go into Castile as Isabella's bridegroom, when there are no more than three hundred *enriques* in the treasury? What sort of figure will you cut!'

Ferdinand looked grave. 'I cannot go as a beggar, Father.'

'I do not know how else you can go. I had hoped that there would be a little respite to enable me to get the money for your journey. I am making you King of Sicily so that you will enter Castile with the rank of King, but how can we possibly send you without the necessary pomp, the glittering garments and all that you will need for your wedding?'

'Then we must wait ...'

'To delay could be to lose Isabella. Villena is working with all his might against the match. I believe his plan is to rid Castile of Isabella – perhaps by marriage, perhaps by other methods – and no doubt set up La Beltraneja in her place. My son, you may have to fight your way to Isabella. ...' John stopped, and a smile spread across his face. 'Why, Ferdinand, I think I have the solution to our problem. Listen to me. I will tell you briefly and then we will lay this plan before a secret council.'

'I am eager to hear what you propose, Father,' said Ferdinand.

'The frontier from Almazin to Guadalajara will be dangerous for you to cross. It is the property of the Mendoza family which, as you know, supports La Beltraneja. If you travelled as yourself, with the embassy, nobles and servants, you would find it impossible to cross that frontier unobserved. But what say you, my son, if you went with a party of merchants? What if you were disguised as one of their servants? I'll warrant then that you would travel to Valladolid unmolested.'

Ferdinand wrinkled his nose in distaste. 'In the attire of a servant, Father!'

John put his arm about the young man's shoulder.

'It is the answer,' he cried. 'You will remember, Ferdinand, that a kingdom is at stake. Now I consider this, I see that it is the only manner in which you could hope to reach

Isabella in safety. And think! It provides us with the excuse we need. What folly to equip you as a King when you travel as a merchant's lackey!'

As soon as the innkeeper received the party of merchants he noticed their lackey. The fellow had an insolent air, and it was clear that he thought himself superior to the position he occupied.

'Here, fellow,' cried the innkeeper when the merchants were being ushered to the table, 'you'll need to go to the stables and see that your masters' mules are being watered and fed.'

The arrogant fellow's eyes flashed, and for a moment the innkeeper thought he struck an attitude as though he would draw his sword – if he possessed one.

One of the merchants intervened. 'My good host, let your grooms attend to our mules ... water and feed them while we ourselves are at table. As for our servant here, he will wait upon us.'

'As you wish, good sirs,' was the answer.

'And,' went on the merchant, 'bring in the dishes. Our man will do the rest. We would be left in peace to eat our meal as we have business to discuss.'

'I am at your service, my masters.'

When the landlord had left them, Ferdinand grimaced.

'I fear I make an indifferent lackey.'

'Considering that Your Highness has never played the part before, you do it very well.'

'Yet I fancy the man believes me to be an unusual servant, and that is what we must avoid. I shall be glad when the role is ended. It becomes me not.'

Ferdinand touched the rough cloth of his serving-man's doublet with distaste. He was young enough to be vain of his personal appearance, and because all through his life he had lived in fear of losing his inheritance, his dignity was especially dear to him. He was less philosophical than his father, and less able to stomach the indignity of creeping into Castile like a beggar. He had to accept the fact that Castile and Leon were of greater significance than Aragon; and it went hard with him that he, a man and prospective husband, should have to take second place with his future wife.

It should not continue to be so, he told himself, once he and Isabella were married.

'It will not be long, Highness,' he was told, 'that you have to masquerade thus. When we reach the castle of the Count of Treviño in Osma it will not be necessary for you to travel thus ignobly. And Treviño is waiting for us with a right good welcome.'

'I can scarcely wait for our arrival at Osma.'

The innkeeper had come in to usher into the room a servant who carried a steaming dish of *olla podrida*. It smelt good, and for a moment the men sniffed at it so hungrily that Ferdinand, who had been leaning against the table talking to the merchants, forgot to adopt the attitude of a servant.

So surprised was the innkeeper that he stopped and stared.

Ferdinand immediately understood and tried to put on a humble air, but he felt he had betrayed himself.

When he was again alone with his friends, he said: 'I hope the innkeeper does not suspect that we are not what we pretend to be.'

'We will soon deal with him, Highness, should he show too much curiosity.'

Ferdinand said it would be better if he were not addressed as Highness until the journey was over.

As they were eating their meal, one of the men looked up suddenly and saw a face at the window. It disappeared immediately, so that he was not sure whether it had been that of the innkeeper or one of his servants.

'Look! The window,' he said quietly; but the others were too late to see the face.

When he explained what he had seen dismay fell on the company.

'There can be no doubt,' said Ferdinand, 'that we are under suspicion.'

'I will go out and slit the throat of the inquisitive inn-keeper and all his servants,' cried one member of the band.

'That would indeed be folly,' said another. 'Perhaps the same idle curiosity is shown here towards all travellers. Eat as fast as you can and we will be gone. It may well be that someone has already sent a message to our enemies, telling them of our arrival at this inn.'

'They could not possibly see anything strange in a party of merchants ... No, it is curiosity, nothing more. Come, let us eat in peace.'

'Eat certainly,' said Ferdinand, 'but there is too much at stake to linger. Doubtless I have betrayed us by my manners. Let us hasten away from this place. We will pass the night out of doors or in some inn which we feel will be quite safe ... but not here.'

They ate hurriedly and in silence, and one of their party called in the innkeeper and settled the account.

They left the inn and rode on, but when they had gone some distance they began to laugh at their fears. The inn-keeper and his servants were oafs who would know nothing of the coming of the heir of Aragon into Castile, and they had allowed themselves to be frightened without cause.

'Spend the night out of doors!' cried Ferdinand. 'Certainly not. We will find an inn and have a good night's sleep there.'

The man who had paid the innkeeper gave a sudden cry of dismay.

He had pulled up his mule, and the others pulled up with him.

'The purse,' he said, 'I must have left it on the dining table!'

They were all dismayed, for the purse contained the money to defray their expenses during the journey.

'I must go back for it,' he said.

There was a short silence.

Then Ferdinand said: 'What if they did suspect? What if they make you their prisoner? No. We are well away from that inn. We will go on, without money. Castile is too big a prize to be lost for the sake of a few *enriques*.'

It was far into the night when they arrived outside the castle of the Count of Treviño.

Inside the castle there was tension.

The Count had given his instructions. 'We must be prepared for an attack by our enemies. They know that we are for Isabella and that we shall offer shelter to the Prince of Aragon when he passes on his way to Valladolid. It may well be that the King's men will attempt to storm the castle and take possession of it so that they, not we, will be here when Ferdinand arrives. Therefore keep watch. Let no one enter. Guard well the drawbridge and be ready on the battlements with your missiles.'

So the castle was bristling with defences when Ferdinand and his party arrived.

They were very weary and exhausted, for they had ridden through the night and the day without money to buy a meal; and when they came to the castle gates Ferdinand gave a great shout of joy.

'Open up!' he cried. 'Open up! And delay not.'

But one of the guards watching from the battlements, determined to defend the castle against the Count's enemies, believed that the King's men were below.

He dislodged one of the great boulders which had been placed on the battlements for this purpose and sent in hurtling down to kill the man who had advanced a few paces ahead of the group.

This was Ferdinand; and the guard's timing was sure.

Down came the massive boulder.

'Highness!' shouted one of the party who were watching Ferdinand, and there was such a shrill note of urgency in his voice that Ferdinand, alerted, jumped clear.

He was only just in time for the boulder landed on the spot where he had been standing, and Ferdinand had escaped death by only a few feet.

Startled into anger, Ferdinand called: 'Is this the welcome that you promised us? I come to you, I, Ferdinand of Aragon, having travelled far in disguise, and you do your best to kill me after promising me succour!'

There was consternation in the castle. Torches appeared and faces were seen peering from the battlements.

Then there was shouting and creaking as the drawbridge was lowered, and the Count of Treviño himself hurried forward to kneel and ask pardon for the mistake which might so easily have turned the whole enterprise into tragedy.

'You shall have my pardon as soon as you give us food,' cried Ferdinand. 'We are starving, my men and I.'

The Count gave orders to his servants; and across the drawbridge and into the great hall went Ferdinand's party; and there, at a table laden with food which had been prepared for them, the travellers refreshed themselves and laughed together at their adventures. For the most dangerous part of the journey was over. Tomorrow they would set forth with an armed escort supplied, at Isabella's command, by the Count of Treviño. Then it would be on to Dueñas, where Ferdinand would cease to be regarded as a humble lackey, and where he would find many noblemen rallying to his cause, eager to accompany him to Valladolid and Isabella.

THE MARRIAGE OF ISABELLA

In the house of Juan de Vivero, the most magnificent in Valladolid, which had been lent to Isabella on her triumphant entry into that city, she now waited.

This was, she believed, so far the most important moment of her life. For years she had dreamed of her marriage with Ferdinand. But for her own determination she would have long since been married elsewhere. And now Ferdinand was only a few miles from her, and this very night he would stand before her.

It was not easy to control her emotion. She must be calm; she must remember that she was not merely a Princess of Castile – she was its future Queen.

She had a large dowry to bring her husband, and on that account she rejoiced. But in spite of her dignity and position she was anxious as to whether she herself would appeal to Ferdinand, for this was to be the perfect marriage. Not only was it to be a welding together of Castile and Aragon, to make a stronger and all-Christian Spain; it was to be the mating of two people, whose interests and affections must be so entwined that they were as one person.

It was this second factor which gave her cause for anxiety.

I know I shall love Ferdinand, she told herself; but how can I be sure that he will love me?

He had lived the life of a man, although he was a year her junior; and she, although she had trained herself to understand state matters, had lived the sheltered life which had been necessary if she were not to be contaminated by her brother's licentious Court.

The Admiral and the Archbishop had talked seriously to

her concerning the impending interview.

'Do not forget,' said the Archbishop, 'that while he can only make you Queen of Aragon, you can make him King of Castile and Leon. What is Aragon compared with Castile and Leon? You must never let him forget that you bring more to this marriage than he does, that it is you who will be Queen, and that his title of King will be one of courtesy.'

'I do not think,' said Isabella gently, 'that a marriage such as this should begin by jostling for position.'

'I trust,' said the Archbishop testily, 'that you are not going to be overpowered by his good looks.'

'I trust,' replied Isabella, with a smile, 'that I am going to be pleased with them.'

The Archbishop regarded her with some sternness. He had admired her very much, and it was for this reason that he had decided to support her, but he wanted her to remember that it was he who was largely responsible for putting her where she was, and if she wanted to retain his co-operation she must listen to his advice – and take it.

He did not intend to allow Ferdinand to assume too much power, to take that place as chief adviser to Isabella which he, Alfonso Carillo, Archbishop of Toledo, had held.

'It might seem advisable,' he said now, 'that Ferdinand should be asked to perform some act of homage – merely to show that, as far as Castile and Leon are concerned, he is in an inferior position.'

Isabella smiled, but her voice was firm. 'I shall certainly not ask my husband for any such homage,' she declared.

The Archbishop left her in a far from pleased frame of mind, and prepared himself to receive Ferdinand, who was shortly to arrive from Dueñas with as few as four of his attendants.

It was midnight when Ferdinand arrived at the house of Juan de Vivero.

Clothes had been lent to him, so he came not as the merchants' lackey but as King of Sicily.

The Archbishop received him and, when they met, Ferdinand was glad that his shrewd father had had the foresight to bestow the title of King upon him, for there was an arrogance about the Archbishop of Toledo which was not lost on Ferdinand. He hoped the man had not imparted the same quality to Isabella. Yet even as this thought entered his mind, Ferdinand smiled. He had a way with women – and Isabella, for all that she was the heiress of Castile and Leon, was a woman.

'The Princess Isabella is waiting to receive you,' said the Archbishop. 'I will conduct you to her presence.'

Ferdinand inclined his head and the Archbishop led the way to Isabella's apartments.

'His Highness Don Ferdinand, King of Sicily and Prince of Aragon.'

Isabella rose to her feet and stood for a few seconds, trembling with the force of her emotions.

And there he was – Ferdinand in the flesh, the dream become a reality, as handsome as she had imagined him (no, more so, she hastened to tell herself; for how could any person – imagined or real – compare with this young man who now stood before her?).

Ferdinand, seventeen years old, with fair hair and a complexion toned to bronze by exposure to the sun and air, a grown man in physique, slender and perfectly proportioned! His brow was high and broad, his expression alert; and he was too young and unmarked as yet for that alertness to be construed as cupidity.

Isabella was conscious of a great gladness, for the Ferdinand she saw before her had stepped right out of her dreams.

Ferdinand was gracious; he took her hand, bowed low over it; then he lifted his eyes to her face and there was a smile in them, for he too was not displeased.

What a joyous thing it was, he thought, when a royal person need not take someone who was aged and ugly. Here she was, his Isabella, the best possible match in Spain, and she was only one year older, and looked younger, than he was.

He saw a young woman somewhat tall, with a complexion as fair as his own, and bright hair with a gleam of red in it which was enchanting. And what pleased him most was the gentle manner, the almost mild expression in the blue eyes.

Charming Isabella, so suitable, so young and – he believed – so malleable.

Ferdinand, in his swaggering youth, told himself that he would very soon be master of Castile, Leon – and Isabella.

'I welcome you with all my heart,' said Isabella. 'Castile and Leon welcome you. We have long awaited your coming.'

Ferdinand, who had retained her hand, with a swift gesture pressed an impassioned kiss upon it which brought a faint colour into Isabella's cheeks and a shine to her eyes. 'I would,' he said, 'that I had come months ago ... years ago....'

'Suffice it that you are here. I pray you sit with me.'

Together they went to the two ornate chairs which had been set side by side like two thrones.

'You have had a hazardous journey,' said Isabella. And when he told her of his adventures at the inn and at the Count of Treviño's castle, Isabella turned pale at the thought of what could so easily have happened to him.

'It is of no importance,' Ferdinand murmured. 'You do not know it, but I have often with my father faced death in battle.'

'But now you are safely here,' said Isabella; and there was a note of exultation in her voice. She believed that this marriage had certainly been made in Heaven and that nothing on Earth could prevent its taking place.

The Archbishop, who was standing by listening to this conversation, was growing a little impatient.

'The marriage,' he reminded them, 'is not yet an accomplished fact. Our enemies will, even now, do all in their power to prevent it. It must take place at the earliest possible moment, and I suggest four days hence.'

Ferdinand threw a passionate glance at Isabella who, taken off her guard by the prospect of such an early date for their marriage, returned it.

'There should,' went on the Archbishop, 'be a solemn betrothal immediately, and it is for this reason that Your Highness has ridden to Valladolid at this late hour.'

'Then,' said Isabella, 'let us proceed with all speed.'

The Archbishop then solemnly declared them betrothed, and there, before those very few witnesses, Ferdinand and Isabella ceremoniously joined hands.

So shall it be until death shall part us, Isabella told herself; and she was aware of a greater happiness than she had hitherto known.

There was great activity in the house of Juan de Vivero. Here was to be celebrated the marriage of the heiress of Castile to the heir of Aragon.

There was need of the utmost haste. There was so little time in which to prepare; and at any moment they might expect interruption by the King's soldiers, come to prevent the marriage which the Marquis of Villena had determined should not take place.

Isabella was alternatively in a state of bliss and anxiety.

Four days seemed like four weeks; and every commotion in the courtyard, any shout from below, set her trembling with fear.

Apart from the fact that her half-brother's men might arrive at any moment, there were other causes for anxiety. She had very little money; Ferdinand had none at all. How could they celebrate a marriage without money?

And this was the most important marriage in Spain.

Celebration there must be, but how could they decorate the house, how could they provide a banquet without money?

There was only one thing to be done; they must borrow.

It was not a very happy start, thought Isabella.

She could not discuss this with Ferdinand, for after that midnight meeting and solemn betrothal he had gone back to Dueñas, there to await the day of his entry into Valladolid as bridegroom at the public ceremony.

But the money was found. That had not been so difficult after all.

Why, reasoned many to whom the problem was put, this is the heiress of Castile and Leon. One day she will be Queen, and then she will not forget those who provided the money for her wedding.

But there was a matter which gave even greater concern.

There was a degree of consanguinity between Isabella and Ferdinand, and therefore, before they could marry, it was necessary to procure a dispensation from the Pope.

Since this had not yet come to her, Isabella appealed to the Archbishop of Toledo.

'I fear,' she said, 'that we must postpone the marriage.'

'Postpone the marriage!' cried the Archbishop in amazement. 'That is impossible. If we postpone it, I can say with certainty it will never take place. Your brother and my nephew will take good care that we never again get as near to it as we are now.'

'There is one thing of the utmost importance which you have forgotten. The dispensation has not yet come from the Pope.'

The Archbishop was genuinely alarmed, but he gave no sign of this. He wondered whether it was possible to get a dispensation from the Pope, who was the friend of Henry and Villena.

'Would you marry Ferdinand if the Pope refused the dispensation?' asked the Archbishop cautiously.

'It would be impossible,' replied Isabella. 'How could I marry without it?'

'The marriage would be binding.'

'We should be censured by Holy Church. How could we

hope for a successful marriage if we began it by opposing the ecclesiastical canons?'

The Archbishop paused. Here was a new light on Isabella's character. Devout, he had always known her to be. Well, others were devout – inasmuch as they attended Mass regularly and did not ignore the tenets of the Church. But who would allow the rules of the Church to come between them and their desires? Isabella would, it seemed.

The Archbishop made a quick decision.

'Have no fear,' he said. 'We shall have the dispensation in good time. I have made all concerned aware of the urgency.'

'My good friend,' murmured Isabella, 'what should I do without you?'

The Archbishop returned her smile. He hoped she would remember those words and not seek to take his power from him and bestow it on Ferdinand.

In his private apartments the Archbishop was writing. He wrote slowly and with the utmost care.

Eventually he laid down his pen and studied what he had written.

It was a perfect dispensation. Isabella would never doubt that it had come from the Pope.

The Archbishop shrugged his shoulders.

There were times when bold men had to take matters into their own hands. He had to lead the heiress of Castile and Leon the way she must go; and that way was through marriage with Ferdinand. And if Isabella was too scrupulous a woman of the Church, there must be times when a little deceit must be employed.

The Archbishop rolled up the scroll and went to Isabella's apartments.

'I have great joy in telling Your Highness that the dispensation has arrived.'

'Oh, how happy that makes me!' Isabella held out a hand and the Archbishop handed her the scroll.

He watched her anxiously while she glanced at it; but she was too happy to study it with very much attention.

He took it from her and rolled it up.

'Is it not wonderful,' she said, 'how one by one obstacles are removed from our paths. I was afraid even at this late hour that something would happen to prevent the marriage. The Holy Father is very much the friend of my brother and the Marquis, and I was filled with fear that he might refuse the dispensation. But God has moved his heart – and we have it. It often seems to me that it is the Divine will that Ferdinand and I should marry, for it would appear that whenever we are faced with what might be insuperable obstacles, miracles happen.'

The Archbishop bowed his head. He was a man who believed that when Divine Providence failed to provide the holy miracle, an earthly one devised by shrewd men could be substituted.

In the hall of the house of Juan de Vivero many had assembled to watch the wedding ceremony performed by the Archbishop of Toledo.

The hall had been as richly decorated as was possible, but this might have been the wedding of the daughter of a petty nobleman. It seemed incredible that it could be that of the prospective Queen of Castile.

But it was the best that could be done on borrowed money and in such haste; and if the radiance of jewels and fine brocades was missing, its absence seemed unimportant on account of the shining happiness on the faces of the bride and groom.

They looked beautiful – so young, so healthy and handsome. Surely, said the observers, this hasty marriage was the most romantic that had ever taken place in Spain. And if there would not be the celebrations which usually heralded and followed such ceremonies, what did it matter? At last Castile and Aragon were united; and the townsfolk of Valladolid shouted themselves hoarse with delight when the handsome pair left the house to go to Mass and later dined in public that all might see them and bear witness to the joy they had in each other.

There came that time when they were alone together, and their contentment with each other was not abated.

Ferdinand, experienced young man of the world, and Isabella a little apprehensive, but so ready to follow where he should lead her!

Ferdinand believed that he would mould this woman to his way of thinking. His Isabella was a paragon of many virtues. She was virginal yet passionate; she was possessed of great dignity, yet she was his to command.

'I did not know,' he said, 'that such good fortune could be mine.'

'I knew,' said Isabella. And she smiled that slow dedicated smile, thinking of all the vicissitudes of her hazardous life which only her courage and her belief in her future had made victory over those circumstances possible.

No, Isabella was not surprised that at last she had married the man of her choice, and that he promised to be all for which she had hoped.

She believed firmly that it had always been intended that this should be so.

'Ferdinand,' she said, 'we will work together always. We shall be as one. All I have is yours; all you have is mine. Is that not wonderful to contemplate?'

Ferdinand kissed her with rising passion and said that it was indeed – for she had so much more to offer than he had.

'Isabella,' he said, 'my wife, my love! What a truly wonderful thing it is that in addition to all your beauty, all your virtue, you should also have ... Castile. But,' he added, 'even if you were not the future Queen of Castile, if you were a serving-wench in a tavern, I should love you still, Isabella.

Would you love me if I could not bring you Aragon?'

He did not wait for an answer. He was so sure of his ability to conquer her.

But Isabella was thoughtful. She loved him with all her heart, but she did not think it would be possible for the future Queen of Castile to love a tavern man.

Ferdinand had lifted her into his arms. He was so strong that he could do this easily; and his warm breath was on her cheek.

There was no need to answer Ferdinand's questions, for she was swept into a new adventure which overwhelmed her senses and subdued her dignity and her love of truth – temporarily.

Ferdinand, the adventurer, the man of action, believed himself to be the all-conquering male to whom the weak female must ever be subservient.

Isabella was subconsciously aware of this. Her marriage must be perfect; in the council and in the bedchamber there must be continued harmony.

Thus at the time she was pliant, so eager to learn, so earnestly anxious to please. It was certain that in the bedchamber Ferdinand must be master; he must be the one to lead her step by step along the diverse sensuous paths.

Ferdinand had often told himself that even though Isabella was the future Queen of Castile she was also a woman. He did not know that although she was a woman, she would never forget that she was the future Queen of Castile.

THE DEATH OF HENRY

THE first news of the marriage which reached Henry was brought by Isabella's messenger.

He read his half-sister's letter and trembled.

'But this,' he moaned, 'was exactly what we wished to prevent. Now we shall have Aragon against us. Oh, what an unlucky man I am! I wish I had never been born to be King of Castile.'

He hesitated before showing Isabella's letter to Villena, dreading the storm that it would arouse.

He let the letter drop from his hands, and fell to dreaming. He wished that he had not rid himself of Blanche. He thought of poor Blanche. How dreadful her last days must have been in the château of Ortes. Did she know that plans to murder her were afoot?

'And if she had stayed in Castile, she would be alive now,' he murmured. 'And should I be worse off? I should not have my daughter ... but is she mine? She is still known throughout the Court as La Beltraneja. Poor little girl! What trials await her!'

Henry shook his head. It was a sad fate to be born as she had been born, to be the centre of controversy over a throne. There had been Alfonso ...

If he had not rid himself of Blanche, if he had tried to lead a better life, he would have been a happier man. Now there was nothing but scandal and conflict.

His Queen, Joanna, had left him and was living scandalously in Madrid. He was constantly hearing stories about her adventures. She had had many lovers and there were several illegitimate children of these unions.

Never had a man so urgently desired to live in peace; never had a man been so consistently denied it.

He could not postpone passing on the news to Villena. The Marquis would hear of it from some other source if he delayed.

He asked the page to bring Villena to his presence, and when the Marquis came, with a helpless shrug he handed him Isabella's letter.

Villena's face became purple with rage.

'The marriage has actually taken place!' he cried.

'That is what she says.'

'But this is monstrous. Ferdinand in Castile! I know what we must expect from that young man. There is none more ambitious in the whole of Spain.'

'I do not think Isabella would attempt to usurp the throne,' said Henry mildly.

'Isabella! What say will she have in affairs does Your Highness think? She will be led into revolt. Holy Mother, on one side this ambitious young husband, and on the other my uncle Carillo who is thirsting for battle. This marriage should have been prevented at all costs.'

'So far there is little harm done.'

Villena scowled and averted his gaze from the King.

He said: 'There is one thing we must do. The Princess Joanna is now nearly nine years old. We shall find a suitable bridegroom for her and she shall be declared the rightful heiress of Castile.' He began to laugh. 'Then our young gallant from Aragon may begin to wonder whether he has made such a brilliant marriage after all.'

'But Isabella has many supporters. Valladolid is firmly behind her. So are many other towns.'

'We have Albuquerque; we have the Mendozas. I doubt not that many others will rally to our cause. Would to God that your Queen would not create such scandal in Madrid! It lends some truth to the slander that the Princess Joanna is not your daughter.'

'My dear Villena, do you believe she is?'

Villena's face grew a shade more purple.

'I believe the Princess Joanna to be the true heir to the crowns of Castile and Leon,' he retorted; 'and by God and all his saints, ill shall befall any who reject that belief.'

Henry sighed.

Why, why, he pondered, were people so tiresome? Why must Villena be so fierce? Why must Isabella make this marriage which was so upsetting to them all?

'Is there never to be peace?' he demanded fretfully.

'Yes,' said Villena contemptuously, 'when Isabella and her ambitious Ferdinand learn that they must stand aside for the true heiress of Castile.'

'That,' said Henry peevishly, 'they will never learn.'

But Villena was not listening. He was already busy with plans.

It was an unusual little Court at Dueñas. There was so little money that it was often difficult to pay for their food and that of their servants. Yet Isabella had never been so happy in her life.

She was deeply in love with Ferdinand, and he was the most passionate and the most kind of husbands. He was delighted that her intelligence matched her physical charms and that she had a deep knowledge of political affairs.

Perhaps those months seemed so precious to them both because they knew that they were transient. They would not always live in such humble state. The day must come when they would leave their humble lodgings and take up residence in one of the castles, and all the pomp and ceremonies which surrounded the sovereigns of Castile and Leon be theirs.

Ferdinand longed for that day; and, in a way, so did Isabella. The delightful intimacies of this life would be lost perhaps, but for all her joy in it, Isabella must not forget that she and Ferdinand had been brought together, not for dalliance in sensuous pleasure, but to make of Spain a mighty country, to unite all Spaniards, to bring them to the true religion, to rid the country of its existing anarchy, to bring back law and order, and to release every acre of Spanish soil from the domination of the Infidel.

And a few months after her marriage, Isabella, to her great joy, discovered that she was pregnant.

Ferdinand embraced her with delight when he heard the news.

'Why, my Isabella,' he said, 'you are indeed possessed of all the virtues. You are not only beautiful and of great intellect, you are fruitful! It is more than I dared hope for. But you look complacent, my love!'

She *was* complacent. She knew that she would give birth to great rulers. It was her destiny to do so.

In the monastery of Loyola, not far from Segovia, the King with the Marquis of Villena, the Duke of Albuquerque and several members of the influential Mendoza family and other highly placed noblemen had gathered in the company of the French ambassadors.

There was one present who was not often seen at such assemblies; this was Joanna, the Queen of Castile, who had come from Madrid to play a special part in these proceedings.

Henry addressed the assembly, Villena on one side of him and his Queen on the other.

'My friends,' said the King, 'we are gathered here for a special purpose and I pray you listen to me and give me your support. We are beset by conflict which could at any moment break into civil war. My half-sister Isabella – as did her brother Alfonso before her – has set herself up as heiress of Castile and Leon. I do not forget that at one time I named her heiress to the throne. That was in the treaty of Toros de Guisando. There she agreed not to marry without my approval. She has broken her word. Therefore I declare that the treaty of Toros de Guisando becomes null and void, and my sister Isabella is no longer heiress to the throne of Castile and Leon.'

There was a murmur of approval in the gathering, led by Villena, Albuquerque and the Mendozas; it quickly became a roar.

Henry lifted his hand.

'There is one whose place she usurps. This is my daughter, the Princess Joanna, now a child in her ninth year. Her mother has come here today to swear with me that the Princess is my daughter; and you will, when you have heard and accepted her testimony, agree with me that there can be only one heiress, the Princess Joanna.'

'The Princess Joanna!' chanted the audience. 'Castile for Joanna!'

'I am now going to ask the Queen to swear on oath that the Princess Joanna is the legitimate heiress of Spain.'

Joanna rose to her feet. She was still a beautiful woman but the lines of depravity were firmly etched on her face now, and there was a certain insolence in her demeanour which was far from queenly. Joanna was aware that all present knew of the retinue of lovers who attended her in Madrid, and of the children who had been the result; and quite clearly she was indifferent to this.

Now she cried: 'I swear the Princess Joanna is the daughter of the King and no other.'

'Castile for Joanna!' cried the assembly.

Then the King rose and took his wife's hand. 'I swear with the Queen that the Princess Joanna is my daughter and no other.'

'Castile for Joanna!'

The King then turned to the French ambassadors, among whom was the Count of Boulogne. The Count came forward.

'It is our pleasure,' said Henry, 'formally to announce the betrothal of my daughter Joanna to the Duke of Guienne, brother of the King of France, and with the approval of the nobles of Castile the ceremony of betrothal will now take place, with the Count of Boulogne standing proxy for his master.'

'Long live the Duke of Guienne!' was the cry. 'Castile for Joanna!'

Meanwhile, in the house of Juan de Vivero, Isabella was preparing for her confinement.

She was in a state of bliss. She shut herself in with her happiness. She was reading history; it was necessary to profit from the experience of others. She was studying state matters; and as usual she spent a great deal of time with her confessor and at prayers. Her life was divided between the study, which she believed to be necessary for a ruler who had a mighty task before her, and the domestic affairs of a wife and mother. Isabella had determined that in neither role should she fail.

It was delightful to sit with Ferdinand and talk of the reforms she intended to bring to Castile. When she heard stories of the terrible state of affairs, which existed in the country districts as well as in the towns, she would work out plans for righting this state of affairs. She planned to bring a new order to Castile; and she would with the aid of Ferdinand.

These intimate little conferences were all the more delightful because they were shared only by the two of them. Previously all political discussions had been presided over by the Archbishop of Toledo. Isabella had turned to him, trusting his loyalty and wisdom. But with the coming of Ferdinand it was with Ferdinand she wished to discuss affairs.

What could be more pleasant than a conference which was also a *tête-à-tête* for lovers!

The Archbishop found it far from pleasant.

On one occasion, when Ferdinand was on his way to Isabella's apartments, he met the Archbishop also bound for the same destination.

'*I* am going to the Princess,' said Ferdinand, implying that

254 CASTILE FOR ISABELLA

the Archbishop must wait awhile.

Alfonso Carillo, always a hot-tempered man, reminded Ferdinand that he was Isabella's chief adviser. 'She herself, I doubt not, will tell you that, but for me, she would never have been proclaimed heiress to the throne.'

Ferdinand was young and also hot-tempered. He said: 'My wife and I do not intend to be disturbed. We will send for you when we need you.'

The eyes of the Archbishop widened with horror.

'I think, Highness,' he said, 'that you forget to whom you speak.'

'I forget?'

'I would ask you to consult the Princess Isabella. She will tell you what she owes to my loyalty and advice.'

Ferdinand retorted: 'You will find that *I* am not to be put in leading strings as has been the case with some sovereigns of Castile.'

The Archbishop bowed his head to hide his smouldering anger, and turned away to prevent an outburst which might have proved disastrous.

He muttered to himself: 'Before you attempt to escape from leading strings, my young cockerel, make sure that you are a sovereign of Castile.'

Ferdinand went on angrily to Isabella's apartment, where she was lying on her bed, her women about her.

Ferdinand stormed: 'I have just left that insolent fellow. One would think he was King of Castile. He will have to learn a little humility if he is to hold his place.'

'Ferdinand . . .' said Isabella, and anxiety showed in her eyes. She held out her hand. 'It would be wise, I think, to go cautiously. He is much older than we are. He is wise, and he has been loyal.'

'I care not!' blazed Ferdinand. 'I would ask him to re-member to whom he speaks.'

'Nevertheless,' replied Isabella, 'our position is by no means stable.'

Some of that indignation which Ferdinand had felt towards the Archbishop was now directed towards Isabella. Was she telling him what he should do? She was only a woman, and he was her husband.

'I think,' began Ferdinand coolly, 'that you may safely trust me to deal with such matters.'

But Isabella had cried out.

'It is the pains, Highness,' said one of the women, coming forward. 'They grow more frequent now.'

Isabella lay in her bed, her child in her arms.

Ferdinand stood by the bed, smiling down at her.

'A daughter, Ferdinand,' she said. 'It should have been a son.'

'I would rather have this daughter than any son,' declared Ferdinand in the first flush of parenthood.

'Then I am completely happy.'

'We shall have sons.'

'Oh yes, we shall have sons.'

Ferdinand knelt by the bed in a sudden rush of emotion.

'There is one thing only that matters, my love. You have come through this ordeal.'

Isabella touched his hair with her hand. 'Did you doubt that I would?'

'Loving you as I did, I must needs fear.'

'No,' said Isabella. 'Have no fear in future, Ferdinand. For something within me tells me that you and I will have many children and that there are long useful years before us.'

'Oh, Isabella, you put me to shame. You think always of your duty.'

'What a happy woman I am when it is my duty to love and serve you ... and Castile.'

He kissed her hand with mingling fervour and tenderness.

'We shall call this little one Isabella,' he said; 'and we shall hope that she will resemble her mother.'

* * *

When King John of Aragon heard of Ferdinand's quarrel with the Archbishop of Toledo he was disturbed.

He wrote immediately to Ferdinand.

'Have a care, my son. You are unwise to offend a man of such influence. I advise you to placate him immediately, and in future act with great caution.'

But John knew Ferdinand. He was impulsive and too young perhaps for the position in which he found himself. He would find it very difficult to placate the Archbishop, and it might well be that the prelate was beginning to waver in his loyalties.

I must be kept informed of affairs in Castile, John told himself.

The situation was full of dangers. Could it be that the young couple did not notice this? Many great families were supporting the claims of La Beltraneja, and Castile was divided on this matter of the succession. What could be more alarming? And here was Ferdinand jeopardizing the friendship of one of the most forceful and powerful of his supporters.

John himself was enjoying a little respite from his troubles.

The Duke of Lorraine, whom the Catalans had appointed as their ruler, had died and all his children were too young to take his place. Thus the Catalans were without a leader, and John saw his chance of settling their differences and restoring order; but the Catalans would not give in so easily. The result of their resistance was the rigorous blockade of Barcelona which eventually brought them to a mood for negotiations.

When John entered their city he was shocked by the terrible signs of famine which he saw, and being as eager for peace as the people of Barcelona themselves he went to the Palace and there swore to respect the constitution of Catalonia.

The ten-years-long civil war was over, and John felt as

though the ghost of his first-born had at last been laid.

This peace was not achieved until the end of the year 1472, and during this time the situation in Castile had continued to give him cause for anxiety.

The daughter of Isabella and Ferdinand – little Isabella – was now two years old; poverty at the little Court at Dueñas was acute, and John was very anxious as to the fate of his son; he longed to have him with him, yet he realized the need for him to stay in Castile. Isabella had her adherents and John had heard that many of them had deserted the cause of the King and La Beltraneja when the Duke of Guienne had died in May of that year. At the same time the situation was alarming.

Then further conflict broke out in Aragon.

When John had borrowed money from Louis XI of France, Louis had taken as security the provinces of Roussillon and Cerdagne, the inhabitants of which now complained bitterly of their foreign masters and sent to John telling him that, if he would liberate them, they would very willingly become his subjects once more.

John immediately rallied to the cause, while Louis, incensed by what was happening, sent an army into Aragon.

The Archbishop of Toledo presented himself to Ferdinand and Isabella.

Ferdinand scarcely disguised the irritation the Archbishop aroused in him.

Ferdinand was worried and, because of this, so was Isabella. She had assured him that his father was the bravest of soldiers and the shrewdest of strategists, and he had no need to fear. But Ferdinand remembered the age of his father, and his uneasiness persisted. They were discussing the new turn of affairs in Aragon when the Archbishop was ushered in.

Carillo was secretly pleased with himself. He was seriously considering whether he would not abandon the cause of Isabella and join that of La Beltraneja. He felt that with the

King and La Beltraneja there would be no interference in the conduct of affairs, except of course from his nephew the Marquis of Villena. But they understood each other; they were of a kind; the same blood ran in their veins; neither would interfere in the other's province. He, Carillo, would be immeasurably useful to the other side if he changed now.

Yet he was not eager to change sides again; he had not his nephew's easy conscience. Yet the need to lead was all-important. He was ready to support a failing cause, providing he might take the lead. He could not endure to be in a subordinate position, and since the coming of Ferdinand he had felt himself to be forced into one.

Now, as he stood before Ferdinand and Isabella, he expressed his deep concern regarding events in Aragon.

Ferdinand thanked him coolly. 'My father is a seasoned warrior,' he said. 'I doubt not that he will be victorious.'

'Yet the French are capable of throwing a powerful force into the field,' answered the Archbishop.

Isabella looked alarmed and glanced at her husband, who had flushed and was beginning to grow angry.

'I would suggest,' went on the Archbishop, 'that if you should decide it was your duty to go to your father's help, we of Castile would provide you with men and arms.' He turned to Isabella. 'I know that Your Highness would put no obstacle in the way of this help to your father-in-law, and that I speak with your authority.'

Ferdinand was torn between his emotions, and he was too young to hide them entirely – much to the amusement of the Archbishop. He was delighted at the prospect of helping his father, and at the same time he was annoyed that the Archbishop should imply that he could only be provided with men and arms at Isabella's command.

Isabella drew a deep breath. She was so happy with her husband and her two-year-old little daughter; and the thought of Ferdinand's going into battle terrified her. She looked quickly at Ferdinand.

He had turned to her. 'How could I bear to leave you?' he said.

Isabella answered: 'You must do your duty, Ferdinand.'

Ferdinand thought of riding into Aragon, where he would not be treated as the consort of the Queen but as the heir to the throne. It was tempting. Moreover he was fond of his father, who was too old to engage in battle.

There was the Archbishop smiling at them benignly. He would delay changing sides for a while. With Ferdinand out of the way he would feel much happier, and Ferdinand would go to Aragon.

'Yes,' said Ferdinand slowly. 'I must do my duty.'

It was long since Beatriz de Bobadilla had seen Isabella, and she often thought of her and longed for the old companionship.

Life had changed for Beatriz since those days when she had been Isabella's most intimate maid of honour. She found herself in a difficult position, because her husband was an officer of Henry's household, and there was such a wide division in the country – on one side the supporters of the King, on the other those of Isabella.

Andres de Cabrera had been made Governor of the town of Segovia, and the Alcazar which he occupied there was the depository of the King's treasure. Andres was therefore in a very trusted position; so it was very difficult for his wife to communicate with Isabella.

Beatriz fumed incessantly about this state of affairs.

She was devoted to her husband, but she had a great affection for Isabella, and Beatriz never did anything by half-measures. She must be a devoted friend as well as a devoted wife.

Often she discussed the country's affairs with her husband and forced him to agree that there could be no prosperity in a land which, while there were two factions disagreeing as to who was the heiress to the throne, must continually be trembling on the brink of civil war.

On one occasion when Andres was smarting over the over-bearing behaviour of the Marquis of Villena, Beatriz seized the opportunity for which she had been looking.

'Andres,' she said, 'it occurs to me that, were it not for this man Villena, now Grand Master of St James, there might be an end to this strife.'

'Ah, my dear,' replied Andres, shaking his head, 'there are still the two heiresses. You cannot have peace when there is a division of opinion as to whether the Princess Isabella or the Princess Joanna has the right to the title.'

'The Princess Joanna – La Beltraneja!' scoffed Beatriz. 'Everyone knows she is a bastard.'

'But the Queen swore...'

'The Queen swore! That woman would swear to anything, just for a whim. You know, Andres, that Isabella is the right-ful heiress to the crown.'

'Hush, my dear. Remember we serve the King, and the King has given the succession to his daughter Joanna.'

'*Not* his daughter!' cried Beatriz, clenching her right fist and driving it into the palm of her left hand. 'Nor does he believe it. Did he not at one time make Isabella his heiress? The people want Isabella. Do you know, I believe that if we could bring Isabella to Henry – in the absence of Villena – we could make him accept her as his heiress, and there would be no more nonsense about La Beltraneja. Would this not be a good thing for the country?'

'And for you, Beatriz, who would have your friend with you.'

'I should like to see her again,' mused Beatriz almost gently. 'I should also like to see her little daughter. I wonder if she resembles Isabella.'

'Well,' said Andres, 'what do you plot?'

'Henry comes here often,' said Beatriz.

'He does.'

'Sometimes without Villena.'

'That is so.'

'What if Isabella were here too? What if we arranged a meeting between them?'

'Isabella! Come here ... into the enemy's camp!'

'You would call my house the enemy's camp? Any who sought to make her their prisoner in my house would have to kill me before they did so.'

Andres laid his hand on his wife's shoulder. 'You talk too lightly of death, my dear.'

'It is Villena who rules this land. He rules the King. He rules you.'

'That he does not. That he never shall do.'

'Well, then, why should we not invite Isabella here? Why should she not meet Henry?'

'It would be necessary to ask Henry's permission first,' warned Andres.

'Well, I would undertake to get that ... provided he came here without Villena.'

'You would play a dangerous game, my dear.'

'That for danger!' cried Beatriz, snapping her fingers. 'Have I your permission to speak to the King when he next comes here alone?'

Andres laughed. 'My dear Beatriz,' he said, 'I know that when you ask for my permission it is merely a formality. So you have decided to speak to Henry at the first opportunity?'

Beatriz nodded. 'I have decided,' she said.

She knew it would not be difficult.

She asked the King for permission to talk with him when next he came to stay at the Segovia palace and Villena was busy in Madrid.

'Highness,' she began, 'will you forgive my boldness in raising a certain question?'

Henry was alarmed, immediately afraid that his peace was about to be disturbed.

Beatriz ignored his worried expression and hurried on. 'I

know Your Highness, like myself, loves peace beyond all things.'

'You are right in that,' agreed Henry. 'I wish for no more conflict. I wish those about me would accept what is, and leave it at that.'

'Some would, Highness, but there are others, close to you, who make strife. Yet it would be quite easy to have peace throughout Castile tomorrow.'

'How so?' Henry wanted to know.

'Well, Highness, I am not skilled in politics but I know this: There are two sides in this quarrel. Part of the country supports Your Highness, and the other part, Isabella. If you made Isabella your heir you would placate those who are against you. Those who are with you would still remain with you. Therefore there would be an end to the conflict.'

'But my daughter Joanna is the heir to the throne.'

'Highness, the people will never accept her. As you know, I served Isabella and I loved her dearly. I know that she longs for an end of hostilities. She is truly your sister. There is not a doubt about that. But as to the Princess Joanna ... at least there are great doubts as to her legitimacy. If you would only meet Isabella ... talk to her ... let her tell you how grieved she is by the conflict between you ...'

'Meet her! But how? Where?'

'Highness, she could come here.'

'It would not be permitted.'

'But Your Highness would permit it – and those who would not, need not know of it.'

'If I sent for her they would hear at once.'

'Highness, if I fetched her and brought her to you they would not hear of it.'

'If you set out for Aranda, where I understand she is now, the purpose of your mission would be surmised; all would know that you proposed bringing her to me.'

Her eyes sparkled. 'Oh, but, Highness, I would not go as myself. I would go disguised.'

'This is a mad scheme of yours, my dear lady,' said Henry. 'Think no more of it.'

'But if I could bring her to you ... in secret ... you would receive her, Highness?'

'I could not refuse to meet my sister. But have done.'

Beatriz bowed her head and changed the subject.

Henry then seemed contented; but he did not know that Beatriz had begun to form her plans.

Isabella was lonely in the palace at Aranda. She was thinking of Ferdinand and wondering how long their separation must last.

Sitting by a great fire stitching with one of her women, and periodically glancing up, she saw through the windows the snow fluttering down. The roads would be icy; and she shivered, wondering what the weather was like in Aragon.

She was working on a shirt. She had been true to her vow to make all the shirts which Ferdinand wore. It was a little jest between them.

'Every shirt of yours must be stitched with my stitches,' she had told him. 'No other woman must make such a garment for you ... only myself.'

Ferdinand was delighted. He was always deeply touched by such feminine gestures. Isabella sighed. Ferdinand loved her femininity more than her predilection for governing. He would rather see her occupied with stitching than with state affairs.

One of her women, who was seated in the window seat, called out that a peasant with a pack on her saddle-bow had ridden into the courtyard.

'Poor woman, she looks so cold and hungry. I wonder if she has wares to sell.'

Isabella laid aside her work and went to the window. She felt it her duty to take a great interest in all her subjects. She was teaching little Isabella to be considerate of all people. They might be her subjects one day, she reminded her; for if she and Ferdinand should have no sons, that little Isabella might be Queen of Castile.

'Poor woman indeed!' she said. 'Go down, lest they turn her away. Have her brought in and fed. If she has goods to sell, perhaps she will have something that is needed in the house.'

Her woman went away to do her bidding, but she soon came back, consternation on her face.

'The woman asks if she may see you, Highness,' Isabella was told.

'What does she want?'

'She refused to say, Highness. She was very insistent. And, Highness, she does not speak like a peasant though she looks like one.'

Isabella sighed. 'Tell her that I am engaged,' she said. 'But ask her business and then come and tell me what she says.'

Isabella paused, and held up a hand to stay her woman for she had heard a voice, protesting in loud tones, which held an unmistakable ring of authority. She knew that voice.

'Go,' she said, 'and bring this woman to me ... at once.'

In a few moments the woman was standing on the threshold of the room. She and Isabella looked at each other, and then Beatriz, throwing off her ragged cloak, held out her arms. This was no time for ceremony. Isabella ran to her and they embraced.

'Beatriz! But why? To come like this!'

'Could we be alone?' asked Beatriz.

Isabella waved her women away.

'It was the only way to come,' Beatriz explained. 'So I came thus ... and alone. Had I come as myself, the news could have reached Villena. As it is, you shall come to Segovia, where the King now is, and until you have met and talked with him the meeting will be a secret. It is the only way.'

'Henry has expressed a wish to see me?'

'Henry will see you.'

'Beatriz, what does this mean?'

'We know, dearest Highness, that reconciliation between you and Henry would mean that the people of Castile could live without the daily threat of civil war.'

'Henry knows this!'

'He longs for peace. It will not be difficult to persuade him to it ... if we can keep him from Villena.'

'Beatriz, you are asking me to go to Henry. Do you remember how they tried to capture me, to imprison me? Do you remember what was done to Alfonso?'

'I ask you to come to the Alcazar of Segovia. No harm could come to you there. Andres guards it ... and I guard Andres.'

Isabella laughed.

'You were always a forceful woman. Does Andres love you the less for it?'

Beatriz looked hard at her friend. 'You, too, are strong,' she said. 'And Ferdinand, does he love you less for that?'

Beatriz noticed that a slight shadow crossed Isabella's face as she said: 'I do not know.'

Isabella rode into Segovia with the Archbishop of Toledo beside her.

Henry received her with warmth, and his eyes filled with tears as he embraced her. 'You know, my dear sister, that all this strife is none of my making.'

'I do know that, Henry,' answered Isabella; 'and the state of our country brings as much grief to me as it does to you.'

'I long for peace.' Henry said this with unaccustomed vehemence.

'And I.'

'Then, Isabella, why should we not have peace?'

'Because there are jealous nobles who surround us ... who jostle each other for power.'

'But if we are friends, what else should matter?'

'It is this affair of the succession, Henry. You know I am the true heiress of Castile. I am your half-sister ... your only relation.'

'But there is my daughter.'

'You do not believe Joanna is that, Henry.'

'Her mother swore it.'

'You do not believe her, Henry.'

'Who shall say? Who shall say?'

'You see,' said Isabella, 'if you would but accept me as heir to the throne there would be no more strife. If you and I were friends and were seen together, how happy all would be in Castile and Leon.'

'I long to see all happy.'

'Then Henry, we could begin to right these wrongs; we could bring back law and order to the country. There is this senseless conflict as to who is the heir, when there are so many important reforms to be considered.'

'I know. I know.'

The Archbishop came to them. He did not wait to be announced. He had assumed complete authority.

'If you would walk through the city holding the bridle of the Princess's palfrey, Highness, in an intimate manner, as brother to sister, it would give great joy to the people of Segovia.'

'All I wish is to give them joy,' Henry insisted.

The people of Segovia had vociferously expressed their delight at the sight of the King, walking through their streets and holding the bridle of his sister's palfrey. Here was good news. The threat of civil war was over. The King had cast off the yoke of Villena; he was thinking for himself; he was surely going to accept Isabella as his heir.

When they returned to the Alcazar, the people gathered outside and shouted: 'Castilla! Castilla! Castilla for Henry and Isabella!'

Henry, with tears in his eyes, saluted the people.

It was long since he had been so cheered.

Late that night Beatriz hurried to Isabella's bedchamber.

Isabella had already retired.

'Isabella,' whispered Beatriz in her ear, 'wake up. Someone has arrived who is waiting to see you.'

Isabella started up in bed. 'What is this, Beatriz?'

'Hush,' said Beatriz. 'The palace is sleeping.'

She then turned and beckoned, and Isabella saw a tall, familiar figure enter the apartment.

She gave a cry of gladness, for Ferdinand had thrown himself upon the bed, and she was in his arms.

Beatriz stood by, laughing.

'He has come at a good moment,' she said.

'Any moment he comes is a good one,' answered Isabella.

'My dear Isabella,' murmured Ferdinand.

Beatriz said: 'There will be plenty of time later to show each other your pleasure. At the moment there is one other matter of importance to settle. Henry has received you, Isabella, but will he receive your husband? That is what we have to consider. And it will soon be known that Ferdinand has returned and that you are both here with the King. Once this reaches Villena's ears, he will do his utmost to prevent the renewal of friendship between you all. Tomorrow morning early, you must seek an audience with Henry. You must persuade him to see Ferdinand.'

'He will do so; I know he will.'

'He must,' said Beatriz. 'It is imperative. He must be reconciled to you both. It will be Twelfth Day ... is it tomorrow, or the next day? That is an excuse for a banquet. We shall give one – Andres and I and when it is seen how friendly the King is towards you two, all will know that he acknowledges your marriage and accepts you as his heirs. I shall leave you now. But until the King has received Prince

Ferdinand it should not be known, except by those whom we can trust, that he is here.'

Ferdinand had thrown off his travel-stained garments, and Isabella was in his embrace.

'It seems so long since I saw you,' he said.

'There should not be these partings.'

'Yet, if it is necessary, they must be. How is our daughter?'

'Well and happy. How delighted she will be to see her father!'

'Has she forgotten him?'

'No more than I could. And Aragon?'

'My father is a mighty warrior. He will always win.'

'As you will, Ferdinand.'

There was need for silence, and after a while she said: 'Was it not courageous of Beatriz to arrange this meeting between the King and ourselves!'

'She is a courageous woman, I'll grant you – but ...'

'You do not like Beatriz, Ferdinand. Oh, but that must not be. She is one of my dearest friends.'

'She is unlike a woman. She has hectoring ways.'

'That is her strength.'

'I like not hectoring women,' said Ferdinand.

The faintest alarm came to Isabella. In her life as a Queen there would be times when she must make her own decisions and all others must respect them.

But Ferdinand was home after a long absence; and she could not think of the difficulties which lay ahead. They were of the future and the present time had so much to offer.

Beatriz was exuberant. Her schemes for the reunion of Isabella and Ferdinand with the King had had as great a success as she had hoped for.

Henry was pliable, subject to be swayed by the prevailing wind; and here in Segovia with the guardian of his treasury,

THE DEATH OF HENRY

and the latter's forceful wife, he appeared to be the firm friend of Ferdinand and Isabella.

He had ridden to the Twelfth Night celebrations between Ferdinand and Isabella, smiling and chatting with them as they rode, to the intense joy of the people. Through the streets they had ridden thus to the Bishop's palace, between the Alcazar and the Cathedral, in which the Twelfth Night banquet was being held.

The banquet, supervised by the indefatigable Beatriz, was a success. Sweating serving men and women waited on the guests and minstrels played in the gallery. At the head of the table sat the King; on his right hand was Isabella, and on his left, Ferdinand.

Beatriz surveyed her beloved mistress and friend with beaming satisfaction, and Andres watched his wife.

He was aware of a certain tension, a certain watchfulness. It was inevitable, he told himself. All the conflict, all the strife, could not be dispersed by one brief meeting. Henry was eating and drinking with enjoyment, and his eyes were becoming a little glazed as they rested on one of the most sensuously beautiful of the women. Henry had not become a wise King in such a brief period of time; Isabella had not become secure in her place.

The banquet over, dancing began.

As Isabella was seated by the King, Beatriz hoped that he would lead the Princess in the dance. What could be more symbolic?

Yet Henry did not dance.

'My dear sister,' he murmured, 'I feel a little unwell. You must lead the dance – you and your husband.'

So it was Isabella and Ferdinand who rose, and as they came into the centre of the hall others fell in behind them.

Beatriz hastened to the side of the King.

'All is well, Highness?' she asked anxiously.

'I am not sure,' said Henry. 'I feel a little strange.'

'It is too hot for Your Highness, perhaps.'

'I know not. I seem to shiver.'

Beatriz beckoned to the beautiful young woman who had caught the King's notice during the banquet; but Henry now seemed to be unaware of her.

'Sit beside him,' whispered Beatriz. 'Speak to him.'

But the King had closed his eyes and had slumped sideways in his chair.

All night long the King lay groaning on his bed. He was in great pain, he declared.

News spread through Segovia that the King was ill, and that the nature of his illness -- vomiting, purging and stomach pains -- pointed to poison.

There were silent men and women in the streets of Segovia; yesterday they had cheered; today they were solemn.

Could it be that the King had been lured to Segovia that he might be poisoned? And who was responsible for his condition?

There were many, who had helped at the banquet, who might wish him dead, for almost everyone present was a supporter of Isabella and Ferdinand.

The people of Segovia did not wish to believe that their beloved Princess could be guilty of such a crime.

When Isabella heard of the King's illness she was horrified.

'He must not die,' she said to Beatriz. 'If he does, we shall be blamed.'

Beatriz recognized the good sense of that.

'Remember,' said Isabella,' the conflict in Aragon when the people believed that Carlos was murdered. How many suffered and died during those ten years of civil war?'

'We must save the King's life,' said Beatriz. 'I must wait upon him. It would not be wise for you to be constantly in the sick room. If he died they would surely blame you then.'

So Beatriz supervised the nursing of the King, and it

seemed that because she so willed that he should not die, his
condition began gradually to improve.

The Marquis of Villena rode with his troops into Segovia
and imperiously presented himself at the Alcazar.

Isabella and Ferdinand received him calmly, but Villena
was far from calm. He was enraged and alarmed.

The King was not to be trusted. As soon as his, Villena's,
back was turned he was consorting with the opposite side.
This would teach him a lesson.

Villena demanded that he be taken at once to the King.

'I fear,' said Isabella, 'that my brother is not well enough
to receive visitors.'

'I demand to be taken to him.'

'You may not make your demands here,' said Isabella.

'I wish to assure myself that he is receiving the best attention.'

'I will send for our hostess and she will tell you that there
is no need for alarm.'

When Beatriz arrived she told Villena that the King's
condition was improving, but that he was not well enough to
leave Segovia for a while.

'I must be taken to him at once,' said Villena.

'I am sorry, my lord,' Beatriz answered, her voice placat-
ing but her eyes belying her tone. 'The King is not well
enough to receive visitors.'

'I shall stay here until I see him,' said Villena.

'We cannot deny you hospitality, since you ask it so graciously,' answered Beatriz.

But even she could not keep Villena from the King. Villena had his men everywhere, and it was not an insuperably
difficult task to get a message to Henry that Villena was in
the Alcazar, and that if the King valued his life he must
insist on seeing him without delay.

Villena sat by Henry's bed. He was shocked by the King's

appearance. His illness had changed Henry. He had become gaunt and his skin was yellow.

Henry thought he saw a change in Villena. There was a certain lessening of that intense vitality, a certain greyish tinge to the skin.

'Your Highness should never have been so foolish as to come here,' said Villena.

'I could not know that I should be smitten with this illness,' murmured Henry peevishly.

'That you should be so smitten was the only reason why you were lured here.'

'You think they tried to poison me?'

'I am sure of it. And they will continue to do so while you are in this place.'

'I trust Isabella.'

'Trust Isabella! She has a throne to gain. It cannot be hers while you live.'

'She is certain that she is the true heiress, and she is ready to wait.'

'But not to wait too long, it seems. No, Highness, we must remove you from here as soon as possible. And we must not allow this attempt on your life to be ignored.'

'What do you suggest?' asked Henry wearily.

'We shall send forces to Segovia. They will enter the town stealthily and take possession of vital points. Then they shall make Isabella their prisoner on the ground that she tried to poison you. We could bring her to trial for that.'

'I do not believe Isabella would try to poison me.'

'Then you do not believe the evidence of your senses.'

'Cabrera's wife has nursed me well.'

'A poisonous woman.'

'A good nurse. She seemed determined to save my life. And, Marquis, do you not think that I should acknowledge Isabella as heir to the throne? She is the one the people want. And with Ferdinand's help she would bring Castile out of its present troubles.'

'But your will, of which you have made me executor, clearly states that your daughter Joanna is heir to the throne.'

'It's true. Little Joanna. She is but a child. She will be surrounded by wolves ... wolves who seek power. I came to the conclusion, when I rode through the streets of the town with Ferdinand and Isabella, that matters would be simplified if I admitted that Joanna was not my daughter and made Ferdinand and Isabella my heirs.'

'I see that some of the poison has been effective,' said Villena. 'As soon as you are well enough to travel we must leave this place for Cuellar. There we will make our plans for the capture of Isabella. We shall not be safe until she is under lock and key. And I tremble for *your* safety while you are in this place.'

'I do not,' said Henry. 'I do not believe Isabella would allow any harm to befall me.'

Villena looked with scorn on the King and, as he did so, he placed his hand to his throat.

'What ails you?' asked Henry. 'You look as sick as I do myself.'

'It is nothing. A certain dryness of the throat. A certain discomfort, nothing more.'

'You have not the same colour that you had.'

'I have scarcely slept since I heard the news that Your Highness was here at Segovia in the midst of your enemies.'

'Ah, if I had but known who were my friends and who my enemies I should have had a happier life.'

Villena looked startled. 'You talk as though you had come to the end of it. No, Your Highness, you will recover from this attempt on your life. And it shall not be forgotten. Let us make certain of that.'

'Well,' said Henry, 'if Isabella was behind a plot to poison me, she deserves imprisonment.'

In the town of Cuellar, whither Villena had taken the King, plans were made for the capture of Isabella.

'Forces shall enter the town,' said Villena. 'Explosives will be thrown at the Alcazar; the inhabitants will be terror-stricken, and then it will be no difficult matter to secure the person of Isabella.'

Several months had passed since the King's illness, but he had never fully recovered and was subject to attacks of vomiting.

As for Villena himself, that great energy which had sustained him seemed to be spent. He still planned; he still had ambitious schemes, but the pain in his throat persisted and he found it impossible to eat certain foods.

In the Alcazar at Segovia, Beatriz and her husband were aware of the plot to capture Isabella, and they doubled the guards at all vital points; thus when Villena's troops tried to make a stealthy entry into the town they were discovered and the plan was frustrated.

Villena received the news almost with indifference.

And the next day even his spirit broke and he accepted the advice of his servants and stayed in his bed. Within a few days he was suffering great pain, and was unable to swallow food. He knew that he had not long to live.

He lay back, considering all the ambitions of his life and wondering whether it had been worth while. He had achieved great power; he had been at times the ruler of Castile; and now it was over and he must lie on his bed, the victim of a malignant growth in his throat which would destroy him, as his enemies had not been able to do.

Isabella remained at large. The people were rallying about her. And he, Villena, who had sworn that she should never come to the throne, was dying helplessly.

Henry could not accept the fact when the news was brought to him. Villena . . . dead!

'But what shall I do?' he said. 'What shall I do now?'

He prayed for his friend; he wept for his friend. He had always believed that he would die long before Villena. He had lost his master and his servant, and he was bewildered.

His secretary Oviedo came to him.

'Highness,' said Oviedo, 'there is a very important matter of which I must speak to you.'

Henry nodded for him to proceed.

'On his death-bed the Marquis of Villena put this paper into my hand. It is your will, of which he was to be executor. I have glanced at it, Highness, and see it to be a document of the utmost importance, since it names the Princess Joanna as your heir.'

'Take it away,' said Henry. 'How can I think of such matters when my dear friend has died and I am all alone?'

'Highness, what shall I do with it?'

'I care not what you do with it. I only wish to be left in peace.'

Oviedo bowed and went away.

He looked at the will. He knew the explosive power of its contents if they became known; they were capable of plunging Castile into civil war.

He could not decide what to do with it, so as a temporary measure he put it in a box, which he locked.

Henry went back to Madrid. He felt not only ill but very weary. He knew that Villena had been self-seeking, a man of immense ambitions, yet without him the King felt lost. He believed that the most unhappy time of his life had been when Villena had sided with his enemies and given his support to young Alfonso. He remembered his delight when Villena had returned to him.

'And now,' murmured Henry, 'I am alone. He has gone before me, and I am sick and tired out with all the troubles about me.'

He was often ill; there was a return of that sickness which had attacked him in Segovia. Indeed he had never fully recovered from it.

Tears of self-pity often filled Henry's eyes, and his doctors sought to rouse him from his lethargy. But there was nothing now which could give him the desire to live. His mistresses no longer interested him. There was nothing in life to sustain his flagging spirits.

It became clear to all in the immediate Court circle that Henry had not long to live. Ambitious noblemen began to court Isabella. The Cardinal Mendoza and the Count Benavente, who had supported first Alfonso and then turned to La Beltraneja, now began to turn again – this time towards Isabella.

Isabella was the natural successor. Her character had aroused admiration. She was of a nature to make a good Queen, and she had a strong husband in Ferdinand.

So, among others, Mendoza and Benavente came to Court, there to await the passing of the old sovereign and the nomination of the new.

On a cold December night in the year 1474, Henry lay on his death-bed.

Ranged round his bed were the men who had come to see him die, and among them was the Cardinal Mendoza and the Count Benavente. In the background hovered the King's secretary, Oviedo. He was uneasy, for he had something on his mind.

Mendoza whispered to Benavente: 'He cannot last long. That was the death-rattle in his throat.'

'He cannot have more than an hour to live. It is time he received the last rites.'

'One moment. He is trying to say something.'

The Cardinal and the Count exchanged glances. It might well be that what the King had to say had better not be heard by any but themselves.

The Cardinal bent over the bed. 'Your Highness, your servants await your orders.'

'Little Joanna,' murmured the King. 'She is but a child. What will become of her?'

'She will be taken care of, Highness. Do not fret on her account.'

'But I do. We were so careless ... her mother and I. She is my heiress ... Little Joanna. Who will care for her? My sister Isabella is strong. She can look after herself ... but little Joanna ... she is my heiress, I tell you. She is my heiress.'

The Cardinal said quickly: 'The King's mind wanders.' The Count nodded in agreement.

'I have left a will,' went on Henry. 'In it I proclaim her my heir.'

'A will!' The Cardinal was startled, for this was an alarming piece of information. He and the Count were only waiting for the end of Henry that they might go and pay their homage to the new Queen Isabella. A will could complicate matters considerably.

'It is with Villena ...' murmured the King. 'I gave it to Villena.'

'There is no doubt that the King's mind wanders,' whispered the Count.

'It is with Villena,' muttered Henry. 'He will look after her. He will save the throne for Joanna.'

One of the attendants came to the two men who stood by the bed, and asked if he should call the King's Confessor.

'The King's mind wanders,' the Cardinal told him. 'He believes the Marquis of Villena to be here in the palace.'

The King's eyes had closed and his head had fallen a little to one side. His breathing was stertorous. Suddenly he opened his eyes and looked at the men about the bed. He obviously did not recognize them. Then he said, and the words came thickly through his furred lips: 'Villena, where are you, my friend? Villena, come nearer.'

'He is near the end,' said the Cardinal. 'Yes, call the King's Confessor.'

* * *

As the Count and Cardinal left the chamber of death Oviedo hurried after them.

'My lords, may I have a word with you?'

They paused to listen to the secretary.

'The King has left in my keeping a document which greatly troubles me,' said Oviedo. 'It was in Villena's possession, until he was dying. He then gave it to me to return to the King, but the King told me to lock it away; and this I have done.'

'What document is this?'

'It is the King's last will, my lords.'

'You should show it to us without delay.'

Oviedo led them into a chamber in which he stored his secret documents. He unlocked the box, produced the will and handed it to the Cardinal.

Had the Cardinal been alone he might have destroyed it; at the moment Benavente was his friend; but men changed sides quickly in Castile at this time, and he dared not destroy such a document while there were witnesses to see him do so.

Benavente read his thoughts, for they were his also.

Then the Cardinal said: 'Tell no one of this document. Take it to the curate of Santa Cruz in Madrid and tell him to lock it away in a safe place.'

Oviedo bowed and retired.

The Count and Cardinal were silent for a few seconds; then the Cardinal said: 'Come! Let us to Segovia, there to pay homage to the Queen of Castile.'

ISABELLA AND FERDINAND

ON the thirteenth day of December, in that year 1474, a procession consisting of the highest of the nobility and clergy of Castile made its way to the Alcazar of Segovia.

There, under a canopy of rich brocade, homage was paid to Isabella, Queen of Castile.

They had come to escort her to the city's square where a platform had been set up.

Isabella, in her royal robes, mounted her jennet and was led there by the magistrates of the city, while one of her officers walked before her carrying the sword of state.

When she reached the platform she dismounted and ascended the structure, there to take her place on the throne which had been set up for her.

When she looked out on that great assembly she was deeply moved. This, she felt, was one of the truly great moments in her life, and it was for this that she had been born.

She had two regrets – one disappointing, one very bitter. The first was that Ferdinand was not here to share this triumph with her because he had, only a few weeks before Henry's death, received an urgent call from his father and had joined him in Aragon; the other was that her mother could not be aware of what was happening to her daughter this day.

And as Isabella sat there on that throne, Queen of Castile by the desire of the people of Segovia, it was her mother's voice which she heard ringing in her ears: 'Never forget, you could be Queen of Castile.'

She had never forgotten.

She heard the bells peal out; she saw the flags fluttering in the breeze; she heard the guns boom forth. All these were saying: Here is the new Queen of Castile.

There were many to kneel before her, to kiss her hand and swear their loyalty; and she in her turn told them, in that sweet, musical, rather high-pitched young and almost innocent voice, that she would do all in her power to serve them, her subjects, to bring back law and order to Castile, and to be a worthy Queen.

The voices of the crowd rang out: 'Castile! Castile for Isabella! Castile for the King Don Ferdinand and his Queen Doña Isabella, Queen Proprietor of the Kingdoms of Castile and Leon!'

She felt warmed by their mention of Ferdinand; she would be able to tell him how they had called his name. That would please him.

Then she descended from the platform and placed herself at the head of the procession, when it made its way to the Cathedral.

Isabella listened to the chanting of Te Deum; and earnestly she prayed for Divine guidance, that she might never falter in her duties towards her kingdoms and her people.

Ferdinand came with all speed from Aragon, and joyously Isabella received him.

Was it her fancy, or did he hold his head a little higher? Was he a little more proud, a little more masterful than before?

In the midst of his passion he whispered to her: 'First you are my wife, Isabella. Do not forget that. Only second, Queen of Castile.'

She did not contradict him, for he did not expect an answer. He had spoken as though he made a statement of fact. It was not true. If she had never known it before, it had become clear to her after the ceremony in the square and the Cathedral.

But she loved him tenderly and with passion. She was a wife and a mother, but the crown was her spouse, and the people of Castile – the suffering and the ignorant – they were her children.

She would not tell him now. But in time he must come to understand. He would, for he too had his duty. He was younger than she was, and for all his experience he was perhaps not so wise, though not for all the world would she tell him so.

He will understand, she assured herself, but he is younger than I – not only in years – and perhaps I am more serious by nature. It will take a little time before he understands as I do.

His grandfather, the Admiral Henriquez, was delighted at the turn of events.

He placed himself at the service of his grandson.

The day after Ferdinand's return he presented himself and embraced the young husband with tears in his eyes.

'This is the proudest moment of my life. You will be King of Aragon. You are already King of Castile.'

Ferdinand looked a little sulky. 'One hears much talk of the Queen of Castile, little of its King.'

'That is a matter which should be set right,' went on the Admiral. 'Isabella has inherited Castile, but that is because the Salic law does not exist in Castile as it does in Aragon. If it were accepted here, you, as the nearest male claimant to the throne, through your grandfather Ferdinand, would be King of Castile – and Isabella merely your consort.'

'That is so,' agreed Ferdinand, 'and it is what I would wish. But everywhere we go it is Isabella ... Isabella ... and they never forget to remind me that she is the *reina proprietaria*. It is almost as though they accept me on sufferance.'

'It shall be changed,' said the Admiral. 'Isabella will do all that you ask of her.'

Ferdinand smiled smugly. He was remembering her passionate reception of him, and he believed it to be true.

'It shall be done. She adores me. She can deny me nothing.'

Isabella listened in dismay.

He was laughing, his arm about her, his lips against her hair. 'So, my love, this shall be done. The King and his beloved consort, eh? It is better so. You, who are so reasonable, will see this.'

Isabella felt dismay smite her, but her voice was firm, though sad, when she replied: 'No, Ferdinand, I do not see it.'

He released her, and his frown was ugly.

'But surely, Isabella . . .'

She wanted to cry out: Do not use that cold tone when you speak to me. But she said nothing. Instead she saw again the people in the square . . . the people who had suffered during the evil reign of her half-brother. And still she said nothing.

He went on: 'So you hold me in such little esteem!'

'I hold you in the greatest esteem,' she told him. 'Are you not my husband and the father of my child?'

Ferdinand laughed bitterly. 'Brought here as a stallion! Is that what I mean to you? Let him do what he has been brought for – after that he is of little account.'

'But how can you say this, Ferdinand? Do I not ask your advice? Do I not listen? Do we not rule these kingdoms together?'

Ferdinand stood up to his full height. For the first time she noticed the lights of cupidity in his eyes, the arrogance of his mouth; yet these faults in him did not make her love him less, although they confirmed her belief that she herself must rule Castile and Leon.

'I am your husband,' he said. 'It is you who should listen to my advice.'

'In some matters, yes,' she answered gently. 'But have you

forgotten that I am the Queen of Castile?'

'Forget it! How can I! You will not allow me to do that. I can see that I demean myself by staying here. I can see that I am of no account whatsoever. Madam, Highness, I no longer wish to remain. Is it necessary for me to ask permission of the Queen of Castile to retire?'

'Oh Ferdinand ... Ferdinand ...' she cried; and the tears started to her eyes.

But he had bowed abruptly and left her.

It was the first quarrel, but she realized how easily there might have been others.

He had believed until this moment that he would have no difficulty in relegating her to second place.

She wanted to go and find him, to tell him that all that she possessed was his. She wanted to say: What do I care for power, if in gaining it I lose your love?

But she remembered his face as he had stood there. Ferdinand, a little vain, a little greedy. Handsome, virile Ferdinand who lacked the modesty, the dedicated desire to serve which were Isabella's.

There would only be one ruler of Castile from this moment until the end of her days; and that must be Isabella.

So she waited, fighting back her tears, trying to soothe her anguish.

It is not pleasure that is important; it is not happiness, she reminded herself. It is doing one's duty in that state of life to which God has called one.

The Court knew of the quarrel between Isabella and Ferdinand.

The Archbishop of Toledo smiled slyly and shrewdly. Here was a situation after his own heart. The Admiral had put these ideas into the head of that young bantam, and the Archbishop was going to vanquish the Admiral; and if it meant Ferdinand's retirement to Aragon in a sulk, that could not be helped.

The Archbishop was delighted at the prospect of dousing the arrogance of master Ferdinand.

'There is no law in Castile,' he told the council, 'to prevent a woman from inheriting the crown. Therefore there can be no question of Isabella's becoming merely the consort of King Ferdinand. It is Ferdinand who is the consort of Queen Isabella.'

Ferdinand was furious.

'I shall not stay here to be so insulted,' he declared. 'I shall return to Aragon.'

The news spread through the Palace, and reached Isabella.

'Ferdinand is preparing to return to Aragon . . . for ever.'

Ferdinand was somewhat alarmed by the storm he had raised.

He was piqued and humiliated, but his father would call him a fool if he returned to Aragon. And a fool he would be.

He was hot-tempered and impulsive. He should never have declared his intention of returning. Now he would either have to go or make his position even more humiliating by remaining.

Already the news was spreading beyond the Palace. A rift between Isabella and Ferdinand, because Ferdinand wishes to take precedence and Isabella refuses to allow it!

He felt bewildered, for the first time realizing that he was after all only a very young man.

Outside the Palace little groups of people had gathered. They were waiting for the news that the marriage, which had seemed so ideal, was broken and that Ferdinand was to go back to Aragon.

He had seen them from the windows. He had seen the sneers on their faces. They would boo him out of Castile, for they were all firmly behind Isabella.

But what could he do?

His servants were waiting for orders.

'I shall return to Aragon,' he had cried before them all. 'I cannot wait to shake the dust of Castile from my shoes!'

And now ... they were waiting.

Someone was coming into the room; he did not turn from the window.

'Ferdinand,' said a voice, soft and very loving.

Then he turned and saw Isabella. She had waved all his servants out of the room and they were alone.

He looked at her sullenly for a few seconds, and her heart beat faster with her love for him, because he looked at that moment like a spoilt child, like their own little Isabella.

'Why, Ferdinand,' she said, 'we should not be bad friends.'

He could not meet her eye. 'It seems to be your wish,' he mumbled.

She came to him and took his hand. 'No, it is far from my wish. I was so happy, and now I am no longer so.'

She knelt at his feet and was looking up at him.

For a few seconds he believed she had come to beg his pardon, to offer him all he asked, if he would stay with her.

Then he realized that until this moment he had not known Isabella. He had known a gentle woman, a woman who longed to please him, who loved with mingling tenderness and passion; and because he had been too much aware of Ferdinand to be aware of Isabella, he had thought he understood her.

She took his hand and kissed it. 'Ferdinand,' she said, 'why should there be this trouble between us? We are quarrelling over power as children quarrel over sweetmeats. One day you will be King of Aragon, and it may be that you will sometimes ask me to help you with some problem in the governing of your country. I know I shall do the same as regards mine. Why, if you had your will in this matter and the Salic law was introduced into Castile, our little Isabella would no longer be heir to Castile and Leon. Think of that,

Ferdinand. Come, my husband, do not, I beg you, I implore you, carry out your threat to leave me. For I need you. How can I rule these kingdoms without you? I shall need you a hundred times a day in our life together. Ferdinand, it is I, Isabella, who ask you ... stay.'

He looked at her then. There were tears shining in her eyes, and she knelt to him; but even as she knelt she remained Queen of Castile.

She was offering him a way out of his predicament. How could he return to Aragon except ignobly? She was saying: 'How can I live happily without you, Ferdinand, I who need you so?'

He said: 'Perhaps I have been hasty. It is not easy for a man...'

'No, it is not easy,' she said eagerly, and she thought of him, Ferdinand, the beloved of his mother and father – and of herself. It was not easy for him to be merely the Queen's consort when he believed he should be King. 'But you are King of Sicily now and one day, Ferdinand, you will be King of Aragon. And Aragon and Castile will be as one. Ferdinand, we must not allow the great happiness we have brought to each other to be spoilt. Think of the great happiness we shall bring to Castile and Aragon.'

'I believe you are right,' he said.

Then she smiled, and her smile was radiant.

'And since you say that you need me so much...'

'Ferdinand, I do, I do!' she cried.

Then she was on her feet and in his arms; and they clung together for a few moments.

She released herself and said: 'You see, Ferdinand, we are so young and there is so much to do, and our lives lie before us...'

'It is true, Isabella,' he said, and touched her cheek, looking at her as though he saw her afresh and that he had discovered something hitherto unknown to him.

'I want everyone to know that all is well,' she said, 'that

everyone can be as happy as we are.'

She drew him to the window and the people below saw them standing there.

Isabella put her hand in that of Ferdinand. He raised it to his lips and kissed it.

There was immediate understanding.

'Castile!' cried the people. 'Castile for Isabella ... and Ferdinand!'

BIBLIOGRAPHY

History of the Reign of Ferdinand and Isabella the Catholic. William H. Prescott. Edited by John Foster Kirk. Two Volumes.

The Heritage of Spain. An Introduction to Spanish Civilization. Nicholson B. Adams.

A History of Spain from Earliest Times to the Death of Ferdinand the Catholic. Ulick Ralph Burke, MA. Two Volumes.

The Soul of Spain. Havelock Ellis.

Spain and Portugal. Edited by Doré Ogrizek. Translated by Paddy O'Hanlon and H. Iredale. Nelson.

Spain: A Companion to Spanish Studies. Edited by E. Allison Peers.

A History of Spanish Civilization. Rafael Altamira. Translated by P. Volkov.

Spain. Henry Dwight Sedgwick.

Christianity in European History. Herbert Butterfield.

Persecution and Tolerance. M. Creighton, DD.

The Story of the Faith. A survey of Christian History for the Undogmatic. William Alva Gifford.

Queens of Old Spain. Martin A. S. Hume.

Spain. Sacheverell Sitwell.

Spain: It's Greatness and Decay, 1479-1788. Martin A. S. Hume.

The History of Spain. Louis Bertrand and Sir Charles Petrie, MA, FR Hist S.